SAVING TIBERIUS

Gordon K. Jones

Copyright © 2020 by Gordon K. Jones

All rights reserved. No part of this publication may be reproduced or transmitted in any form or by any means, electronic or mechanical, including photocopying, recording or any information storage and retrieval, without the written permission of the publisher. Names, characters, places and incidents are either the product of the author's imagination or used fictitiously, and any resemblance to actual persons living or dead, events or locales is entirely coincidental. All trademarks are properties of their respective owners.

Published by BookLand Press Inc.
15 Allstate Parkway
Suite 600
Markham, Ontario L3R 5B4
www.booklandpress.com

Printed in Canada

Front cover image © Juliasha and Jackie2k

Library and Archives Canada Cataloguing in Publication

Title: Saving Tiberius / Gordon K. Jones.
Names: Jones, Gordon K., 1954- author.
Identifiers: Canadiana (print) 20200235079 | Canadiana (ebook) 20200235109 | ISBN 9781772311228 (softcover) | ISBN 9781772311235 (EPUB) | ISBN 9781772311242 (PDF)
Classification: LCC PS8619.O53255 S28 2020 | DDC C813/.6 – dc23

We acknowledge the support of the Government of Canada through the Canada Book Fund and the support of the Ontario Arts Council, an agency of the Government of Ontario. We also acknowledge the support of the Canada Council for the Arts, which last year invested $153 million to bring the arts to Canadians throughout the country.

This book is dedicated to our late tabby, Morgan, who for 16 years, bravely fought diabetes, never ran when we pulled out a syringe and who inspired this book. I've always felt that pets are not "just like family"… they are family.

Chapter 1

Beth Poole smirked as she looked across the table at the man who had just issued one of the most absurd statements she'd ever heard.

"Really! You're really asking me to believe ... it just disappeared?"

Morgan Watson smiled and nodded to her. He didn't know why he had brought it up. Supper had been excellent, he loved pub grub, plus the conversation had been flowing very easily between them. It had been quite awhile since he had been on a first date and had always followed one rule when on one: never to bring up the subject of his cat, Tiberius. He knew many women enjoyed hearing people talk about their cats but whenever he spoke of his, he ended up telling the entire story. Although true, it sounded so far fetched and unbelievable he felt he came off as just another bullshitter trying to impress a woman. In the past whenever he had brought the subject up on a first date, there never was a second.

"Really?" Beth repeated. "It just disappeared, and you expect me to believe that ... that your cat cured itself ... completely ... of diabetes!"

Why did he have to go and break his rule? He knew he should've never mentioned he had a cat which seemed to have entirely beaten the disease until after maybe a few dates, probably more than a few and certainly not on a first date.

Perhaps it was because he had already known her for awhile. He had met Beth in a yoga class he took every Wednesday. Although his buddies kidded him about his weekly classes, he felt he really needed them. Morgan was a fencer and the footwork involved really tightened up his body, especially his hips. Yoga helped open them back up and he felt stretched and loose when class was over.

It seemed no matter how many people had shown up for class, Beth always managed to be on the mat beside, in front, or behind him. He found her so easy to talk with, so after five weeks of chatting before and after class he finally decided to ask her out. Dinner and drinks for a first date was a natural. She had said yes, and they decided to hook up at a downtown craft beer pub after work the next night.

She was thirty-two, just a couple of years younger than Morgan, dark blonde hair touched with champagne highlights, exuberant in nature, and her skin-tight yoga outfit did not hide what Morgan considered to be a very nice figure. Morgan had stood up and smiled when he saw her entering the pub. It was the first time he had seen Beth in street clothes. She looked stunning in her dark dress pants and blue top. Now instead of enjoying the evening with her, he found himself on the defensive.

"Well, it sure seems that way," Morgan said knowing he had to do his best to explain and make it sound like the truth and not some pile of horseshit. He picked up his beer, took a sip and looked around as if seeking help. "You see, Tiberius has, no sorry, I mean once had diabetes. Again, it's really hard to explain.

"I adopted Tiberius from a cat rescue when he was just a little kitten and a year later he developed diabetes. I had to test his blood sugar twice a day and give him a shot every two to three days to keep his glucose levels below ten. Then after about two and a half years his levels seemed to stabilize on their own. It's been three years now since I've given him a shot."

"And you're sure he had diabetes to begin with?"

"That's what Dr. Everingham, his vet, said. For two and a half years I had to give him insulin and it's not cheap. If I went away for a three day weekend, his glucose levels would shoot through the roof and I would have to give him a shot the moment I got back, the next day and sometimes three days in a row to get it back down to where it should be."

"Interesting," Beth said while giving him a look which said she really wasn't sure whether she should buy into his story or not. She changed the subject slightly, "So, why the name 'Tiberius'?"

"I'm a bit of a *Star Trek* fan. If you know the franchise *James T. Kirk* was the captain. The 'T' in the name was short for Tiberius."

Damn! This could be strike two, thought Morgan right after answering. *First, she hears what she considers a bullshit story and now thinks I'm a full out Trekky. Next, she'll be asking me if I live in my parents' basement!*

Beth looked down at her watch and then back at Morgan. "It's almost eight-thirty. I've got to get going. Remember I told you I had plans at later on tonight?"

"Yes you did," he answered and managed to stop their server on the way to request the bill. "I'll pay so you can get going. Your get-together is at nine-thirty if I remember right and I don't want to hold you up."

"No, we're splitting the bill. Maybe I'll let you pick up the tab next time. Let's talk about it next Wednesday after yoga."

Bingo! She wants to go out again. She doesn't think I'm a dick.

Morgan walked Beth out to the sidewalk and hailed a cab for her. They said their goodbyes with a hug outside and she gave him a kiss on the cheek before she climbed into the rear seat and sped off into the night.

The next day, Friday, when Morgan walked into his third floor Toronto condo after work, Tiberius was there as usual, waiting to greet him. Morgan was always amazed by an animal's internal clock. Every morning, Tiberius seemed to know minutes before the alarm went off it was just about to. He stationed himself in front of Morgan's face accordingly so he would be the first thing Morgan saw when he opened his eyes. When Morgan arrived home from work, he was always sitting in the same spot, staring at the door

"Hey Tiberius! How's my boy?" he said bending over to give him a pat. Tiberius never acknowledged the question as he was too busy purring away. After a few pats, Tiberius always flipped over onto his back to get his belly rubbed. Morgan would then scoop him up and walk over to the window so they both could look out. Same routine, every single night after work.

After giving Tiberius a can of cat food for supper, he popped a meatloaf he had made the night before into the oven and went to pack up his fencing bag for practice the next morning. He came back into the living room, dropped his bag by the front door and saw Tiberius sitting in the middle of the room smacking his lips. Obviously, he had enjoyed his supper.

Morgan grabbed a replica early 1800s British sword he had hanging by the door and sliced through the air with it a few times. Tiberius came trotting over as he usually did when Morgan did this, stopped and sat in front of Morgan and watched the blade of the sword. It was knighting time.

"I hereby dub thee, Sir Tiberius of King Street," Morgan declared and tapped the blade of his sword, the edge pointing away from the cat's neck, just in case, on both shoulders as he spoke. This little ritual was something he would never tell his male friends about. Probably not any women either.

Friday nights were pretty much all the same. He would feed Tiberius, change and meet up with some buddies for supper and a few beers. The rest of the weekend would speed by as weekends usually do. He had chores, grocery shopping and fencing practice before he met up with some more friends for Saturday night. He looked forward to Sunday. Usually it would have been a lazy day on the couch, having a couple of craft ales while watching his Blue Jays beat up on the Orioles but instead there was a large fencing tournament he had entered.

When Sunday was over, he would be sore and tired but it would be a good sore and tired from a great workout and hopefully a new gold medal to hang on the wall with all the others.

♦ ♦ ♦

Tiberius was happily digging into his breakfast when Morgan left for work where he was the Procurement Supervisor for a large Canadian wide insurance firm. Many would find his role boring but he quite enjoyed it and found it a challenging position.

He loved living close to the downtown core of the city. It was far enough away from the constant hubbub, noise and action which was downtown Toronto but close enough so it was a short walk to go see the Jays, theatre, movies or hit the many pubs, bars and restaurants plus he was only a twenty minute walk to the office.

After walking about ten minutes, he realized he had forgotten his lunch. He loved cold meatloaf sandwiches and didn't want to waste time lining up for an expensive foodcourt meal which would only be half as good as the sandwiches packed and ready to go in his fridge. So he turned and headed back. Still he wouldn't be late for work, as he always gave himself plenty of time to get there but would now have to grab a streetcar in order to get there on time.

As he stepped off the elevator and walked down the hall to his condo, something didn't feel quite right to him. When he reached the door, he knew something definitely was wrong. The door was not completely closed. The catch rested against the doorframe keeping it slightly ajar and the sound of muffled voices came from inside.

"Just grab the fucking thing and let's get going!"

"God damn it, I'm trying for fuck's sake!"

Morgan dropped the keys back into his suit pocket, gave the door a push and took a quick step inside. Two men were by the bookcase Tiberius glared down from. He was hissing and lashing out at them with his claws fully extended. As both men turned towards Morgan as he came though the door, Tiberius seized the opportunity to escape. He scampered across the top of his protective perch, leapt down onto the back of the chair by the window and raced between the legs of the larger of the two men into the bedroom.

Morgan stood in the doorway for a moment not really knowing what to do and didn't realize he was blocking the intruders' exit. One was quite brawny and the other tall and slight. He was in trouble and had no idea how to handle it.

"What the hell's going on in here?" Morgan asked in a voice full of fire.

"Fuck, get 'em'," the slight man said to the brawny one. Instantly, the large man turned and made a couple of quick steps towards Morgan while pulling something out of his jacket pocket.

Morgan turned and grabbed the replica sword from its mount on the wall. He wheeled around to see the brawny man was almost on him, a long-bladed knife in hand, held high in the air and plunging down toward Morgan's chest.

Instinctively, Morgan's sword cut across the width of his body and with full force slammed into his attacker's wrist. Although the blade had never been sharpened, it did its damage and slashed through the skin and nerves right down to the bone. He heard a loud crack of the bone shattering, followed closely by a loud painful howl. The knife which Morgan's assailant once held fell to the floor.

    Just as in a fencing competition, the move was not yet competed. As the man attempted to grab his smashed wrist, he never saw the blade of the sword being backhanded towards his head. Block the attack and strike. Parry and riposte. It was what Morgan had been taught and had practiced over and over again for years and here, in real life, those moves were saving his life. His attacker had leaned in after being struck on the wrist so Morgan's backhanded slice struck the assailant hard against the side of the man's face with the steel guard instead of the blade and sent him crashing to the floor.

    Morgan spun and saw the thin man coming quickly towards him and was horrified to see he had pulled a handgun from his pocket and was raising it to take aim.

    "Shit!" Morgan yelled as once again his well-practiced reflexes took over. With another yell, he extended the point of his blade fully in milliseconds. He drove off his back foot with explosive speed in a long perfectly executed lunge forward which took his attacker totally by surprise. Unlike a tournament, though, where he felt the satisfaction of his thin blade bending against a heavy Kevlar jacket, he instead felt his hardened military blade drive deep into his attacker's stomach. Blood appeared instantly as the man looked at Morgan in disbelief before he dropped his gun and clutched his oozing wound with both hands.

    Morgan yanked out the blade and turned towards his first attacker, slashing out with his blade as he did in case the man was coming at him again. As he did, he felt something heavy slam into the side of his head.

    The brawny man had recovered enough to clamber to his feet and had grabbed a small brass cannon Morgan had on display on a small table. Holding it by the barrel with his good hand he had swung it blindly in Morgan's direction. The cannon had found its mark and Morgan stumbled sideways against his TV stand, knocking the large screen TV over so it leaned against the wall. Groggy, but still on his feet, he had the presence of mind to keep hold of his sword.

Morgan's eyes watered, his head pounded plus he found himself dizzy and suddenly a little weak. Still he managed to pull himself up straight and held up the sword with the tip of its blade pointing directly at the two injured but still dangerous figures. There seemed no further danger of attack from them, however, as he viewed the surreal scene in front of him.

Both men were standing. The large man was bent over holding his shattered wrist, which was dripping blood onto Morgan's freshly shampooed carpet. More blood was being spilled from the gash in the other's stomach, which he tried to stop by holding the length of arm against the slash as he stumbled towards the door. He yanked down one of Morgan's sweaters which hung on a hook by the door drying after Morgan had washed it and jammed it against the wound saying, "Let's get the fuck out of here!"

The brawny man held onto his bleeding shattered wrist as he looked back across the room. Blood trickled down the side of his head, "What about ..."

"Fuck it!" gasped the other as he lurched clumsily towards the door, "I'm not bleeding to death for that thing."

Morgan made no move to stop them from leaving. *Just hurry up and get the fuck out*, he thought.

When both had left, Morgan moved quickly to the door, slammed it shut and locked the deadbolt. He was shaking and felt as if all the energy had left his body. With his back to the door, he slid down it until he was sitting on the floor using the door as a backrest. His sword lay across his lap and as he reached into his pocket for his phone, he saw Tiberius poke his head around the corner and look at him. The cat warily turned his head back and forth to check out the rest of the room to ensure it was safe before he trotted over to Morgan and onto his lap.

"Shit, Tiberius. We're in big trouble," Morgan said as he picked up the tabby and held him against his shoulder even though he barely had the energy to lift him. "Somebody's found out about you."

Chapter 2

Morgan sat at his small kitchen table with Tiberius in his lap. Across from him, a uniformed police officer sat and after taking sip from his water bottle, summed up what he thought had happened.

"Okay, you walked in on a B and E and the two men you encountered felt trapped. Their fight or flight response kicked in and they decided to fight. From the sounds of it, you're really lucky to just have that bruise on the side of your head. You really should have somebody take a look at it to make sure you're not concussed."

The officer stood up, smiled and gave Morgan a friendly nod before he walked into the living room. "Jeez, there's a shit-full of blood out here!" Morgan heard the officer exclaim.

Although small, the kitchen had two entrances and he heard somebody come in behind him. Startled, he jumped up and turned while Tiberius leaped onto the floor, raced to the other door, stopped and turned around. Once he determined it was still safe, he returned back to Morgan's lap.

"Hey, it's alright," said the woman who had entered the room. She was obviously a detective or something as, although she was not in uniform, Morgan could see a badge clipped to the top front of her pants and a gun in its holster rested up against her side.

Morgan sheepishly sat back down. "Sorry. Still a bit jumpy."

"No doubt. You've had quite a morning," she said as she placed a reassuring hand on his shoulder. "Detective Rogers, Major Crime Unit. Mind if I sit down?"

"Sure." Morgan motioned to the chair just vacated by the other officer. Detective Rogers took the offer and sat down. "I've already talked to three of you, all with the same questions. Are you going to put me through this again?"

"No, we're done with all that. They just wanted to confirm your story is straight. It's a hell of a mess out there."

"Sorry, I didn't have time to clean up," Morgan chuckled as he lowered his head into the palms of both hands. The detective looked at him, then down to her small notebook.

"Well, it looks like they didn't knock the sense of humour out of you."

Detective Rogers got up and walked over to the fridge and opened the door. She saw full drawers of vegetables, a package of chicken breasts, two of rows of diet cola, a dozen or so craft beer from four different breweries, three refillable full water bottles on the door and a jug of water with a filtering system in it.

"Looks like you eat healthy for the most part," she said picking up a can of Black Oak Pale Ale. "Hey, one of my favourite breweries. This one's particularly good." She put it back, looked over to where Morgan sat and saw his empty glass. "You should have something more to drink. How about some water?"

"No but go ahead and grab something for yourself or the boys in there." She ignored his offer, took one of the water bottles from the door and handed it to him. Morgan screwed off the top and gulped down a quarter of it. Some spilled onto his chin.

"Damn it," he muttered as he wiped it away with his hand. Now she was closer he could read her badge which was good as he had already forgotten her name, "thanks Officer ... Rogers, is it? I guess I was thirstier than I thought ... a little more rattled too."

"Detective. Detective Rogers."

"Sorry."

His head was starting to clear from the pain killers he had taken just before the police arrived. For the first time since he saw her when he answered the door to let everybody in, he noticed how attractive she was. Dark, slightly mussed shoulder length hair framed an attractive face and set off her sapphire blue eyes. There was a small scar on her left cheek which only added to her good looks instead of taking from them. Hidden underneath her no nonsense outfit, she looked to have a very firm, in shape body which one would expect of someone in her line of work.

"No problem," she answered, while tearing a sheet of paper towel off a roll which sat on the counter and handing it to him. "The consensus we've arrived at here is this was a normal everyday break and enter, a B and E, which escalated when you walked in on them. I've been told though, you think differently."

"Officer Rogers ... I mean Detective ... sorry," he said as he set the bottle of water down and leaned towards where she was seated across from him. She spoke with an air of authority but there was something about her which made him believe he might at least be able to sow a seed of doubt in her that this was not indeed a typical break and enter. He sighed and continued, "When I walked in, the two of them weren't ransacking the place looking for money or valuables or any shit like that. I know it sounds crazy but they seemed to be after Tiberius. They had him trapped up on the bookshelf. He was what they wanted!"

"Tiberius. Your cat?"

Morgan nodded.

"Why?"

"How the fuck should I know?" He stopped for a moment. "Sorry."

"For what?"

"For swearing. Using the "F" bomb. I should be able to control my language more."

"Because I'm a woman?"

She didn't look annoyed when she asked but her question did have a slight bit of tone to it. "Yes ... no ... fuck, I don't know."

"So why do you think they wanted your cat?"

"I have no idea," Morgan said as he looked down at the floor and saw a small coffee stain. For some reason, he wished it was cleaner right now, even though he was sitting there in a blood-stained shirt and pants." He's a cat. A tabby. Special to me, of course, but why anybody would want to take him, I don't know."

"Mr. Watson…"

"Morgan, please."

"Okay. Morgan, if you think they were after your cat, there must be a reason. Some little detail you don't think is important but could help us in our investigation."

Morgan didn't answer. Detective Rogers leaned back in her chair. Something in his story didn't seem right about the series of events.

"Maybe your cat, what's his name? Tiberius?"

Morgan nodded. He was becoming too tired to speak much more and his head started to pound.

"Let's go back and reconstruct what could have happened. These two strangers break in. They startle Tiberius, who in self-defence, lashes out with a paw and scratches one of them. Thinking you're gone for the day, they figured they had time for some revenge. Catch him, hurt him, kill him. After all, they didn't hesitate to try to kill you."

Morgan absentmindedly rubbed the side of his head where he was struck with the cannon. "No. the more I think about it, I'm sure they were after him!"

"Did they say anything, something which would make you believe that?"

Morgan sat and replayed the events in his mind.

"Now I think of it, yes, they did. On the way out, one of them said something about not wanting to die for him or something like that."

A uniformed officer stepped into the kitchen and interrupted. "Are you almost finished here, Detective? The forensic guys have everything they need and are packing up. Mr. Watson, off the record, they want to thank you for your blade work. Lots of great blood samples around. Made their job a lot easier but, damn it, this place of yours is going to take some time to clean and sanitize. I'd think of a new carpet rather than having it cleaned if I were you."

The detective nodded and the officer stepped back out. She looked at Morgan and smiled for the first time, "It must have been quite the surprise for those two who broke in. They weren't expecting a visitor, especially one with a sword and who really knows how to use it."

"Funny, when I first took up fencing it was to get myself up off the couch at night and away from the TV. Who knew one day it would save my life?"

The detective walked around the table and gently grabbed the side of his face to give his injury a closer look. "You have a nasty welt on the side of your head. You should have looked at."

"First I want to get Tiberius over to his vet, Doctor Everingham, to make sure he's alright."

"The vet clinic on Queen by Niagara?'

"That's right. Why?"

"No reason. Just wondering."

The detective stood up and walked through the door behind her and into the living room. By the time Morgan had drained the last of his water, Detective Rogers had returned. Morgan sat down his bottle and looked up as she put her hands on the table across from him and leaned towards him. Even in a fully buttoned-up top, she gained his full attention and for a moment, he forgot about his sore head.

"Here's what's going to happen. You and Tiberius are coming with me. We're going to drop Tiberius off at the vet and then I'll run you over to the hospital. The fact this is a police case will get the both of you looked at a lot quicker."

Morgan got up and with Tiberius in his arms followed her into the living room. This was the first time since this all happened that he had a chance to really look around and it was a mess.

Splashes of bright red movie-style blood decorated the walls. There were a few dark red, sticky-looking areas in the carpet, and a large smear by the front door. The floor was littered with various items which had been knocked off his shelves. His large flat screen TV was knocked over and leaning against the wall with its glass shattered. For some reason, the blue latex gloves the investigators wore seemed so bright and jumped out at him.

One of the gloved officers was holding Morgan's bloodied sword and seemed to be studying it. He looked up at Morgan. "So, you fought off two men, one with a military grade knife and another with a gun with this? Great work, Swordsman."

Morgan looked down and chuckled a little sheepishly.

Detective Rogers came up beside him. "What do you want to do after the two of you are checked out? You probably don't want to come back and stay in this mess. Do you have somebody to stay with?"

Morgan thought for a moment. Most of his friends didn't have cats. He didn't want to bother those who did as their cats might not get along with having a strange cat in their domain. There was also the fact he didn't want to put any of his friends in the danger he thought he and Tiberius might be in.

"I think Tiberius and I will just grab a hotel for a night or two, at least 'til I can call my insurance company and get somebody in to clean this place. "

"Good idea. Take a moment, grab some of your things and something to put Tiberius in. Once you two have been looked at, I'll run you over to a hotel."

"Sounds like you're going way above and beyond. Thank you."

"Usually we'd just call a paramedic for you and be done but you've had one hell of a day." Rogers stepped closer, smiled and stroked Tiberius. "And we need to have this guy looked after too and there's no way an ambulance would detour to a vet. Just don't tell my boss!"

Morgan returned her smile and walked across the living room to his bedroom, doing his best not to step in any of the blood patches along the way. He closed the bedroom door, sat Tiberius on the bed. After he had changed into some clean clothes Morgan sat down beside him and ran his hand down Tiberius's head and along the top of his back a couple of times, which started some loud purring. Morgan then scooped up Tiberius and deposited him into the collapsible canvas pet carrier which he always had open by his closet in case of an emergency. Tiberius looked up unhappily at him through the mesh.

"Yes, you were a brave boy with those assholes. They didn't know what they were up against with you and me." Morgan picked up the carrier and peered in closer. It was like he was talking to a child as he explained, "No need to be nervous. The detective's going to take us for a ride so we can get ourselves looked after."

Hmmm, I wonder what it would be like to date a cop?

Chapter 3

The first stop was to the Queen West Animal Hospital. Although the clinic was busy, when Dr. Everingham heard what had happened, he immediately took Tiberius's carrier, held it up and peered inside. Tiberius stared back and pressed his nose against the mesh.

"He doesn't look to be in any distress considering what he just been through," the doctor reported. "I want to take him to the back, though, and give him a thorough going over to ensure he's one hundred percent. No hidden scratches, cuts, bruises, anything unusual. I also want to take a blood sample to ensure he wasn't slipped anything. Could you come back in about an hour or so?"

"Sure, "confirmed the detective. She turned to Morgan. "Alright, there's one down Gives me enough time to run you over to the hospital. If it looks like you're going to be long, I'll come back for Tiberius, then head back for you. We still need find a hotel for you too, one which allows animals."

"I don't want to leave Tiberius alone," Morgan pleaded. "He's not safe. Somebody's after him, for whatever reason."

"Hey, you need have that welt on your head looked at. You might be concussed." Seeing Morgan was visibly upset at leaving Tiberius behind, the detective reached out and placed her hand on his shoulder in a reassuring manner. "Look. Tiberius will be fine. He's in a safe place. Just to be sure, I'll let the staff know not to release him to anybody but you or me."

"So you think there's something going on too!"

"No. I just want you to relax."

They climbed into her unmarked squad car. Morgan was glad she was letting him ride up front, rather than in the back like a criminal. It was a short ten-minute drive to Toronto Western Hospital. His silence concerned her. Maybe he was injured more than she originally thought.

The detective looked over at Morgan, his head being held up by his arm, which was wedged against the car window. She had been promoted to the Major Crime Unit just three weeks before. It was a lot of hard work and long hours of study to get there and now here she was chauffeuring around this guy and his cat. Not the dream case she had envisioned when she received her new badge but then again, she was the one who suggested it.

He seems to be a nice enough guy, she thought looking back to the road. Queen Street was jammed with traffic. *But man, he can sure handle himself in a crisis. I've never heard of guy with a sword taking down two perps. Of course, I've never heard of a guy defending himself with a sword at all! Damn it, one even had a gun and got the worst of it.* She chuckled softly. Morgan didn't seem to notice. *He sure loves that cat. I have to figure out a way to convince him this was just a B and E. I've got a job to do and it's not baby sitting a cat.*

Paula didn't have any cats of her own. She thought they were okay but didn't like how aloof they could be. One day she hoped to get a dog, but only if her hours ever became normal but never would think of having a cat. Despite this, she liked how Morgan, who was a good looking, well built guy, tough enough not to back down from a fight, was comfortable enough with himself to show the soft side of his persona with Tiberius.

She pulled into emergency and guided Morgan inside. After years of working in the division, she came to know many of the emergency room doctors and looked for a familiar face. She spotted Dr. Campbell, waved him over, explained what had happened and asked if he could take Morgan in fairly quickly. The doctor looked around and saw there were no life or death cases waiting for him.

"Sure, I don't see a problem Paula. Everything's under control here at the moment. Mr. Watson, could you come with me please."

As they passed the detective, Morgan looked her way and smiled, "Paula. Nice name. I like it."

"Detective Rogers to you," she replied back with a slight smile on her lips. For some reason she liked that he now knew her first name.

Although she knew all the hospitals in the area would be canvassed to see if any patients had come in with the kind of injuries Morgan had dished out, Paula went to the emergency check in desk and asked anyway. The answer, as expected, was negative.

She stepped outside into the shade of the canopy over the main entrance. Something was bothering her, and she couldn't put a finger on it. Paula headed back out to her squad car and flipped open the laptop attached to the front seat. After scrolling through some area incidents from the night before, one caught her eye. She pulled out her cell phone and called into the station.

"Hey, Jim. Paula. Didn't I see something about a break in over the weekend at the Queen West Animal Clinic?"

"I don't know, I just came on duty. Let me have a look," Jim replied. There was a short pause. "Yup, here it is. There was a break-in on Saturday night. Time unknown.

It seems the clinic was well-secured, all windows barred. Apparently, somebody managed pull the bars off of a small basement window in the back. Turned out they were quite rusty. Alright, it says here some drugs were taken and things were messed up a little. They unlocked and left via the rear door. Nothing really special. Why?"

Paula sat quiet for a moment. "Not sure. I'm working a case in that hood and was just there on something different. Thanks Jim." She put the phone back into her pocket and headed back into the hospital.

She had an uneasy feeling. Something was coming together in her mind, but she didn't know what or why. Inside the hospital, Paula asked to see Morgan and was led to his bed in the ward. She had to be cool about this.

"How's the head?"

"Sore. Your doctor friend gave me a quick going over but was called away. Look, I don't know how long I'm going to be here, and I don't want Tiberius left alone for too long. I know you don't believe me but somebody's after him. I'm sure."

"Look, I know you're worried. I'll head over now and get him. Then you can relax. Sound good?"

"I really do appreciate it."

"You're probably overreacting but then I might too in your situation. It might take me a little while with traffic so don't panic if I'm not back right away. In the meantime, just relax and try to get some rest. Tiberius is in good hands." She turned to walk away, stopped for a moment and turned slightly back towards him, "I may not have a sword like you but I do have a gun."

He smiled.

Once outside the emergency ward, Paula rushed over to her car and headed back to the clinic as fast as she could. She found a half a block from the clinic under a 'no parking sign' went inside and saw Dr. Everingham coming out of an exam room. He motioned for her to follow him to an exam room near the back. Before going inside, he asked a nurse to get Tiberius.

"He's fine," the vet said. "He was probably scared at the time, but he has no physical injuries. No cuts, welts, sores of any kind. We're sending out some blood for testing just in case."

"I'm glad to hear it. Mr. Watson will be too. By the way, I was told this clinic was broken into Saturday night."

"Yes, it was. We do our best to keep everything locked up tight, but the junkies still find ways. We had somebody come in to fix the bars and check the one's on the other windows."

"Let me ask you something. If somebody broke in, just how easy would it be for them to find information on a pet and it's owner?"

"What do you mean?"

"Okay, let me start by asking what kind of drugs were taken? Was there anything which value on the street?"

"No, not really. It just looked like a grab and go. Nothing anybody would want or could use to get high. We keep that stuff locked up tight and not in an obvious spot. My guess is they were just amateurs."

The door slid open behind Paula and the nurse handed Tiberius in the carrier to the doctor, who set it on the table. Dr. Everingham took Tiberius from the case and cradled him against his chest.

Paula reached out and stroked Tiberius. "Maybe they weren't. Let's say a person wanted to find somebody and where they lived but," she held up a finger as she worked the idea out loud, "they don't know the name of the person they are after. They just know the name of their pet and its vet. Wouldn't this be the best place to find the name, address and phone number of that person? Just make it look like a robbery and nobody's the wiser?"

"They don't know the persons name?" Dr. Everingham was cut off before he could say more when the door behind Paula slid open part way and a nurse leaned her head inside. She looked troubled, "Doctor, somebody's here wanting to pick up Tiberius."

Paula looked at the vet. "Put him back into the carrier and stay here." She stepped to the door and quietly asked the nurse, "Don't point but where is he?"

"He's the one beside the desk by the door."

Paula leaned out into the hall and took a look. "Brown shirt and pants? The one with his back to us looking outside?"

"Yes."

The detective stepped into the hall and walked as naturally as she could past the two exam rooms which separated them. So far she was lucky. He was still looking away. When she was about six feet away the man turned and saw her approaching. It wasn't her demeanour which alerted him but the badge which hung from her hip. He turned to his left, grabbed the computer monitor on the desk, threw it in her direction and headed to the door, knocking aside a young couple who were coming in, each holding a carrier.

The young woman managed to remain upright with her carrier in hand but her male friend had violently smacked the back of his head hard against the door frame and tumbled forward towards the street, dropping his carrier and the howling cat it contained as he did.

Paula pushed the door open as far as she could. The woman with the carrier had quickly recovered from her shock and moved to see if her friend was alright. His feet were sprawled on the bottom step and his body lay across the sidewalk. He was conscious and rolled over across the entrance holding his head. The two people and their carriers made it difficult for Paula to pass. She half climbed, half leapt over them all, turned and started to pursue. She barely had a glance at the suspect's face and really only knew he was dressed in brown with brown shoes.

Although he only had a five or ten second head start on her, she ran a dozen or so steps east along Queen Street looking at both sides of the street as she went but found he was nowhere in sight. Paula dashed down the sidewalk, slowing at each alley she passed to take a look down. At the first street corner, she turned south and jogged to the first laneway which ran parallel to Queen Street. Paula stopped and looked first right and then left before she swore and swung a fist through the air as she did.

"Shit!"

The laneway was completely empty. She had lost him.

She quickly made her way back to the clinic where she found the two cats and people who were knocked out of the way during the escape were alright. The man held a hand to the back of his head while he was being looked after by Dr. Everingham and one of the nurses. She stopped to take a look herself. It was nothing serious, just a little bump. Plus, he would have a story to tell all his friends for weeks to come.

Damn it, she thought. *There's going to be a lot of paperwork to do tonight.*

She tapped Dr. Everingham on the shoulder and motioned for him to the same exam room where they had left Tiberius. They found him still safe in his carrier, his nose pressed up against the mesh.

"Okay, doctor. What's so God damn special about this cat?"

"Tiberius ... why?"

"Because there was a break in at Morgan Watson's condo this morning a day after there was a break-in here. Because, he keeps insisting, they were focused on grabbing Tiberius. Because just now, somebody we don't know tried to pick up Tiberius to take him to who knows where. So, tell me. What the hell's so unusual or special about this cat?"

Everingham unzipped the carrier, took out Tiberius and cradled him, "Detective, I've been treating this guy since Mr. Watson first picked him up from a cat rescue. He came down with diabetes, which we treated for a couple of years. Then it went just disappeared."

"Disappeared?"

"Yes, that's right." The vet handed Tiberius to the detective and called up Tiberius's file on the room's computer terminal. Paula was quite surprised when Tiberius snuggled close against her. "He had insulin shots almost every other day for thirty-one months and then for the next few months his level remained below but close to ten. No shots were required. After about nine months his glucose dropped down around five and stayed there. Below seven is normal."

"And he's been at that level for how long?"

"A little over three years now. I consider him cured although the experts don't, at least not yet."

Tiberius shifted and now had a paw on each of Paula's shoulders and started to purr. She smiled as she petted him. "He is a sweetie."

"Oh, yes. The nurses here all love him, and he eats it all up."

"Let's say he did somehow cure himself. Is there a way this could be adapted as a treatment for humans?"

"Possibly but I doubt it. Animals have amazing recovery systems, totally different from a human. It's not really unusual for a feline to go long periods of time without a shot. Many cats, for instance, from about twenty to fifty percent or more, can go into remission a few weeks after receiving insulin. In fact, complications people with diabetes have such as diseases of the kidney, coronary arteries and blood vessels rarely happen with diabetic cats.

"Tiberius is different because of the length of time he was dependant on insulin before going into full remission. What we did after a year when we felt he was no longer insulin dependent was report the case to the JDRF." He saw she did not understand the acronym, "The Juvenile

Diabetes Research Foundation. They appreciate any feedback which may help them to find a cure. They said to just keep monitoring and send them blood samples every quarter. You have to realize for humans, if something special could come of this, they would let me know. They definitely would want to study Tiberius more closely."

Paula pondered for a moment what the doctor had just explained and the events which had unfolded in the short few hours since she came on the case. She turned her head and looked into Tiberius's eyes. *Okay, so you are special. Medically special but it seems from what I've heard here, not special enough, she thought. But what if ... shit! What if somebody had heard about this cat? What if THEY think they can get a cure from him? Oh damn! What if Morgan's right? What if somebody is after Tiberius? If that's the case, then they're both in danger!*

Chapter 4

Not only did he have a fitful sleep but during the night Morgan had been awakened a couple of times by noises in the hall. Both times he had quickly reached over and grabbed the seventeen-inch, 1907 British Enfield bayonet he had lying on the covers beside him. The police may have had taken the sword he defended himself with in the attack but there was no way he was going to leave his condo without a weapon. The bayonet, which an uncle had left to him when he passed away, would do just fine.

Both times he had thrown back the covers and swung his feet to the floor. Then he would sit, staring at the hotel room door with beads of sweat forming across his forehead. Although he tried to breathe as quietly as he could, he could hear each breath which sounded shaky and panicked. The rhythm of his heartbeat seemed to fill the room. For five minutes he would just sit and stare intently at the door as if it would swing open at any second and he would have to defend himself once again. Meanwhile Tiberius, startled from his deep sleep, would leap off the bed and scramble up to the safety of the top of the armoire which housed the TV, sit and stare back down at Morgan.

He had to remind himself over and over he was in a hotel room and a hotel had people who would be returning to their rooms after a night out. *Why do people have to be so God damned noisy? Crap, this is a weeknight. Party on the weekend, Assholes,* he thought each time before he would hear a door close farther down the hall. *Relax Asshole. They're not partying, just going back to their rooms. Relax, damn it. Relax!*

Detective Paula, which was how he referred to her in his mind, had assured him they would be safe. Still he didn't sleep easy. At least now after the second attempt to take Tiberius, she believed him, believed that he and Tiberius were in trouble. He guessed it was why she accompanied him and Tiberius up to their room. How did she put it after she had unlocked, then opened the door and handed the key back to Morgan? "I know you're nervous. I would be too but you're safe. This is one hotel room. One single hotel room in all of Toronto, the fourth largest city in North America ... a city with hundreds of hotels and thousands of rooms. Now do you really think anybody could find you tonight?" He remembered how he liked it when she had placed her hand reassuringly on his arm as she spoke.

'You're safe, Morgan. You're safe. Detective Paula was right. Just try to get some sleep,' he thought before he laid back down and pulled the covers over him. In many ways, he was glad Tiberius, being a tabby, was quite dog-like. All he had to do was pat the bed a couple of times and Tiberius would jump down from his perch and onto the bed where he would curl up against his feet. *We're safe, we're safe, we're safe,* Morgan thought over and over before he drifted off into another fitful sleep.

♦ ♦ ♦

Paula Rogers gave her pillow a punch before setting it down at the head of the bed and tossing the covers over it. The day before when she returned to the station, she was called in to see her commander regarding Morgan and Tiberius or what was simply called the 'Watson home invasion', she had received what she considered a total overreaction from him regarding the days events.

"What in hell were you even doing at the vets?" Detective Sergeant Andrew Lin had asked the moment she stepped into his office. His eyes pierced hers while awaiting an answer, "Well? Why were you there? The cat wasn't injured at all. Shouldn't he have been just locked in the bedroom while the paramedics took Watson to the hospital?"

"In my defence, Sir, they arrived at the scene the same time as we did but I felt the victim didn't need immediate medical treatment requiring an ambulance."

"You didn't answer my question. Why were you at the vet?"

"It's in my report." Paula knew she wasn't going to win this one but had to defend herself. Deep down she knew she was right.

"I want you to explain it to me," the sergeant had said slowly and quietly.

"Mr. Watson received a nasty welt and cut on his head and I felt he should go to the hospital to check for concussion. He felt Tiberius was the target of the robbery and might have been drugged or injured. He wanted him checked out at the vet before he would agree to go to the hospital. It turned out his instincts were right. The cat was the target. If I hadn't been there, who knows what might have happened to Tiberius."

"It seems like you've become quite fond of this Tiberius. Most would refer to him as 'the cat'. You're talking about him as if he were human."

"No, Sir. I just spent some time with it." She was grateful she came out quickly with "it" and not Tiberius.

She remembered how the sergeant had leaned back in his chair, folded his arms together and looked down. For what seemed like an hour but was probably only ten seconds or so, she waited and shifted her stance.

"Detective, I know you're new to this department and so far, I've had great reports about you. Yesterday was your first day solo and this incident turned out to be an unusual situation. You have to realize you didn't stop this attempt because of your instincts. You stopped it because you happened to be doing a nice thing and got lucky. Ninety-nine percent of the time doing something like this would be a waste of your time, the departments' time and the taxpayer's dollar."

"I thought our duty was to the public."

She remembered how the Detective Sergeant slowly rose from his chair before shouting, "Not as a God damn fucking chauffeur! You're a detective remember that. You want to drive people around this city, get a job with Uber. Now get the hell out of here!"

She had turned to the door when the sergeant beckoned to her. His voice had returned to normal, "Oh, one more thing. You're off the Watson case. We have very little resources to utilize and having you guard a cat is not a very effective use of our time. We're not forgetting about the assault. Not for a moment. It's a serious matter but not one for you to be focused on. Tomorrow I'm putting you out there with a partner. My feeling is you became attached to this case too quickly and will find it hard to let go."

Her mind drifted back to the present. *Too attached! I've been a cop for 10 years and I've never let myself get too close to any case. Hell, he probably thinks that because I'm new and a woman. Asshole!* She punched the covered pillow a few times, then threw back the covers and picked it up and fired against the wall.

It was three hours before she was to report for duty. She knew she wasn't too close to this case and could let it go. First though, she thought before she reported in she would pay Morgan a visit and explain what her department knew up to this point and what would be happening from here. *It's my duty and only proper it comes from me. Besides, they can't give me crap for what I do on my own time.*

♦ ♦ ♦

When Morgan woke up the next morning and raised his head, he saw Tiberius, who had been sleeping at his feet, lift his head and stare right back at him. Then they both looked around the strange hotel room to remind them as to where they were. *Damn, it wasn't a dream.*

"Hey, Tiberius, how's my boy? How'd you'd like sleeping in this strange room?"

It was the cue for Tiberius to give a massive yawn before he got up to his feet, stepped across Morgan's legs and walk slowly up the side of the bed so he was close enough to receive a few pats. He then fell over onto his side, received a few strokes across his rear haunches and with another strange sounding meow, flopped over onto his other side to get another few pats. Back and forth he flip-flopped until after a minute or so. Morgan finally decide to get his day going so he sat up, swung his feet off the bed and felt a throbbing pain in the side of his head, a reminder of the events the day before.

"Okay my boy. Let's see. I've already told my office about the break-in, minus some of the gorier details and now we have the rest of the week off. The cleaners are coming in to clean up the mess at noon and we need to be there. After that, I don't know." He kept running his hand down Tiberius's back as he spoke. Tiberius looked up at Morgan like he understood but like most tabbies he was really just enjoying the attention. "I'm not sure how today is going to play out but what I do know is as much as you hate being hauled around in your carrier, I'm not leaving you alone."

Before he showered, Morgan set out some wet food for Tiberius. After checking into the hotel, he and Tiberius had dropped into a pet store a couple of blocks away for some food, a litter box and cat litter. Morgan was glad Detective Paula had brought them to this hotel. It was a three star, clean but didn't allow pets. Paula had convinced them otherwise, and for an extra twenty-five dollars a night, Tiberius was reluctantly allowed in as a guest.

After showering and changing, Morgan suddenly noticed how hungry he was. The hotel didn't have room service and although it offered a continental breakfast Morgan figured it was probably cereal, dry muffins, packaged cream cheese, peanut butter, jam and toast, none of which appealed to him. He didn't want to cram Tiberius into his carrier just for some crappy food and he couldn't take Tiberius to a restaurant. He thought about hitting a drive-through before he realized he didn't have a car. It was back at the condo.

A knock at his door took him away from his pondering and when he opened the door he was surprised to find Detective Paula standing there holding a coffee shop bag and a tray with two coffees, a small pile of sweeteners and sugar. Morgan smiled and invited her in.

"I'm glad to see you, Detective," he said as she made her way to a table by the window. She set down the tray and removed a couple of freshly made bagels and butter from the bag. He could tell from their aroma they were made sometime in the past couple of hours.

"Only because I have food."

"No. You could be empty handed, and I would still be glad to see you." He pulled out a chair for her and then moved to another. "Of course, the food sure does help. Have a seat, Detective."

"I'm off-duty at the moment so please call me Paula. Now dig in. You're probably starving."

"Oh yeah. You got that right," he said as he opened up a bagel and spread some butter on it. He noted she added just a little cream and one sugar pack to her coffee. He might have the occasion in the future to buy her, or better yet, make her a coffee and now he knew how she liked it.

They talked sipped coffee and ate bagels while Tiberius lay on the bed and watched. Yesterday Paula's tone was far more formal, professional and serious than this morning, he thought. After about five minutes of pleasant chatter of the day's weather, the Blue Jays win, *oh my God, she's a fan*, and other impersonal things, Paula looked over to the bed at Tiberius. "He hasn't taken his eyes off of us since we sat down."

"He's a cat. He's nosey."

Paula looked past Tiberius to the bayonet which was still lying on the bed. "How many swords do you own?"

"The one your police friends took and this one, although it's not a sword but a bayonet. After yesterday I felt better having it here with me. After all, I didn't have you and your gun around to protect me." He smiled as the last sentence came out. "However, you did save me from starvation this morning coming here with all this."

"Well, I thought bringing you something to eat might also take the edge off of some bad news I have," she saw his smile fade as she spoke. "I'm off the case."

"Why? What the hell's going on? What about Tiberius? Is it because he's a cat and not a kid?"

"No it's not that. No, no. We have people digging around about this. Just not me." Paula noticed how Morgan had a slight look of alarm on his face and knew she had better show he and Tiberius were not being forgotten. *Tiberius! Yesterday he was just a cat. Now I think of him as Tiberius.*

"Look, we found out a lot yesterday, more than we usually do on day-one of a home invasion," she explained in a low reassuring voice. "There were fingerprints all over the gun and knife. They may have been wearing gloves when they broke in but they never expected to lose their weapons, so their old prints were all over them. We also have their blood for the trial when we do catch them, and we will, to really nail down a conviction."

"You know who they are?"

"Yeah. They're small time hoods with a history of break and enters, small store robberies, muggings, that sort of thing. They've been locked up before. This time with an assault charge added, they'll be put away for a lot longer."

"Great. Once you guys catch them, we can find out who hired them and why."

She reached over and took hold of his hand which was resting on the table. "That's the hope."

Suddenly realizing what she had done, she slowly leaned back in her chair so her hand slipped out of his. There was silence and for a moment their eyes locked. *Christ Paula,* she thought, *how unprofessional!*

She got up from the table and unconsciously reached into her jacket pocket and touched her badge. "I don't have to be in for another hour so why don't I drive you back to your place to pick up some more things if you like, plus you can get your car? Tiberius should be fine here."

"Thanks, I appreciate it but for the next few days, at least till I get some things figured out, Tiberius goes where I go."

"I understand."

He went over and sat on the bed and ran his hand down Tiberius's head and across his back a few times before scooping him and with an apology, placed him in the carrier. He placed the carrier on the bed and as he sat back in his chair and put on his shoes, he watched from the corner of his eye as Paula went over and started running her finger along the carrier mesh and up against Tiberius's nose. "Hey little guy, how about another ride in my car?"

Morgan picked up the carrier bag and followed Paula to the elevator, which they took to the lobby. It was a small, crowded area with a reception desk with a clerk behind it busy assisting a couple checking in. Three chairs and a small table were set by the window, with one of the chairs occupied by a man reading a newspaper. It was funny to Morgan. He usually didn't pay much attention to details. Now he seemed wired into the world around him.

They stepped out into the bright sun. As she walked, Paula pointed in the direction she was parked. Morgan, who awkwardly held the carrier out from his side as he walked so it wouldn't bounce up against his leg caused him to move much slower and he started to lag four or five feet behind.

He had just cleared the driveway when something hard slammed into the back of his neck and he felt the carrier being wrenched from his hand as he fell against the side of a parked car.

"Get back here you bastard!" he cussed loudly as he stumbled forward in an attempt to stop his assailant.

Alerted by Morgan's panicked yell, Paula turned in time to see Morgan take a few steps forward before falling hard to the pavement. The attacker, who was in full flight, carrier in hand, was just a few steps away from her. Instead of stepping in front of him and trying to take him down in a head on collision, one she was bound to lose, she stepped quickly to the side to seemingly let him continue. As he was about to pass, she drove into his side with all her weight, her shoulder coming in under his armpit which sent them both off their feet.

The assailant hit the ground hard with loud grunt with Paula landing on top of him. In the collision he had let go of the carrier. Tiberius let out a howl as his case landed and tumbled end over end a few times.

Morgan looked up in time to see the two go sprawling. *She got him!* He thought as he watched as Paula grabbed the man by his right arm and lever him over onto his belly with the arm pulled up his back. Handcuffs seemed to appear out of nowhere and she snapped one cuff over the wrist she held, before reaching for the other arm.

As Morgan scrambled to his feet, he was horrified to see a second man come up behind her, hand raised, holding a knife. He was still a couple of steps away from being able to strike when Morgan shouted out a warning.

Paula spun her head around and realizing what was about to happen, rolled off her prisoner, onto her back and kicked out hard against the knife man's left knee with her right foot. The man screamed as he crumbled to the ground in pain.

It was enough of a distraction for the original attacker, who with only one hand cuffed, to roll over and send an elbow hard against Paula's upper chest just below her throat, which sent her onto her back as she yelled in pain. The man clambered to his feet, took a quick look over at Tiberius in his carrier and then to Morgan who was coming at him. The man then decided it was best to get away and tried to run but Morgan was already on him.

Morgan grabbed him and the two kept their feet as they struggled, cursed and stumbled onto the sidewalk. Finally, Morgan managed to force him off balance and threw him up against the rear of a parked van.

"Fuck this!" the attacker growled. With his free hand he pulled a revolver and was about to fire when Paula came charging in with a loud yell. Distracted, the gunman turned in her direction but was too late as Paula moving as fast as she could, hurled herself into his side, knocking him backwards onto the street. Her momentum sent her into Morgan who grabbed onto her waist and stopped her from sprawling into the busy street.

There was a loud screech of tires, followed by a sickening crunch and thud. Both Morgan and Paula turned in time to see the man's body end its short flight through the air, hit the road hard and flop like a rag doll as he rolled a few times down the pavement.

The driver sat behind the wheel in shock as Morgan and Paula raced over. Paula knelt over the still body while Morgan could only stand and stare down. Blood covered the man's face. His forehead had sustained a huge gash and his skull looked to be caved in slightly over his left eye, plus his neck was grossly twisted in a very unnatural way, a sure indication he was dead.

Paula stood back up and looked back over to the grassy area where this all started. The man with the shattered kneecap had the carrier and was trying to limp away. Paula held up a finger to the driver motioning him to stay and raced back to stop the attempted escape, followed a few steps behind by Morgan.

The man stopped for a moment reaching into his pocket, came out with a gun and immediately fired. The bullet missed Paula and smashed the window of a parked car. There was no time for a second shot as Paula grabbed the man's gun arm, yanked it upwards, then sent a crushing knee to his groin. The man dropped his gun, howled and grabbed his crotch with both hands as he sank to the ground. A second set of handcuffs came out and this time Paula was successful in cuffing both wrists behind him.

The shot had stopped Morgan in his tracks. He stood frozen for a moment, watching as the second attacker cursed and wailed in pain as Paula roughly slapped the cuffs on. Then he heard a loud cat howl and he raced over to the carrier which held Tiberius. Morgan picked it and carried it back to where Paula sat beside her prisoner in her dirty, grass stained pants, with her ripped pant legs stretched out in front of her. He flopped to the ground beside her.

"You alright?" he asked.

"Yeah, thanks ... You?"

"Rattled but still in one piece."

For a moment they sat quietly as a crowd started to form around the broken body on the street. Many looked at the dead man, then over to the two figures sitting with an animal carrier and a cuffed cussing man on his stomach. Sirens could be heard in the distance.

"Morgan."

"Yes Paula?"

"When my people arrive, please call me detective."

Morgan understood and nodded. "This just became a very long day."

Morgan, without taking his eyes off Paula pushed the hair back off his forehead, then wiped the sweat and grit from it with the back of his hand, "You saved my life detective. Thanks."

"Mr. Watson. You saved mine. Thanks."

She gave a small chuckle then her face turned serious as she got up and made her way over to greet the officers getting out of the squad car which had just arrived.

Chapter 5

Halina Shimon sat in the small undecorated boardroom and waited. The room was devoid of any furnishings except for a boardroom table and a dozen chairs. No paintings, art or corporate morale boosting banners hung on the walls. Known as the bunker or the paranoia room, it was windowless and swept daily for bugs, recorders and listening devices. This was the only room where company secrets were allowed to be shared.

The Constance Addison Research Laboratories was a privately funded research facility looking for a way to cure for diabetes or at least to develop a drug which could be taken orally instead of by insulin injections. While alive Constance Addison was a diabetic, one who also enjoyed a good party. She had come from old money and was the last surviving child of the family line. Constance had started up a trust to fund private diabetic research at her facility three years before she died of diabetic complications due to her lifestyle. As she had never married, her will had bequeathed her fortune to the facility.

Halina was an endocrinologist with the company, one trained to deal with and research diseases related to glands. In Halina's case, her focus was on the pancreas and hormones which might be used to replace the insulin the pancreas produced. She had bounced around as a researcher for various laboratories, mostly for cancer, but her passion was developing a cure for diabetes. Finally, she was hired by 'Connie labs' as it was nicknamed, as a junior researcher.

For six months she had been with the lab which had made great inroads in assisting in solving a major problem, developing an insulin pill which could be taken by diabetics instead of injection. The problem with taking insulin orally was the acids in the stomach broke down the oral insulin before it could be absorbed into the stomach lining and make its way to a person's liver. Halina's contribution to this research was so valuable she had risen quickly to senior researcher and in the process had gained the ear of Dr. Leo Sturgess, the man in charge of the entire operation.

Halina sighed, pushed aside her tea, stared at the door of the bunker and waited. She had to give an update and was not sure exactly how she could explain it. Finally the door opened and Dr. Leo Sturgess came through and sat down at the end of the boardroom table so he was close to the end and on an angle to her.

He wore a white lab jacket with three different coloured pens sticking out of the front pocket. In his early sixties, his thinning curly grey hair wrapped itself around a large bald area. Always serious, his piercing brown eyes always looked even more intense through the wire rimmed glasses he wore.

"Halina," he said in an even tone. He never was one for small talk,

"Doctor Sturgess."

"What's the news? I thought were going to be having a cat join us. So ..." He held out his arms and looked around. "Where is this little feline?"

"I don't have him yet," Halina said quietly as she looked down at the table.

"I'm sorry. I must have heard wrong. Did I hear you say you don't have him?"

"No, I don't. Not yet."

"Stop using the word "yet". You either have him or you don't. Or are you inferring the feline is now on its way to us?"

She'd grown to love the people at the clinic but hated the man in front of her. He was abrupt, arrogant and condescending, poor traits, she thought, for a person in charge of the operation of the entire facility, including research, hiring and firing. It was the firing part which had Halina worried at the moment. "I'm still working on it."

"You're working on it," Dr. Sturgess said flatly as he sat with his eyes fixed on hers. Halina just nodded.

"Dr. Shimon. You are the one who came to me with this incredible story of a cat who had beaten this disease. You said you could get him. You said it wouldn't cost too much and it could be done in a way our clinic would never be suspected." Dr. Sturgess removed his glasses, looked down and rubbed his eyes for a moment.

Before he continued, he put them back on and again looked at Halina as he spoke, his eyes never seeming to blink. "You know I would not have given you any money or had allowed you to put your plan into motion on just your word alone?"

Halina's hand started to tremble slightly. She opened her purse and started to dig around.

"Low sugar?'

"Unfortunately, yes," Halina answered as she continued to search her purse. "I was late, skipped breakfast and took just a small shot. I guess it was a little too much."

"That was quite stupid Dr. Shimon. As an endocrinologist and diabetic you should know to test your glucose properly. You don't guess. You don't assume. You also should always have hard candy close by in an easy to find place, say in the pocket of your lab jacket, not sitting at the bottom of an overly cluttered purse," the man in charge said as he leaned back in his chair with a hint of a smile on his face as he watched her search a little more frantically through her purse.

Halina knew how he loved to lecture, loved to talk down to and belittle others. She hated it even more when he did it to her but at the moment all she could do was to rummage around and try to tune him out as he continued. "After all, you know as well as I, handling diabetes is a balancing act. You've had it all your life. You know you must be always ready for a drop in glucose. What if you're driving when hypoglycaemia kicks in? What if…"

"Stop lecturing me!" Halina said sternly, trying not to shout. Having finally found a candy, she quickly unwrapped it and popped it into her mouth. Although her hands were still trembling, she was starting to feel better. Maybe it wasn't low sugar but just her nerves. "No I haven't got the damned cat but I'm going to get him. I promise you."

"And, of course, you'll be keeping our company's name out of it, should anything go wrong," the doctor said very smooth and calm.

"Yes, of course!" Halina sternly replied. She stopped herself for a moment and thought of what he had said before her hands interrupted them. "Dr. Sturgess? What other information did you have or get when I came to you about the cat?"

Her boss took off his glasses but kept his eyes on her while he tapped the side of his face. She could tell he was pondering on whether to answer her question or not, so she prodded him some more. "I would like to know or I shut it all down right now. Oh, I know you could fire me and there would be nothing I could do about it. Yes, you have been shielded from this quite well so there is nothing I could use against you on this if you did. If you really do want this cat, I would like to know what makes you so sure about it."

Dr. Leo Sturgess looked down towards the table, nodded, then looked up and started to explain. "We have a contact who works in the main lab of the Canadian Juvenile Diabetic Research facility. A mole, if you will. We pay him well. He's fairly high up in the organization. High enough to know they have been receiving reports from a vet about a suspect cat. My man hasn't been able to put a name to either.

"They've been receiving blood work from its vet for a couple of years. Tests have revealed this cat somehow may be creating a hormone, one yet not known to science."

"What? A new hormone? I don't understand."

"Dr. Shimon," he said using his same professional voice he used in the labs, "You obviously know it's the beta cells in the islets of the pancreas that produces the insulin a person needs"

Halina nodded.

"And how a diabetic's immune system, for some reason, will go and destroy these beta cells and keep others from forming."

Again, frustrated at hearing him to go about a subject she could teach, she nodded.

"Well, this cat in question has been monitored for a few years. At first researchers in the JDRF labs only found traces of this hormone in the cat's blood samples but as time went on, this hormone seemed more prevalent in each sample. Researchers there then started to look to find a link between the hormone and this cat's success.

"So when you came to me about this cat, knowing its name and the name of the vet, it was information my mole couldn't get. The last time he contacted me a couple of weeks ago he had informed me the JDRF had put a seventy-five percent chance of success this creature would lead to a cure."

"But how?"

"We don't know yet and likely the JDRF doesn't either. They would have a much better clue than us, as they have been getting all the blood samples. Either this hormone brings the cat's immune system under control or it is capable of producing, nurturing and protecting new beta cells."

"Wow!" exclaimed Halina who was sitting bolt upright in her chair, absorbing every word.

"Yes. 'Wow' indeed." Sturgess said in a very plain monotone tone. He stopped for a moment and again removed his glasses. His expression was dead serious. "Dr. Shimon, we need that cat. This animal looks to be the diabetic Rosetta Stone to a complete cure. We need it and need to get it before JDRF does."

"Dr Sturgess. We've had a setback. The cat wasn't delivered last night as it was supposed to be. I'm going to…"

"I don't want to know," he retorted as he raised his hand for her to stop talking. He leaned forward in his chair so his face was close to Halina's and continued, but in an extremely low and menacing tone. "Whatever's happened so far is your business, not ours. We didn't have a set back. You and your people had a setback. As you have already said, there is no trail to me or this lab and there had better not be one in the future, which is why you received cash from me. It's why we meet in this room and only talk about it in this room because as you know, it can't be bugged.

"You need to make this disappearance look as unsuspecting as possible. Should anything happen and the police come to investigate me, I will totally disavow you and your actions in every single way. You were a poor junior researcher trying to make a name for herself. A lone wolf. A woman seeking personal glory. I gave you a chance and then you pull this cat heist of yours, betraying the trust between us I thought we had. More than anything else, remember that!"

"Doctor, you have explained all this before."

"An hour ago, I received another report from my contact. JDRF feels with the latest sample they just finished analyzing there now is an eighty-five percent chance of success with this hormone. You get me that cat before they get it and you'll not only be paid handsomely but I promise you'll be working along side me and I'll ensure your name will be included on the research papers we submit. We'll cure diabetes, make a fortune and," he let the word "and" hang in the air for a couple of seconds, "and we'll receive a Nobel as icing on the cake."

"What about the cat?"

"Dr. Shimon, that's a very stupid question. Do you really think we have plans to kill it? We require it be alive for study. I assure you that once we have it that it will live and live quite well and happy. Now, go out and find me that cat." Finished, Sturgess stood up, put on his glasses, turned his back and left the room.

It was a long day afterwards for Halina. She tried to keep her mind on the tasks at hand, but she kept drifting off thinking of the call she had to make. Once she considered leaving the lab, going for a walk and calling as she walked, but managed to talk herself out it. She wanted a place secure and private. Phone calls could not be made or received from the boardroom where she had spoken to Sturgess earlier. The room was shielded from phone calls, texts and the internet. Sturgess had ensured the room was of the highest security. She would have to wait until she was home and could call without anybody being able to listen in.

Finally, the day had ended and after a twenty-minute transit and short walk, she arrived home. She walked in the door and found her sitter/housekeeper, Nicole, in the spacious kitchen putting away what looked to be the last of the dishes. As she put away the last plate, Nicole asked Halina if she could go. Halina told her she was in for the night and Nicole could take off.

Halina was happy to have the place to herself. She poured herself a glass of water and was about to head upstairs when the phone in her purse rang. She knew the ring.

It wasn't the ring of her regular phone but the phone she had recently bought. The ringtone told her she no longer had to call the man she hired. He was calling her. She sat in a kitchen chair, put the phone to her ear, but said nothing. Instead she waited for the other party to speak.

"Halina," asked the male voice at the other end. It was Oscar, the man who told her to buy a phone with prepaid time on it from a variety store and pay with cash. He had called it a burner phone, disposable and nearly impossible to track.

"Oscar?" she asked.

"Yes. Can you talk?"

"Yes I can. First question, do you have the cat?"

"No. We've had some problems."

"Problems! You're stealing a god-damn cat. How hard is that? When I gave you the cat's name and the name of its vet, you said it would be a piece of cake. You break into vet's clinic, hack their computer and easy peasy, you get the address. You break into his place, grab the thing and drop it off where I told you to. You yourself said it would be the easiest money you and your men ever made."

She heard Oscar sigh at the other end of the phone before he spoke. "It should have been. Breaking into the clinic was easy enough but when my boys broke into the guy's home, he came back and surprised them."

"So your people screwed up? He came home and surprised them. Them ... as in ... how many? Obviously more than one? So how many? Two? Three? Four?"

"Two."

"Two of your tough men against one downtown city boy?"

"He was trained, maybe in martial arts. He cut them up good."

Halina voice was starting to rise. "You grab the kitty, put it in a box and bring it to me. It's the opening scene to hundreds of fucking kid's movies."

"People aren't killed in kid's movies!"

Halina was stunned by the statement and for a moment sat silent not believing what she had just heard. "Killed? You mean dead? How ... what's going on? What happened? This was supposed to be easy."

Oscar explained, "Yesterday after the break in didn't work out and with all the blood which had to be in his place, I figured this guy would check him and his cat into a hotel room. I have a guy who I've used many times to track credit cards. We got Watson's from the vet file when we broke in. I don't know how the guy does it, but he's the best, and sure enough, he found out the hotel. Even the room number.

"We had him. If he left the room without the cat, we'd go get the cat from the room. If he took the cat with him, we just whack him and grab the cat. The only thing is, when he left with the cat, it turned out he had a cop with him. A female cop in plain clothes."

"So?"

"So, according to what I heard from the lawyer..."

"LAWYER?"

"Lawyer, yes, I'm getting to that. My guy who was arrested has a brother who's a lawyer. He called me. It turns out the guy left with the cat, but he and the cop weren't walking together, so nobody noticed her. When they went to grab the cat, one of my boys was killed by the cop and the other arrested."

"Arrested? Good God! This whole thing's coming apart. You promised me you'd get the cat and keep my name out of it. 'Easy', you said. Now I might be going to jail?"

"No, you're not going to jail. I know he won't talk, he knows better. But with everything which has happened, if you call this thing off, I expect a lot of hush money just to be sure he keeps quiet."

"We agreed on five thousand. It can come out of your end," Halina said as she noticed her voice rising again. "Or are you keeping the half I fronted you and splitting?"

"It'll take ten to keep him quiet. After today, the cops are going to be keeping a close eye on this now. It simply makes this operation much more difficult to pull off."

"Cops? More difficult?" Halina sighed. This had become far more complicated and dangerous to her than she had originally thought, "Hush money would be wise. What about the one who was killed?"

"He's a loner. No family I know of. That's what I hire. Now about the new pricing? If you want out, it's ten G's for my boy to keep his mouth shut and you still pay up the two and a half you still owe me."

"Because your people screwed up!" she growled back.

"Shit happens, Lady," Oscar stated firmly. "Now, getting that cat is going to be much more difficult. Fifty thousand should do it, oh and that's on top of what we just spoke about. So that makes it, what, sixty-two thousand, five hundred. Hey, to keep this simple, why don't we just round up to sixty-five?"

Halina thought for a moment. She wondered if Sturgess would go for this. He didn't even want to know the details, so she couldn't explain why. She still had twenty-five thousand in the bank left over from the inheritance she had received when her mom had passed away a year before and her mom's home where she now lived, "I could do for twenty-five, all in."

"Lady this isn't a fucking negotiation. You want to keep me damned quiet too, right? Twelve thousand five hundred ... no fifteen thousand for us to walk away and keep quiet or sixty-five to get the cat."

Halina sat silently in her chair. Never did she ever contemplate having to go to jail. She looked around at the walls of her overly large kitchen and out through the arched opening into living room where she could see the huge saltwater aquarium. Then she turned her head and looked out the window at the green leaves rustling gently in the breeze on the trees which ran down the property line of her one-acre estate. *Jail ... or all this.*

"Okay. Deal. Get me that cat but no more screw-ups."

"Sure. You know lady it's a lot of money for a fucking cat? Why's this thing worth so much?"

"None of your business. To me it is and that's all you need to know," she said as she ended the call and tossed the phone back into her purse.

She felt parched and drained the water from her glass before she headed upstairs and slipped quietly into a nursery, where she found her two-year old son, Shane, sound asleep on his stomach. Halina reached into the crib and placed her hand on his back, feeling it rise and sink with every breath. She let out a sigh.

"You're not going through life the way mommy had to Sweetie," she said in a very quiet caring voice, "Trips to the hospital. Three operations to save a failing eye and still losing it. The fear of total blindness. Foot issues. No, Shane, this is not the life I want for you. I'm going to get the cat and you're going to get you a cure. They promised me a share of the fame but I don't care about that. Mommy just wants you all better. Mommy can get this done. Mommy has to get this done"

Halina took her hand off Shane's back and pulled his blanket up over him. She felt his warm cheek with the back of her hand and rested her hand on as his back again for a few more moments. She smiled as she drew it away and as quietly as she had entered the room, she slipped back out.

Chapter 6

It was a long day as Paula had promised it would be. Hours went by until Morgan was finally finished answering all the questions, many times, the same questions over and over regarding the day's events. He divulged Tiberius's apparent cure in the process. When asked why he didn't mention it after the first attack, he could only answer honestly how he never though of it at the time. After all it wasn't every day a person found themselves in a fight for their lives.

Paula was put through a different interrogation by the Special Investigations Unit, the SIU, who questioned her actions, motives and reasons for being there. Neither Morgan nor Paula had an easy time of it.

Tiberius, to Morgan's relief, was being well-looked after. Worried he might stroll and get lost in the wide-open divisional office, he was set loose in an Inspector's empty office who had the day off

The office was set up with food, water and a litter box. This caused the other officers to joke they would wait till the next day and let the Inspector clean out the dirty litter, not that they would let that happen. Tiberius, though, seemed content to jump up to the highest place in the office to curl up and nap between two sets of books.

When it was all finally over, Morgan put Tiberius in his carrier, grabbed the bag of food and went to the front desk, "Have you seen Detective Rogers?"

"She left about fifteen minutes ago."

He sighed, looked into the carrier at Morgan and said, "Let's head outside, get some fresh air and figure out what we do next."

At the moment, he wasn't sure what to do. He knew there was no way he could go home after what had happened that morning. He was very wary about booking into a hotel as he had no idea on how they had been found. The best idea he could come up with was to hit an ATM, grab some cash and book into some lower end joint.

As he stood there pondering his next move, he heard a car close by honk its horn. He held a hand over his eyes while they adjusted to the early evening sun and was delighted to see Paula sitting in the driver's seat motioning for him to come over. She hadn't abandoned him after all.

"Put Tiberius in the back seat and get in," she said in a manner more of a command than a suggestion. Once in she pulled away. "I don't know why but I was uncomfortable walking out of the station with you."

Morgan nodded he understood. He wondered what kind of questioning she had to endure.

After a few minutes, Paula turned onto Eglinton Avenue where heavy traffic and construction slowed the pace down to a crawl. Morgan looked around, "So, where're we going?"

"For the moment, my place. We need to talk and figure things out."

Morgan felt the phone in his pocket vibrate. He pulled it out and looked at it. It was Beth. He dropped the phone back into his pocket.

"Anything important? Do you need to take that?"

"No. It's a woman I went out for drinks with last week. For some reason I told her about Tiberius's condition. I don't know why."

"What condition."

He went though the same thing with her which he explained in his interrogation.

"Shit! Why didn't you tell me about that before? It could be important."

"I never thought about it until I was being grilled today. Your people are quite good by the way. We were in a bar talking. It was our first time out together and I was running out of things to say. So I told her about Tiberius. Maybe somebody overheard."

"Maybe she told somebody!"

He shrugged. "Who knows? Anyways, as soon as I remembered, I told them about her."

"Did she leave a message?

Morgan pulled the phone out and looked. "Uh-huh. Hmmm, a voicemail and a text."

"See what she had to say." Paula said in her professional tone.

Morgan looked down and chuckled. "Her text is quite short actually ... fuck you and your fucking cat!"

Paula looked over at Morgan and laughed. When she spoke next, the hard, official edge she had had left, "I'll bet there's no soft sexy talk in that voicemail. Come on, let me listen to it too."

What the hell? Morgan thought. He turned on the speaker, and then pressed play.

Morgan turned up the sound as the message played, "Morgan! Hey Asshole. Pick up the phone. Come on, pick up!

"What the fuck are you doing? I'm home, for like a minute, when two cops come to the door wanting to ask me about you and your stupid cat and that bullshit story of yours. They were here for an hour. Just left. What the fuck! Somebody's trying to take your precious little cat? Fuck you, you demented, attention craving jerk-faced asshole! Go see a shrink. Only a real sick fuck does these things.

"Oh, and in case you aren't getting the message, DON'T FUCKING CALL ME! And another thing. I like that yoga class so stay the hell away. If you show up, I'LL HAVE A RESTRAINING ORDER PUT AGAINST YOU SO GOD DAMED FAST ... FUCK!"

The call ended abruptly. It was a good thing they were stopped at a red light as Paula had her head resting on the steering wheel as she looked over at him, laughing so hard she seemed about to lose her breath.

"That's one very pissed woman! She actually thinks you made this all up to get attention and sent us out to talk to her. Like we have the time! I hate to tell you, but somehow I don't think you've got a shot with her anymore!"

Morgan just shrugged. He really had nothing else to say to but was glad it seemed to lighten Paula's mood for the final few minutes of their trip. Finally, she turned down a side street just before Yonge Street and pulled into a parking garage beneath a condo building. They gathered up Tiberius and his belongings and headed up to her place.

Once inside, he placed the carrier on the floor and unzipped it. A brown stripped tabby head appeared from out of the carrier, looked about cautiously, then made its way out. Tiberius walked or rather slinked in a crouch with his tail firmly held low so it almost touched the floor as he slowly made his way around exploring yet another new place. Morgan cringed when Tiberius leapt up onto the couch where each cushion and blanket had been placed with care in a strategic and stylish manner.

"It's alright ... jut as long as he doesn't scratch," Paula said doing her best to appear nonchalant about it. She explained where the bowls were and when Morgan went to the kitchen area to grab a couple, she disappeared into the bedroom. He filled up one bowl with water and another with crunchy food, which Tiberius strutted over to and started to munch away.

"Looks like he was hungry," Paula commented as she came back into the room. Morgan looked away from Tiberius and saw she was wearing a loose white top and jean shorts. It was a great look for her, and he couldn't help but notice her shapely legs. "Now Tiberius has been looked after, let's look after ourselves. Wine?"

"Please."

She motioned for him to the couch, the same couch Tiberius wasn't really too welcomed on. "Sorry, but my clothes were ripped and dirty and I didn't have anything much to change into. Haven't had a chance to do any laundry lately and didn't expect to have any company over."

"No problem," Morgan said as he made his way to the couch but never sat. He watched as she went to the kitchen and pulled a Riesling from the fridge. "My clothes are filthy too. Perhaps I shouldn't sit here."

Paula said it was okay and he sat. She didn't say that having Tiberius tear apart her couch was what she was really worried about. Arriving back, she made her way around the coffee table, handed Morgan a nearly full wineglass and instead of sitting at the opposite end of the couch, she sat in the middle. She held up her glass signalling a toast, "to the two of us ... I mean the three of us still being alive and well this evening." She extended her arm so they could ting glasses.

Strangely, instead of talking about the day's events they went into small talk mode. They talked about the neighbourhood her condo was in, her upbringing in North York, his life growing up in Aurora and what had motivated them both to move downtown. Each had the same answer. Downtown Toronto was where life happened.

Finally after half the glass of wine was gone, they sat in silence. It wasn't an awkward quiet but more of a rest. Paula closed her eyes and leaned her head back onto a cushion which sat on the back of the couch and crossed her legs. Morgan looked over at her as she did. Even though she looked completely exhausted, she also looked so incredibly beautiful. He didn't want to be caught staring so instead he followed her lead, closed his eyes and leaned his head back too.

For a few minutes they silently stayed that way until he felt her hand slip into his. Still, neither said a word. They just stayed that way, connected through each other's touch. Finally, she broke the quiet of the room, not squeezing but tightening her hold on his hand as she did, "You know, as officers we're taught to react without emotion. We're run through a thousand and one scenarios. How to fight. How to shoot. When to shoot. We need to take the emotion out of it. Emotions can get you killed out there.

"Then you and your damned cat come along. It's only been a couple of days, but when I saw that gun ..."

She fell silent. Morgan gave her hand a squeeze.

"When I saw him pull a gun on you, I screamed inside. God, I thought there was no way I could protect you. I thought you were going to be dead."

"Sure glad it didn't work out that way."

She opened her eyes, turned towards him, placing her hand on the back of his head as she did and pulled herself towards him to where their lips finally met. The kiss was long and lingering but soon the two mouths started to explore. Tongues met and lips searched. Lips met and parted, each needing air as their breathing became more rapid.

Morgan felt Paula remove her hand from the back of his neck and run it slowly down his arm to his hand which he held firmly against the wonderful curves of her body. At first, he was disappointed when she removed it, thinking maybe she was now having second thoughts which proved to be untrue when much to his delight, she placed it on top of her blouse and onto her breast. It was as firm as he had expected, and he let his hand and fingers wander and explore. She shuddered slightly, gave a little, moan and her lips became more passionate when he ran his thumb around her nipple. *Too many clothes* he thought.

"Too many clothes," he heard her gasp as she broke away from him. He watched as she pulled her top over her head and undo the front of her bra. Paula gave her head a short shake so her hair fell down and played on the top of her shoulders, then stopped and looked deep into his eyes. She was naked from the waist up and Morgan was too busy taking it all in to return her gaze which made her smile.

Her breasts were slightly upturned, and he could see a twinkle of sweat between them. In her work clothes, she looked as if she had a really nice figure. The top she just removed, loose as it was, had showed it off. He reached out and pulled her towards him. Her arms encircled him while his hands ran themselves along her sweeping feminine curves.

Morgan stopped and pulled back a little and saw her shorts, unbuttoned as they were, accented a body any woman would kill to have. He had been with some very beautiful women before but nothing like the sensational woman before him now.

"I'm waiting!" she whispered.

He moved in closer and kissed her again fully on her lips before making his way down her neck and body, kissing, caressing and running his lips over her silky skin as he did. He took his sweet time when he reached her breasts. His fingers lightly touched and played with one breast while his lips fully explored the other. He loved their slightly salty taste, the way her body moved and her arms held him when his mouth found her nipples.

It had been a long day and Morgan hoped their night would be even longer.

♦ ♦ ♦

Dr. Everingham sat in his office, pushed the end call button on his phone and set it on the desk in front of him. He turned his computer monitor towards him, tapped in his access code and pulled up the Tiberius file. The light from the screen flickered off his face as he flipped through page after page of notes from Tiberius's visits.

His clinic was always busy. At first when he contacted JDRF about Tiberius, they had not dismissed him as he thought they would but requested his clinic send bimonthly blood samples for them to test. At first, he had always kept a small sample for himself to analyse but had quit doing so after a few months as he figured he would be called if the lab found something unusual or a pattern. Now he could see why they insisted on regular samples. It was the reason why a director, June Farnsworth, from JDRF had called.

The researchers only ever had the blood they sent to test. Now they wanted to have a close look at Tiberius. As Farnsworth had explained, Tiberius just might have the cure for diabetes.

Everingham turned off his monitor and put his face in his hands. The pieces had all fallen in place for him. He now knew why the detective had asked all those questions, why Morgan was attacked and why Tiberius was almost kidnapped.

And most scary to him, Everingham realized that this likely was only the start.

Chapter 7

Mitt Pin looked down at the body wrapped in a large industrial plastic bag he had helped place in the freshly dug hole in the forest floor. With his broken wrist, he had not been much of a help in digging the makeshift but permanent grave but had insisted on carrying the body on his own from the truck of the car to its final resting place. He closed his eyes and although he wasn't religious said a very short prayer before awkwardly helping to bury the body of his former partner, Jonny.

The man he had come with to help bury or rather, to hide his body forever, worked fast. Mitt couldn't remember his name and really didn't care but it seemed like only a few minutes for the stranger to fill in the hole, roll a fair-sized boulder over the grave and make the area look as natural as possible. He picked up his shovel, threw it up over his shoulder and looked over at Mitt.

"Hey, don't just stand there. I know he was your buddy and all but let's get the fuck out of here. Ain't no place to be hanging around."

"Head back to the car. I'll be there in five."

"No, two. Two fucking minutes! I'm not sitting in a car in the middle of nowhere close to where I just dumped a corpse. Two minutes or you walk."

Mitt nodded his head as his associate walked off and waited for him to be out of sight before he looked downward at the grave. "Jonny. Christ man, you had a gun. He only had a sword. He's the one who should be dead, not you. Buried here with no marker way out in the middle of a bloody forest. Shit buddy, you deserve better. I don't know why the fuck the doc couldn't save you.

"You're the only person I ever liked. Really, the only friend I ever had. Never had nobody growing up. No friends. Shit man, you came along and it was like having a brother. You're the only person I ever liked, ever trusted. Damn it!"

Mitt looked up to the stars but found only the forest canopy above him. He looked down and propped his shovel up against the cast of his broken right wrist. He leaned over picked up a couple of rocks and tossed them onto the leaves and branches which covered the newly turned soil.

He crossed himself, picked up the shovel with his good hand, tossed it onto his shoulder and started to walk away from the grave towards the sounds of a car in the distance which had just started its engine.

♦ ♦ ♦

Morgan opened his eyes. He had been sleeping on his back and could feel Tiberius lying against his feet. The room smelled nice, like perfume. He could feel his left arm resting on top of the covers and ran along the contours of Paula's back to where his hand cupped itself around one of her very hard buttocks as she slept.

The night before had been great. He hoped there would be more like it, rather than just the once. The events of the day before had had caught up to them and they both had crashed into a deep sleep just a minute or so after they were done. Not that he was complaining. Paula was as fabulous a woman as any man could ever want.

He carefully removed his hand off her cheek and did his best to slide out of bed without waking her. Having coffee ready and some eggs cooked up would be a pleasant way for her to wake up. Morgan looked back to be sure he hadn't wakened her. She was asleep on her stomach, her shapely right leg sticking out from under the blankets with her left calf also exposed. Morgan smiled as he slipped out of the room with Tiberius trotting along side of him.

Once out of the bedroom, he found his pants on the floor in front of the couch and pulled them on. As usual he would feed Tiberius first before putting on a pot of coffee. Suddenly though, he heard a thud against the door followed by a man's quiet curse and he froze.

Shit! They found us again! Damn it, I don't have my sword either.

He heard another thud against the door which caused it to press against the lock, followed again by a man's curse, this time louder. Morgan looked for something to grab. As he did, he saw Paula leaning against the frame of her bedroom door, naked except for her panties, holding a gun pointed upwards with one hand, her other hand clamped to her gun hand wrist.

Screw the sword, this is better!

She nodded at Morgan, who quickly and quietly as possible slipped off the door's security chain, unbolted the deadbolt and on her signal, flung the door open. Paula stepped out into the room, saw what was happening in the hall, turned and made a rapid retreat back to the bedroom.

In the hall, kneeling on one knee, was an older man who held an open a cloth bag with a broken strap, attempting to gather up the newspapers which were strewn all around him. He looked up at Morgan. "Sorry Sir. The strap broke and the papers all fell out. Almost got them all now. Very sorry to wake you."

"No, it's alright. I was up anyways. I hope your day improves," he said as he closed the door, twisted the dead bolt, slid the safety chain into place and leaned back against it.

Paula came back into the living room, this time without her gun and wearing a robe. Her face wore a huge smirk, as did Morgan's. She walked towards him and when she was just a few feet away they both broke into laughter as they fell into each other's arms.

"A hell of a way to start the day Detective. One hell of a way."

♦ ♦ ♦

The two phones rang almost simultaneously. Paula picked up hers from the small table by the door, while Morgan went to the kitchen area to grab his which was plugged into the charger. They both spoke for a few minutes before hanging up seconds apart.

"Christ, you won't believe this!" Morgan said first.

"Not sure if it'll top mine."

Morgan held his hand out in a signal for her to go first.

"Alright," she complied, "You know the perp who made the grab on Tiberius yesterday ..."

Morgan nodded, only he thought "asshole" suited the guy better than perp.

"They're letting him post bail today."

"What ... what the hell?"

"Yup. Some guy named Glen Stutz. His bail hearing is at one today."

"How? He assaulted me, assaulted you a cop and tried to take Tiberius ... and the next day he's out. That's bullshit!"

"His story was he and his partner were informed you had thirty thousand bucks hidden inside the carrier with the cat making it all look so innocent. That's all my people could get out of him. His lawyer had a judge grant him a bail meeting for today."

"So obviously they have an address for him?"

"Yeah but it probably won't help. I have an idea, though," Paula said as she turned and headed to the bedroom. She stopped and turned back around. "Sorry, Morgan. What's your news?"

"That was Dr. Everingham, Tiberius's vet…"

"I know who he is."

"He just called to say he was contacted by the head of the head of the diabetic research department."

"And?"

"And they want me to bring Tiberius over to their lab for testing. Apparently, their latest results show there's some unknown hormone or something which has been getting stronger in his bloodstream which they think cured him. They don't know how it's produced but apparently whatever it is, holds the key to permanently cure diabetes. Not just treat it. Cure it."

"Holy shit!"

"Exactly!"

Chapter 8

Morgan was in the living room putting on his shoes when he looked up and saw Paula came out of the bedroom. She was dressed in black slacks and wearing a form fitting, short sleeve, light blue button up shirt with the top two buttons undone. A camera was slung around one shoulder and a holstered gun rested on her hip. To Morgan, no other woman could look as kick-ass as she did right then.

Paula had confirmed the SIU wasn't going to need anything from her, at least for a few days and she had been granted seven days off before reporting back to work. She would be on desk duty until the investigation into their attacker's death cleared her fully of any wrongdoing. She had the time and was not about to hole up and wait to be jumped again. As she had told Morgan earlier, it was time to go on the offence.

"Explain this to me one more time, please," Morgan asked. "I'm all for following this Stutz asshole when he gets released. It's better than just waiting for shit to happen to us. What about Tiberius?"

Paula stopped him with a quick kiss." Don't worry. It's all arranged. He'll be in good hands."

"Good. The JDRS are looking forward to examining him."

"No way. I'm not comfortable with them having him."

"Why?"

"Because you were staying at a three-star hotel in a huge city and they managed to find you in a single night. If the people after him have those kinds of connections and resources out there, they surely have somebody on the inside of JDRS. Like I said, he'll be in good hands with people I trust the most in the world."

A knock on the door made him jump.

"It's alright Morgan," Paula said holding up a hand to him indicating there was nothing wrong. Paula walked over to the door and opened it up to a tall casually dressed, black woman, who looked to be in her forties. She was a good-looking woman with black hair with a single red streak running through it which fell over her shoulders. "Morgan, this is Grace. Grace Upton."

Grace walked in, gave Paula a hug, then greeted Morgan with a handshake.

"Grace and Jim are going to look after Tiberius today."

Morgan turned his head and gave Paula a questioning look.

"Paula," said Grace releasing Morgan's hand, "I don't think you've explained to Morgan who Jim or I are."

"Goodness, I guess I didn't," Paula answered. "Jim is Grace's husband. He's a dispatcher down at the station. I've known Jim for what seems like forever. We partnered when I was just a rookie. He taught me almost everything I know about working the street. He's always had my back. Still does to this day. I would say other than Grace, he's my best friend.

"When the other guys were being assholes about me being a woman on the force, Jim would always step in. He took a lot of flack for protecting me and a lot of innuendo went around about the two of us being partners. Some guys are assholes you know and I'm working in a very macho world."

Grace interjected, "Jim would come home so pissed off. He's an honest guy, one you can always trust. I heard the rumours but know Jim through and through. He would never do anything to hurt me. Jim told me everything. Still I was a little apprehensive.

"Then one evening he suggested we invite Paula over for supper. She was such a sweet girl. That night I could see how close they were. I could see the bond the two of them had together."

She placed her hand on Paula's face, then let it fall to her shoulder, "What I could also see was a person who would always have his back and would be there to protect Jim with her life, if need be."

"I wasn't there the night Jim got shot," Paula added. "Oh God I wish I had've been. They partnered him with a rookie. If I'd have been with my experience it never would have happened. Now he's got that bum arm and has been on dispatch ever since. I know a little part of him died when he was told he couldn't work the streets anymore."

There was a short silence in the room.

"Anyways," Paula said changing the subject, "when I go away, Grace looks after my place. She has a key for parking and to my door. We can't leave Tiberius alone here, so I gave Grace a call. I figured while we are out, Grace could take Tiberius back to her place. She'll simply take Tiberius down to the underground, put him in her car and off they go. If in fact we are being watched, nobody would suspect a thing."

Morgan looked down and saw Tiberius stroll over to Grace without hesitation and rub up against her legs.

Grace bent down, picked him up and held him out in front of her so the two of them were looking at each other face to face, eye-to-eye.

"What a sweetie!" she exclaimed as she put him against her shoulder. Tiberius reacted with some loud purring. "Morgan don't worry. He'll be just fine with us."

Morgan looked over to Paula, who added one final point to reassure him, "Morgan, there's nobody in the world I trust more than Grace and Jim. Jim's got the day off so Tiberius will be spending the day at a cop's house, so stop worrying. He couldn't be anywhere safer!"

"Well, Grace, you also seem to have Tiberius's vote too," Morgan said as he went over to grab the now all too familiar carrier. He could see Tiberius fuss a little in Grace's arms having seen the carrier, so he handed it over to Paula and walked over and took Tiberius from Grace. "His back claws scratch sometimes when you put him in the carrier. He doesn't like going in there in the first place and lately he's been in there a lot. My chest is full of scratch marks. They can hurt and I want you two to start off on a good note."

With Tiberius kicking and twisting, he managed to get Tiberius inside and quickly zipped up the bag. He looked over at Grace and thanked her. He held up the carrier to where he could see Tiberius, "You'll be okay, my boy. I just hope these good people don't fall in love with you too much," he said softly.

They said their goodbyes and then Grace headed off with Tiberius in hand.

Paula took a quick check of her camera, turning it on and off, then reached into her pocket to ensure she had an extra battery. She pulled her revolver from its holster, gave it a quick check over, snapped it back into place and looked over at Morgan.

"OK, let's roll. Hopefully Stutz leads us somewhere interesting which can provide some answers."

♦ ♦ ♦

Paula found a decent place to park, close enough to watch the entrance but far enough away not to be noticed doing so. Morgan sat a copy of Glen Stutz's mug shot in his lap, while Paula ensured her camera was ready to go. Morgan quietly watched the courthouse door, glancing down occasionally at the picture, then back to the door. Paula, slumped in her seat behind the wheel, keeping a continuous view of the courthouse, noticed from the corner of her eye Morgan's continuous motion of looking up towards the courthouse, then down to the picture, then back up again.

"Morgan, it's the only exit from the courthouse. We're not going to miss him. Besides, you hardly look natural doing that head bobbing thing. You realize we're not supposed to attract attention. We're supposed blend unnoticeable into the scenery."

"Oh ... right," he replied. He was still for about a minute or so, before he looked down at his watch, then back to the door. Thirty seconds later, he repeated the action.

"Stop it. He'll be out when he's out," said Paula not taking her eyes off the courthouse doors. "These things hardly ever run on time. You just have to be patient."

"Sorry. I've never been on a stakeout before."

"You'll see that it gets really old, real fast."

"Yeah, I can see that already."

Once again she spotted Morgan looking down at the mug shot, then to his watch, then back to the courthouse door. She saw he wasn't going to relax and figured he might settle down more if she could get him talking. She picked what she knew would be a favourite topic, "So, how did you end up with Tiberius?"

Morgan smiled for a moment as he thought back to that day, "A girl I was dating at the time heard a pet shop was having an adoption day for a local cat rescue and wanted to go and adopt one. You've heard stories of animals picking you, not you picking them. Well, it's what happened here. I would go by his cage and he would stick a paw out and try to grab me. He never did it to anybody else. Just me. So I walked out with this little tiny two-week-old fur ball in hand and she came out with nothing. Funny, I wasn't even a cat person at the time. Guess I am one now!"

"What happened to the girl?"

"Oh, and this is dumb. Shows you, I mean it showed me what kind of demented person she was. She kept insisting I got the cat just to impress her. Tiberius and I obviously worked out." He laughed. "She and I? Hell, we were finished a couple of weeks later."

"Good story," Paula chuckled. "You know, I always think of cats being a woman's thing. You always hear of crazy cat ladies but never a crazy cat man. It's quite obvious, though. You're very attached to him."

"Yep, sure am," Morgan replied then paused for a moment. He wondered how he could explain it to her. "You see, no matter what has happened in my life, good or bad, Tiberius has always been there. He doesn't offer comments or advice, just comfort. If a day has been bad, I just flop down in my chair and Tiberius will come, jump up and sprawl across me and the arm of the chair. Suddenly everything is alright with the world. Tabbies are big sucks. I love that about them. Love that about him."

Paula took her eyes off the door and looked at him seriously for a moment, "What if ... because of all of this ... you had to give him up?"

"What…"

"There he is," Paula interrupted as she pulled up her camera and took a burst of shots. She was glad their target came out the door when he did. It was a question which might need to be asked at some point but not at the moment.

Morgan looked over and easily picked him out. He was too far away to really see if he looked like his mug shot but the man's left pant leg was cut away and he was sporting a cast which started from above the knee, down to his ankle. He looked a little awkward with his crutches.

"Looks like you did a great number on his knee," Morgan exclaimed with a look of satisfaction, "Looks painful."

"Always go for the knee, shin or groin," Paula replied coldly as she started the car. "Works every time."

Stutz stopped, let go of the right crutch handle, reached out and shook hands with a man Paula assumed was his lawyer. *Oh, how I'd love to smash that phoney smile of yours, you slimy snake*, she thought. As much as she understood the law and reasons behind the mechanisms of justice, she hated defence lawyers with a vengeance.

The lawyer turned and headed back into the building leaving Stutz to hobble his way downstairs to the curb where he hailed a cab. Paula took a picture of its license plate. As the cab drove off pulled out, they started to follow it from a safe distance.

After about ten minutes, the cab pulled into the parking lot of a run-down apartment building. They watched as Stutz leaned forward, said something to the driver, before getting out and heading into the building. The cab stayed where it was and it looked like the driver had turned off the engine.

"That's where he lives," informed Paula. "We're in luck, though. The cabby's waiting for him. Guess after spending a little time in jail he needs to change before heading out wherever. I was hoping he had places to go and wasn't just going to go home and sit on his ass."

It took about five minutes for Stutz to reappear and climb back into the cab. The cab pulled away and again Paula and Morgan followed. The cab made its way to an industrial neighbourhood where it pulled up and stopped across from an old three-story building. Paula passed by the stopped cab and pulled into the drive of a row of industrial units and out of site of the cab.

"Hey, we're going to lose him!" Morgan said with a little panic in his voice.

"No we won't. We can't be seen, and he needs to pay the cabby," Paula answered before she pulled quickly into a parking area of the industrial unit next door. She quickly drove halfway along the length on the building, stopped, turned around and drove back towards the street. Most of the units where empty which allowed for many open parking spots which included an ideal one in front which Paula pulled into.

The cab had pulled away and Stutz slowly crutched his way to the entrance of the building. Paula smiled, "And you thought we might lose him. Look at him limp. He's way too slow to lose. I'll have to be careful not to run over him when I follow."

"Follow him?"

"Yes. We need to find out what he's doing in that building. Who he's meeting with, maybe overhear a conversation?"

"He's seen your face. It'll be too dangerous. He won't know mine."

"Morgan, I'm trained and you're not…"

It was too late. Morgan had already jumped out of the car just as Stutz entered the building.

"SHIT!" Paula swore loudly as she pounded her steering wheel. She watched as Morgan made his way quickly over to the entrance. He didn't run and draw attention to himself, which she half expected he might do and made good time in reaching the door. She saw Morgan hold a hand up to the door's glass to cut the glare so he could see through it. He grabbed the door handle, opened the door halfway and slipped inside, out of Paula's sight.

"Be careful, you asshole!" she whispered quietly to herself.

Morgan stepped inside the door and waited a moment to let his eyes adjust from the brightness of the outside.

He could hear the sound of somebody awkwardly making their way up the stairs with the metallic clang of the crutches followed by a hard thud of a step. The sound stopped for a moment. From above he heard Stutz complain aloud in an exhausted gasping voice to no one in particular, "Fuck! These stairs are killing me. How the hell could they build a place without an elevator anyway? Assholes!"

He heard Stutz resume his climb. It was only two sets of stairs in a typical zigzag pattern to the second floor. Stutz had already rounded the corner of the first set when Morgan had come in, so Morgan knew he hadn't been seen. Finally, he heard Stutz reach the second floor and start to make his way down the hallway.

Morgan worked his way quietly up the steps, hoping there was a place to keep out of sight once he was on the landing. He was in luck. The door had been removed from its frame and there was an area on each side of the doorway big enough for Morgan to hide. Morgan peaked around the corner and down the hall in time to see Stutz, stop and turn towards a door to his right.

Morgan ducked his head back and mentally counted the number of doors to the one he had seen Stutz stop in front of. He heard the creak of the door open, the thud and clump of Stutz entering, then the creak of it closing and the click of the latch.

After unconsciously taking a deep breath, he peeked around the corner and saw the hallway was clear. Quietly he made his way along the wooden floored hallway, staying close to the wall, hoping it would stop any squawking from the floor. It seemed to work. He stopped in front of a door with a 2F above it and a Security Detective Agency sign on it. As he was about to put his ear to the glass to listen in, he heard voices coming up the staircase at the far end of the hall.

He remembered an open door he had noticed across the hall and diagonal to the detective office and took three long, quiet steps to the door and slipped inside. His heart was racing while he smiled to himself. *Looks like I was born to do this stuff!*

The voices came from a man and woman who had climbed the stairs to his floor and were in the hall. Morgan looked quickly around in case he was in the office they were heading for and was happy to see it devoid of any furnishings. He heard the couple stop far down the hall, keys rattle and a door open and close. Slowly he leaned his head out into the hallway to ensure it was empty.

Again, he silently crossed the hallway on the balls of his feet in four short steps. Morgan placed his ear as close to the door as he could in hopes of making out what was going on inside. The conversation was muffled.

"Ten grand," he heard a man say from inside. "It's all here, right Oscar?"

"Stutz gets ten? Oscar, what the fuck? What about me? I almost had my hand fucking chopped off by that asshole and he guts Jonny in the process, God rest his soul."

Shit! This is the guy who attacked me. I killed his partner. What the hell do I do now?

"What? You want me to pay you as much he gets when you screw up the simplest of assignments? You two had the easy job. Nobody even knew you're coming, and you still fuck it up. Against my better judgement I'm letting you keep the original amount I fronted you. It'll be enough to get you out of town but I'm sure not paying the rest.

"Let me get this right. I don't get the job done and get twenty-five hundred. Stutz blows it and gets ten g's?"

"Stutzy kept it together when they nabbed him. Never talked, which is why he's getting ten."

"Ah to hell with this. I'm out of here."

Morgan heard steps coming to the door. He froze not knowing whether to quickly get the hell out or nonchalantly saunter down the hall like he belonged. Maybe he wouldn't be recognized.

"Hey Mitt. Get back here," Morgan heard the one he figured was Oscar say. He looked down and saw the door handle start to turn. Instinctively, he lightly made the dash to the empty office he was in before, slipped in behind the door and waited.

He heard the doorknob being released but not the door opening. It was his chance to leave, so he quickly and quietly made his way along the hall down the stairs, out the door and back to a very relieved Paula.

"You stupid jerk! What did you think you were doing? Don't you know how dangerous that was?"

"I do now. For a moment there I thought I was going to get caught," Morgan said as he tried to catch his breath. "The bastard who attacked me at my place was coming out. I thought I was dead, but he was called back."

"Are you sure it was him? What did you hear?"

"They were arguing over money," Morgan said still breathing heavy, "Stutz was going to get more. The other one, the one I chopped in the wrist, they called him Mitt or maybe Matt, sure wasn't happy about it. His voice though. I'm positive it was him!"

"Mitt Pin. Makes sense. How many are in there?"

"I heard three voices."

"Where are they?"

"Second floor. Security Detective Agency, 2F."

"Detective agency? Well that's quite the cover," Paula replied as she pulled out her phone. She stopped to think for a moment. If she was going in, she should request backup. The problem was they may be gone by the time any units arrived, plus she would be in so much shit for tailing a suspect when she was supposed to be on leave.

Better to come back with an arrest and ask for forgiveness, she thought as she pulled out her gun, snapped the safety off, gave it a quick check, and returned it to its holster. She couldn't arrest Stutz but could haul him in for more questioning. Mitt Pin was in there justifying her barging in without a warrant. Although she didn't know anything about the third man, it sounded as if he might be the one behind the whole thing.

"I'm going in. You stay here," Paula said. When she saw Morgan reach for the door handle, she grabbed him by the shoulder and barked, "Listen, I said you stay here. If you go in there with me, I'll likely lose my career. You won't be any help and could get yourself hurt or killed. I'm going to have enough to look after in there without looking after you too, SO STAY!"

She took a moment to let herself calm down a little. "Oh, if you see units arrive, I would appreciate it if you made yourself scarce. You can't be anywhere around this or I'm in deep shit, got it?"

"Okay, Okay. I understand. Just be safe."

Paula climbed out of the car and hurried over to the building. Quickly and quietly she made her way up the stairs and down the hall. She stopped in front of the detective agency's door to find it wasn't completely closed.

She took a deep breath as she drew her gun from its holster. After a short pause she hollered 'POLICE' before bursting through the door and quickly stepping to her left in case somebody decided to shoot. There was nobody inside to take a shot at her, however. Nobody to arrest. Just a body lying on the floor in a pool of blood, their shirt stained crimson red.

It was the dead body of Glen Stutz.

Chapter 9

Oscar sat on a rusty old fold out chair behind a scratched metal desk which had seen far better days. The two were the only pieces of furniture in the room. Dust floating through the air bothered his sinuses. He had been there for fifteen minutes and as much as he hated waiting, he always wanted to be there first. It cut down on surprises.

Unconsciously he pressed his hand on the outside of his sport jacket against the envelope inside and waited. Stutz was due to arrive soon. It would be a short meeting. Oscar planned to thank him, pay him off and then get the hell out of there. He sneezed, pulled out an ironed folded handkerchief and blew his nose. When he lowered the handkerchief, he found Mitt Pin standing in the doorway. Pin's right wrist was in a cast and held up by his partially zipped up jacket as only his left arm could fit in a sleeve.

"Mitt, what the hell are you doing here? How's the wrist?"

"It hurts but its fine. I figured you'd might be meeting Stutz here."

"So?"

"So, I wanted to see what he's getting. I want to be sure we're all being treated fairly. You know ... equally."

"Mitt, you and I have settled up. We're done."

"Not hardly!"

The conversation was interrupted by a light knock on the door. Both turned and saw the door open wide followed by Stutz on his crutches, who made his way over to the desk, sighed and sat on it.

"Want a chair?" Oscar offered picking up the rusty fold up and holding it out to him. Stutz shook his head no.

"Just came to settle up."

Oscar reached into his jacket pocket, took out the envelope and sat it on the desk. "Sorry about your knee. I know it must hurt like hell but thanks for keeping your head in the game. We never gave you a back-up story to use. Figured it would be easy and you'd never get caught. Hidden money in the carrier ... beautiful!"

Stutz just smiled and nodded once.

"Look, we haven't a clue where the guy and his cat might be holed up. Any idea?"

Stutz reached over and picked up the envelope, "That cop who got me, damn, I still can't believe I missed the bitch. I'm usually a much better shot than that. Anyways, when they were taking me in I heard some of her cop buddies calling her Rogers, others Paula. But you know when I was cuffed and on the ground, I looked over and saw the cat man and her sitting on the grass together. It wasn't like they were cop and victim. There seemed something more to it. I have an idea if you find her, you'll find him and his critter."

Stutz's leg throbbed and there was little else he really could concentrate on. He really just wanted to get his money and leave. He stood up, picked up the envelope and looked inside.

"Ten grand, it's all here right, Oscar? My lawyer said you promised me ten. You said it yourself. I kept it together and came up with a damn good story too."

"Stutz gets ten? Oscar, what the fuck? What about me? I almost had my hand fucking chopped off by that asshole and he guts Jonny in the process, God rest his soul."

"What? You want me to pay you as much he gets when you screw up the simplest of assignments? You two had the easy job. Nobody even knew you were coming, and you still fuck it up. Against my better judgement I'm letting you keep the original amount I fronted you. It'll be enough to get you out of town but I'm sure not paying the rest.

"Let me get this right. I don't get the job done and get twenty-five hundred. Stutz blows it and gets ten g's?"

"Stutzy kept it together when they nabbed him. Never talked, which is why he's getting ten."

"Ah to hell with this. I'm out of here."

"Hey Mitt. Stop!" Oscar pleaded as Mitt turned the handle. He wasn't sure what Mitt would do once outside the door. He was in a rage. Would he go to the cops or just wait and attack him once they left? "Mitt, I only have so much. How about seventy-five hundred?"

Mitt let go of the door handle. He turned back to see both Oscar standing behind the desk with his hands open looking for Mitt to accept his offer and Stutz who was in front of the desk folding the envelope to put in his pocket.

"Fuck this bullshit," Mitt muttered as he quickly moved across the room reaching into his jacket pocket with his good left hand as he did. At first there seemed to be nothing in his hand when he pulled it out, then a blade flashed in the light which a moment later was imbedded in Stutz's stomach.

Stutz's eyes went wide. He was too surprised and paralyzed by Mitt's action. He could not scream, could not fight. As much as Stutz wanted to back away and get the blade out of him, instead he found himself doubling over. With extra effort, Mitt dug the knife further up and in almost lifting Stutz off the ground. Stutz's eyes grew as wide. His mouth was open but no sound came forth.

Then in one movement, Mitt yanked the knife out and with his casted forearm shoved Stutz into the wall. Stutz bounced off the wall, managed to keep his balance for a moment before his knees gave out and he fell in a crumpled heap at Mitt's feet. His eyes were still wide but with very little life left in them.

"Jesus Christ, Mitt! What the hell's gotten into you?" Oscar exclaimed as he backed away from the bloody scene. He quickly looked from where he was in the room, to where Mitt stood and realized he was cut off from the door.

"So, Oscar," growled Mitt, "I guess there's enough for me now right? Oh, I'll be taking the entire fifteen."

"Okay, Mitt. You got it. Let's wipe down this place and get the hell out of here. There's people working on this floor and who knows what the hell they heard."

Mitt stepped scooped up the cash filled envelope from the floor and jammed it into his pocket. He held out his hand for the balance and after Oscar pulled out the remainder of what he had, they went to work quickly wiping down anywhere there might be prints. The doorknob was the last to be cleaned as they left. Oscar motioned Mitt to follow him down the hall to the back of the building.

Seeing the door had not completely closed Mitt reached for the handle but was waved off by Oscar who just whispered "Hands" at him. Mitt looked down, realizing he would be leaving fingerprints, so he let the door be and followed Oscar down the hall. At the end they heard somebody ascending the stairs quickly and ducked into an abandoned office just before the exit.

A woman rushed past them. Ten seconds passed when they heard a female's voice yell "POLICE!" and a door crash open. Oscar looked and saw the opportunity for them to race down the stairs.

Oscar's mind raced. He wondered how the cops could have known so fast. What could have possibly drawn them to this meeting? He realized it didn't matter. The important thing was to get the hell away from the place. He tapped Mitt on the shoulder and instead of heading straight outside, went down a hall to an exit to the back parking lot. Both expected the police to meet them as they entered the sunshine and were relieved to find none. Oscar led Mitt to his car and the two drove off, as slow and natural as any other car leaving the parking lot on any other day.

◆ ◆ ◆

Morgan sat in the car and continued staring at the entrance. Damn, he wished there was something he could do to help. Paula was right, though. He'd be in the way and a liability. But to just sit, wait and stare? It had almost been five minutes of waiting, worrying and staring.

He reached in his pocket and pulled out his phone. Immediately it rang. Startled, he let go and the phone went flying into the windshield, bouncing off and ending up on the floor under the brake pedal. He swore as he leaned over and made a long stretch to reach it. Finally he had it and put it to his ear.

"Jesus, Morgan! What the hell you doing? What took you so long to answer?"

"I'm sorry I ... I just had some ..." he gasped. "Never mind. What's going on in there?"

"I've got a dead body. Look Morgan, I can't have you around. They'll have my ass if they find I had a civilian on a stakeout, let alone you. Leave the car and walk normally. You can't be seen or noticed. Get back to my place. NO CABS! When you get there, buzz 6902, then go to the seventeenth floor, unit 1709. My friend, Nancy, has a key. Hopefully she's home. I'm calling her now."

"Are you okay?"

"You're kidding right? I have a dead body in front of me in a place I'm really not supposed to be. Morgan, just get going! Oh, and don't call me. I'll call you."

Morgan didn't get a chance to wish her luck as she had already hung up.

♦ ♦ ♦

Oscar was furious. "Jesus Christ Mitt, what the hell was that all about? You know we could have worked something out."

"Had to be done," Mitt replied calmly. He looked straight out the front windshield never turning his head in Oscar's direction as he spoke.

Oscar drove keeping pace with traffic, not wanting to draw any attention to them. His original anger was beginning to turn into a little fear, now he was aware of what Mitt was capable of. Mitt was not the big dumb break and enter guy he originally thought him to be. He had just witnessed Mitt's violent and explosive anger. He looked at Mitt who sat calmly in silence, showing no remorse for his actions. Oscar realized he had to deal with Mitt carefully. He also knew he wanted Mitt out of his car as fast as possible.

"Mitt, we have the name of the cop who might be able to put us on to this guy and his cat. Do you want in?"

Mitt said nothing. He turned his head towards Oscar and waited for more.

"Here's what I figure," Oscar said as his mind raced to find a way to keep Mitt calm and get him out of the car. "We find this cop and put a tail on her. Not sure if she knows who you are or not, so I'll get somebody else, but I want you in on this. You're a good man and I'm sure you want to see this thing through.

"Once we find him, I'll put together a plan for you and whoever I have tailing her to grab that cat. You keep the fifteen you already have. I'll have another ten for you when it's done ... so?"

It made Oscar even more nervous when Mitt didn't answer right away. Instead he turned his head and stared out the windshield. A long thirty seconds passed before he finally simply nodded and said in a flat monotone voice "Sure."

"Good," Oscar replied. Up ahead he saw a strip mall coming up on his side of the road. "I'm going to drop you off here. I have some things to do to get this thing going and we really shouldn't be seen together. It wouldn't be good for either of us."

When Oscar saw Mitt nod his approval, he wheeled into the parking lot and stopped. Mitt climbed out. Before he closed the door, he leaned back inside and with an emotionless voice warned, "Stay in touch. Screw me over and you'll die. You'll die painful. Got it?"

Mitt stepped back and swung the door closed. It had barely shut before Oscar had the car in gear and back onto the road.

Chapter 10

Morgan sat in the back of the eastbound Eglinton Avenue bus and stared out the window, deep in thought. It was at the most five minutes, probably less, from the time he left the door of the detective agency to when Paula found Stutz dead. Morgan had no idea how Stutz had died and at the moment didn't care. He only knew Paula was at a murder scene for no other reason than trying to help him and was probably in deep shit with her bosses as a result. For the moment there was nothing he could do except to wait and worry.

The bus pulled over at a stop and Morgan sat bolt upright not believing who he just saw at the stop. It was a heavy-set man with a cast on his right wrist. The same man who had attacked him in his condo. The same man he heard in the office with a now dead Glen Stutz and someone else he knew only as Oscar. Mitt Pin!

He watched as Pin entered the front of the bus, drop some coins in the fare container and walked towards the back. *Shit! What if he recognizes me? Oh shit! What do I do?*

Morgan looked downward doing his best to keep an eye on his assailant without being obvious. He saw Pin sit in one of the seats which ran along the side of the bus. So far, Pin hadn't noticed him. Morgan wondered if Pin would remember what he even looked like. A few more passengers got on and with the bus full, they grabbed onto the bars and straps to steady themselves as the bus lurched back onto the road, their swaying bodies hiding Pin from Morgan and Morgan from Pin.

When he and Paula had woken that morning, Stutz was their only lead. When she had found him dead, Morgan felt they had nothing to go on. Now, Mitt Pin had suddenly just fallen into his lap. Morgan pulled out his phone but remembered Paula had told him not to call. He stared at it for a moment. If it rang, Mitt might look his way and perhaps recognize him. Morgan set it to vibrate and slid the phone back into his pocket.

For a moment, Morgan thought about making a move to grab Pin. When he tried to work out a plan to do so, he was forced to remind himself this man had just walked away from a murder scene and was probably armed. Morgan was not. In the end he figured the best decision he could make was to attempt to be invisible and follow him.

Mitt Pin only had fleeting looks at him when they fought, so probably would not be able to recognize Morgan in a crowd, even though he sat exposed in the front row of the raised back portion of the bus. Morgan, though, had the advantage having seen several mug shots of Mitt afterward their run-in plus Mitt's cast made him more noticeable. Morgan could pick him out of a crowd but figured it didn't work the other way. He hoped when they both got off the bus he could follow without giving himself away.

People got on and off at each stop. Morgan was a little nervous each time the bus emptied and the two could see each other. He was thankful Pin seemed content to keep looking out the front of the bus. At one stop, however, Pin did glance over his way, but then turned back to staring out the front again, much to Morgan's relief. It was a much longer trip than Morgan liked but he felt better when the passenger sitting beside him got up to leave and left their newspaper behind. Morgan took it and pretended to read but kept a close eye on his target.

Finally when the bus pulled into the Laird Drive stop, he watched Pin rise and head to the front of the bus with a few of the other passengers to get off. He waited for Pin to exit out the front before he climbed down the two steps to the rear door and stepped off.

Pin crossed at the lights to the east side of Laird. Morgan hesitated at the light, wondering how to follow on foot at a safe distance, when the light turned red. He was in luck, as Pin started across Eglinton to head north up Laird. It allowed Morgan to cross Eglinton on his own side of the street and follow from twenty or so steps behind and on the opposite side. He saw Pin look over his shoulder but Morgan new he was too far behind to be seen.

To look natural, Morgan pulled out his phone, put it to his ear to hide his face and bowed his head a little. It was likely a very improper way to follow somebody, but it was all he could think of. He was glad he taken the action, however, as when Pin turned right at a side street, he slowed as he did to take a good look behind him. Morgan had to act natural, so he tried to keep the same steady pace he was walking and turned slightly away from his target.

As he reached the street, he saw Pin turn right and head down the driveway of a house second from the corner. With the phone still to his ear, Morgan crossed the street and walked past the house. He saw Pin on the driveway at the side entrance to the house, turn the knob and enter.

Gotcha, Asshole! Now I know where you live!

Morgan walked back to the corner, still with the phone to his left ear so it was shielded from the windows of the house. He turned left at the street and took just a couple of steps so he was out eyesight from where Pin was. Despite Paula's instructions he pulled her police card out of his wallet, making note to program it into his phone later, and punched in the number.

When she answered, Paula sounded tired and never gave Morgan a chance to speak, "Morgan, I told you not to call. What if I..."

"I know where he lives," Morgan declared cutting her off.

"Who?"

"One of the guys I heard in that room with Stutz this afternoon. That Pin guy. You know, the guy whose wrist I broke."

"Mitt Pin? Morgan! Slow down. Tell me what happened."

He never realized how fast he was speaking and breathing. He took a moment to take a few slow deep breaths before explaining what had happened, where he was and most importantly the address of the house.

When he was done, there were a few moments of silence as Paula absorbed all of what she had just heard and thought she should do next. "Okay Morgan. Stay out of sight. I'm just outside my station right now and I'm going to get the guys out there to set up a perimeter to contain him. Then we can take him down.

"Damn it! It's going to take me ten minutes at least to get there. Look, Morgan, remember you weren't with me. You just stumbled upon him. You'll have to make up some story as to why you were on that bus cause when this is all over, they will ask you."

Morgan quickly tried to relate a story back to her, but she cut him off, "Morgan, I don't know the story. I wasn't with you today!"

"Right."

"It's important, so don't forget. We weren't together!"

"Yes, I got it."

"Now stay out of sight. My guys will be there in a few minutes to lock down the area. Morgan, for God's sake, keep out of sight until they arrive."

"I will."

"And Morgan ..."

"Yes?"

"This is dangerous. He's dangerous. I can't stress this enough. If this guy leaves, just note which direction and head the other way. Got it? Morgan, please, you gotta stay safe!" and the phone went silent.

Disregarding what he just agreed to, Morgan moved the phone over to his right ear, again to block the view of his face from the house and walked to the northwest corner of the street so he had a good view of the house. Although the wait seemed long, it was only a few minutes before he saw four squad cars motoring quickly up towards him. One turned right, a street before which Morgan guessed was to ensure there would be no escape out the back. On the same corner another stopped, he assumed again, to block any traffic from the south while another drove past him a block north and stopped to stop traffic coming from the north. The last car turned down the street, drove past the house and stopped three doors down. Two uniformed officers got out. He could see one speaking into his shoulder mike.

One of the two officers from the car which had passed him a moment earlier came over quickly and ordered Morgan to move on.

"I'm the guy who found him," Morgan explained. "I called this in."

"Come with me then," the officer ordered. He led Morgan over to his squad car. "Sir, please stand on the other side of the car so your protected and don't move. Larry, make sure this guy stays put."

Larry, the younger officer who stayed behind, moved over close to Morgan, who still had a view of the house and was happy to watch from that distance. Nothing seemed to be happening. For the moment no one approached the house.

"What's going on? Why isn't anybody doing anything?" Morgan asked the officer with him.

"Perimeter's still being secured. Nothing we can see from here. Don't worry. He's not going anywhere."

Morgan then saw a car, Paula's, drive up and stop in front of the unit which was parked crosswise blocking both lanes of the street. She spoke to him for a moment and then pulled off to the side of the road. Morgan watched as she got out, walked over to the cruiser and was handed a protective vest with "Police" stencilled across the back. She slid it over her shoulders, did it up and tugged hard downwards on the bottom. He was unsure if he felt better seeing she had on protection or if it made him even more nervous knowing she was preparing for a fight.

Paula crossed the street and walked along close to the side of a tall hedge which lined the street to the corner. Once she reached the corner, she stopped, making sure she kept herself hidden from the house. She looked over to the where Larry and Morgan stood, raised her hand slightly and gave a quick wave. From the corner of his eye, he saw the officer wave back, but he was sure he knew who the wave really was for and smiled nervously.

To Morgan, it looked as if everybody was in place. He saw both officers who had parked just past the house start towards it. One went to the side door and the other stopped a few feet behind him. Paula came out from behind the hedge and positioned herself at the end of the driveway.

"What happens now?" Morgan asked Larry. He felt Larry move in a little closer to his side.

"Any number of things once we knock and identify ourselves. Hopefully he's in there and comes quietly."

"Yeah, I'm with you there."

Although he was almost a block away, Morgan had an excellent view of the house from behind the police cruiser. He saw two uniformed officer approach the side door. One opened the screen door, knocked, then stepped quickly to the side. A few seconds later, the inside door opened.

There was a shout and whoever was inside attempted to slam the door shut. The officer who had knocked threw his weight against the door which sent the door flying open and the man tumbling down the basement stairs.

A thunderous boom of a shotgun blast followed immediately from inside and Morgan saw the officer struck and fall to the ground half in, half out of the house His wounded body kept both the inside door and screen door slightly open.

Morgan jolted straight up, paralysed by what he just saw. The second officer moved quickly to the door to rescue his comrade. With a glance to his right he saw Paula by the hedge, draw her weapon and head towards the driveway. Morgan instinctively took a step forward to go help. Before he could take another step, Larry grabbed his arm, twisted it up behind his back and in one motion spun him around, opened up the back door to the cruiser and heaved him inside. Morgan felt the door bang his leg as it closed. In the back of the cruiser, he was trapped and could only helplessly look on.

Another shotgun blast sounded which took a huge chunk out of the wooden door and shattered the glass in the screen door which blew shards of glass everywhere. The second officer who had moved in to grab his partner appeared to be hit by the shot and had taken a heavy dose of glass to his face. He staggered backwards a few steps before he too fell to the ground.

The first officer who had been hit rolled over onto his side, which dislodged a large chunk of glass which still had remained in the frame. It split as it toppled then shattered as it landed on the officer's side.

Morgan watched in horror as Paula and another officer raced up the driveway with their guns drawn. It definitely wasn't what he wanted to see, especially when he saw the front window of the house shatter and a figure from inside take a couple of shots at them.

"No, Paula! No!" shouted Morgan. He grabbed the door handle pulled it up and rammed his shoulder against the door again and again. More shots rang out from inside so he stopped, pounded the window with his fist and resigned himself to be a spectator to what was happening.

More shots quickly sounded, this time from the team outside, which either struck the new shooter or at least drove him back inside. Once Paula and her partner reached the door, he saw her take command and bark out instructions. She pushed the screen door out of the way with her shoulder, then with her pistol at the ready, kicked open the inside door, stepped back and took two quick shots. She never retreated for cover but stood there in the open doorway until her partner managed to pull out the injured man and drag him aside on the driveway against the relative safety of the wall of the house. Morgan was surprised Paula did not join them. Instead she stepped back from the door with her gun slightly lowered. Three more uniformed officers raced up the driveway to assist.

For a moment all was quiet. Then the sound of a shot came from inside which missed everybody and sent pieces of brick flying off the wall of the neighbour's house behind them. An armed figure burst through the door and fired at Paula. The shot would have struck her if she had not twisted and dropped to one knee after the first shot.

Morgan screamed and pounded the window with his fists. "Paula, get out of there! Get out the hell out of there!"

He watched as smoke burst from Larry's pistol followed immediately by the sound of a gunshot, but his shot obviously had missed. The gunman's arm swung around to return fire, but Paula reacted first. She spun on her knee and swung her pistol up. Morgan saw her gun kick and watched the gunman go sprawling backwards, his gun clattering to the ground, his hand clutching his chest.

Morgan was surprised and fearful when he saw Paula still had not moved from her position. Shouts came from inside the house and more gunfire erupted. Paula let go a couple more rounds as her support formed up behind her. He watched four more racing up the lawn towards the front entrance of the house.

More panes of glass were smashed from the front windows and a roar of gunfire exploded. Larry took cover in the culvert from the bullets which kicked up dirt and grass in front of him. A cruiser raced around the corner and skidded to a stop in front of the house. Two officers jumped out the protected side, took up positions behind the cruiser and opened fire at the house.

Morgan slammed his fist against the window of his small prison again and shouted "NO! NO!" As he did, he saw Paula take a deep breath then rush through the destroyed side door followed closely behind by the other three officers. A barrage of shots from different calibre guns could be heard, then the curdling sound of a woman's scream.

At the sound, Morgan stopped hitting the window. Horrified, he placed a hand over his mouth while the other pressed hard against the window. He could feel himself shake.

The two officers who had taken cover behind the cruiser in front of the house followed Larry up the front lawn and in through the front door. The shooting stopped and for a moment, all was quiet.

More police cruisers pulled up in front of the house parking haphazardly. Some officers ran crouched towards the house and entered through the front and side doors. Others with their guns drawn took positions in front and behind the house. Two attended to the wounded officer while another kneeled beside the downed gunman, placed his index fingers against the side of his neck. He felt around a few places, stood up and shook his head. Morgan guessed the man was dead. He felt damn good about it.

Morgan waited in worried silence, hoping for any sign Paula was alright. The fingers of the hand against the car window, gently rubbed up and down against the window. His breathing was short and shallow.

A smile broke out on his face when he saw Paula step through the door onto the front porch. Her gun was back in its holster signifying the battle was indeed over. Her face was dead serious when she looked over to where Morgan sat in the back of the cruiser. As she looked, she raised her right hand slightly and gave it a single quick wave to let him know she was alright.

Morgan saw her smile slightly and wished he wasn't trapped in the cars backseat jail so he could go and hold her. He knew however, even if he was out it was something he wouldn't be able to do. He also knew it would be many more hours before he would have a chance to so.

Chapter 11

Halina sat on the couch of her large living room and bounced Shane on her knee, holding him by his hands as she did. He giggled and urged her on, "Mommy, Mommy, more, more!" he laughed wearing a big smile on his face. She continued on but soon was exhausted. *You'd think after doing this for almost forever I'd have a lot more stamina*, she thought as she stopped and lifted him up to her chest for a hug.

"Mommy has to rest. You've worn me out Sir,' she said as she gave him another squeeze and kiss. She set him on her lap and checked the insulin pump Shane constantly wore to ensure it was still set correctly. Then she ran her fine fingers along the cannula, a thin plastic tube which attached just under Shane's skin to deliver doses of fast-acting insulin when the monitor registered his glucose levels had risen above a certain point. She found it firmly in place.

Satisfied everything was in order, she sat Shane amongst a small pile of toys in the middle of the room. She grabbed a Wet Nap from a dispenser and wiped down her hands. Halina felt very relaxed. Being home alone with her son always put her there.

Halina knew how lucky she was and wasn't. A week after graduating high school, her parents were both killed when a drunk driver took the wrong ramp onto the 401 highway and hit them head on. The insurance settlement was huge, which allowed her to graduate from medical school without needing to get a student loan, which she did anyway on the advice of her parents' accountant, due to student interest rates being so low.

With just one term left before graduation, she discovered she was pregnant. Halina never told the father as she had broken up with him before she found out and decided to raise him on her own. Once Shane was born, she bought them a very nice home in a good neighbourhood. Because of the inheritance and excellent advice from her accountant, she had the money to ensure Shane received the best care and medical devices.

She knew she was lucky money-wise. Her job at the clinic paid well but not well enough for what she wanted for Shane. Her parent's death may have provided for that but it hurt her they died so young and never had the chance to set eyes on their beautiful grandchild.

Shane was playing contently as she picked up her china cup of Earl Grey tea from the saucer which sat on the end table. Before she could take a sip, the doorbell rang. She sighed, sat it down without taking a sip and crossed the room to the front door. Halina smiled when she took a look through the peephole and quickly opened the door.

"Beth!" Halina exclaimed as she took a step outside and gave her cousin a hug. "What are you doing here? I wasn't expecting you. What a nice surprise!"

"Well, cuz, I know we're going out Friday night, but I wanted to see my nephew. Hope I'm not interrupting anything."

"No, come on in," Halina said as she motioned with her arm for Beth to enter.

Beth entered and followed Halina into the living room. Shane's face lit up when he saw her and she scooped him up in her arms. He laughed as she bounced him and when she stopped, he leaned back a little in her arms so he could see her face better and asked a most popular kid's question. "Candy?"

Halina sighed. "Every time you come over, he expects some. You've made it a trained response."

Beth moved Shane to one arm and reached into her pocket with her free hand and pulled out a sucker. He clapped his hands together. "And what do I get for this?"

Shane gave her a hug, then pulled back and reached out to grab it. Beth quickly pulled the sucker back and unwrapped it before she handed it to him. "He's not going to do without the things kids love just because he's diabetic."

"You know, Beth, I just don't want him to get used to candy. When he's in school…"

"When he's in school, he'll always be tempted, whether I give him candy now or not. It's only once in awhile, it's sugar-free and made for diabetics. Later when candies are handed out in school, he won't be left out or try some which he shouldn't have. Not saying he won't. You're going to have your hands full for sure."

Halina left it at that. The topic was always a short conversation and, although she never treated Shane to such goodies, she was actually happy somebody did. For Shane it was a treat and not a habit.

Saying to heck with her tea, Halina offered Beth some wine, which she of course accepted. For the next hour they chatted and played with Shane until he started to show signs of sleepiness. It was an advantage of diabetic candy. No sugar rush. They both went upstairs and tucked him into bed. Halina took care to check the pump and cannula one more time. Shane's eyes were near closed when the lights went out and the two women returned downstairs to their wine.

There was only a sip remaining in each glass. Halina walked over, picked it up and drained it without sitting. "Let's go to the kitchen. I'll open another bottle."

Beth sat at the kitchen table and watched as Halina uncorked a bottle of what she knew would be an excellent Riesling, grabbed two clean glasses and filled each about halfway up. Halina handed Beth hers and sat kitty-corner to her at the table. They tinged glasses and took a sip.

"Halina?" said Beth in a questioning tone.

"Yes, dear."

"I have something to ask and I don't want you to get defensive."

"Okay." Halina said leaning forward.

"Remember last week I told you I had a date with a guy who had a cat which he claimed had cured itself of diabetes?"

Halina nodded and took a short sip of her wine. She wondered where Beth was going with this.

"Well, I had the cops pay me a visit this week. They were asking about that same cat."

"Really? Why?"

"It seems somebody broke into the guy's house a few days after our date and the police suspect it might have had something to do with them trying to take the cat."

"Sounds ridiculous."

"It gets better. He was attacked again the next day. They're unsure if the two incidents are related but the second attack was definitely an attempt to grab the guy's cat."

"Wow, interesting. But why did the cops want to talk to you?" Halina asked horrified by what had started out to be an easy theft now had implications against her cousin and best friend.

"The guy has never spoken to anybody else but me about the cat. Suddenly after he does, I'm a suspect."

'That's awful!"

Beth paused before continuing. "Halina, I have to ask. It's a difficult notion for me to even consider, let alone ask you about. But after I told you about my date did you, um, ah, did you ... have you ... did you try to have make arrangements to steal the cat?"

"What?" Halina exclaimed. She sat stunned for a second and took a sip of wine. The question was totally unexpected, and she needed a moment to think.

"Beth, what you are suggesting is incredible. You tell me something Friday night and Monday morning your date's place is broken into and they think it was to steal the cat ... and you think I was the one who organized it all plus another attack the very next morning?"

"It's just that, you know, you work in diabetic research. Shane has diabetes. A cat might have cured itself. Look, I know you're not an evil person. I just had to ask. After all, it's not everyday cops come beating at my door to question me."

"So, you're out on a date with some guy who's trying to impress you with wild, improbable tales about his cat and on this one flimsy piece of information, I hire some thugs to steal it. Do you hear what you're asking?"

"I know. I'm sorry. After the cops came, I called that asshole Morgan and gave him shit, then I stewed about it for a few days. Last night I remembered telling you and I really just had to ask. I know you're not that type of person, but I had to ask."

Halina reached out, took Beth's hand in hers and held it. "It's alright. I think if things were reversed, I'd be asking you the same thing. No need to apologize."

Beth smiled, relieved Halina wasn't mad or upset. With her free hand, she picked up her glass and took a long sip of wine. Suddenly she pulled her glass quickly away from her mouth, spilling wine on herself as she did.

"Halina ... Halina, how did you know Morgan's place was broken into on a Monday morning? I never told you what day."

Beth watched as fear took over Halina's face. "And how did you know it was in the morning he was attacked the next day?"

No answer was offered by Halina who just sat with her head bowed staring down at her wine.

"Oh God, it was you wasn't it, Halina. Holy shit, you're the one behind all this!"

Chapter 12

Morgan sat quietly on Paula's couch and slowly sipped on a bottle of beer. Between sips he absentmindedly picked at the corners of the bottles label and carefully worked at tearing it off cleanly. The TV was on, but he had the sound muted. He had turned the ringer of his phone back on. So far there were no calls, no texts, no messages.

He was many things at the moment. Wired up, exhausted, worried, confused, unsettled and alone. The day's events ran through his mind. Everything was moving way too fast for him. It was only the week before when his two biggest worries were keeping his department at work operating efficiently and learning to perform a proper counterattack on the fencing strip. Suddenly he found himself caring for somebody, saw them put in harm's way, not once but twice because of him. People had been killed, deservedly so but the fact was they too had died because of him.

He glanced around the room which felt library silent and spiritless.

Damn, I don't even know where to sleep tonight, He thought. *After last night, do I just assume I'm sleeping with*

Paula ... or is this couch going to be my bed? Maybe last night was a one-time thing. Maybe it happened because we were out there defending each other as well as ourselves. It got our juices going and they never stopped. Maybe it was just a release for her after.

Morgan smiled as he thought back about the two of them in bed. *It was a great night, though. Paula really knows her way around a bed. Hope it's not our only time.*

Sure, can handle herself in a fight too. God, the bastard never had a chance when she slammed into him.

The smiled slipped away from his face.

Today, though, I've never seen anything like it. Felt so useless. Shit, all I could do was sit and watch. That was so brutal but hey Asshole, what could I have done if I had managed to get out of that damned cop car? Rush in? Get in the way? Be a distraction for her and her buddies? Hell, you would've got her, yourself or somebody else killed.

He drained the rest of his beer and headed to the kitchen for another.

She's probably in deep shit because of me too, although I'm sure nobody saw me when I left her with Stutz's body. They all seemed to buy my story about why I was on the bus when I saw Pin. That's gotta help.

He twisted the cap off the beer and without a thought, flipped it onto the kitchen counter instead of the garbage. He walked to the kitchen doorway and leaned up against the narrow wall of the entrance.

Hell, I don't even know where Tiberius is. Amazing how quiet and empty a place can feel without an animal in it. I don't even have their damned phone number to call to see if everything is okay with him. Shit, of course it is. If anything, they're probably spoiling him to death. I'm just too damned busy feeling sorry for myself. Where the hell is Paula anyways? Why doesn't she call?

Just then there was a knock on the door. Morgan's first instinct was to head to the kitchen for the chef's knife out before answering the door. He considered it for a moment but instead just asked loudly who was there.

"It's me, Morgan. Grace Upton and I've got a little guy here who's dying to see you."

Without hesitation, Morgan pulled the door open, then stepped back to make room for Grace and the all too familiar carrier which contained Tiberius.

"I have a key but knew you were here and didn't just want to barge in on you," she explained as she stepped inside. Grace walked over to a chair in the living room and unzipped the end of the carrier. Tiberius scampered out and jumped up onto the couch where he started chirping at Morgan to come pick him up. Morgan quickly complied.

"Paula called and told me about today. She thought you could use some company until she gets home," explained Grace. Then with a smile, she added, "Not mine of course, but this little furry one."

Grace reached out and stroked Tiberius "He's such a lovable, sweet boy. We're going to make sure nobody, and I mean nobody, hurts this little cutie."

Morgan thanked her for bringing Tiberius over for him and asked if she wanted anything to eat or drink. She declined. He then asked about Paula and how she sounded on the phone.

"Debriefings can take some time. I would never say this to any cop but they're almost as hard on us waiting as it is for them going through it. Be patient, though. She's fine. She's tough. I've known her for years and she can handle herself with her superiors."

Grace reached out and placed her hand on Morgan's arm. "I think the world of Paula. You've got yourself quite a catch there Morgan. I hope you realize it."

Before he could reply, Grace swung around and left.

Got myself quite a catch? Does it mean what I think? Maybe I'm not on the couch tonight. Quite a catch? Damn, things are happening quickly lately.

He put Tiberius down, pulled open a tin of cat food, emptied it onto a small plate, and set it on the floor. Tiberius tore into it right away. "Hey, boy, it's not like you haven't eaten. I know they would have fed you well. You're just a little pig."

Hearing the sound of food eagerly being licked up suddenly made the place feel much homier, warmer, more alive and comfortable to Morgan. While Tiberius ate, Morgan returned to the couch, picked up the remote, turned up the sound and flipped between news channels to find any reports of the shootout. Most had on the weather, so he leaned back, relaxed and waited.

For the next hour, Morgan enjoyed his time with Tiberius as he waited for Paula to return home. When Tiberius wasn't in Morgan's lap purring away while being stroked, he was fetching small soft balls which Morgan tossed from the couch into the kitchen. Although he still was worried about Paula, he felt more settled having Tiberius around while he waited.

He tossed the ball again for what seemed to be the hundredth time. Tiberius never tired of playing fetch. Morgan drained what was left of his third beer, set it down and leaned his head back. He was tired and could easily fall asleep where he sat, when he heard the sound of a key turning in the lock of the door. Quickly he stood up and took a few steps to the door which swung open just has he got there. An exhausted Paula, pulled out the key, stepped inside, tossed her keychain onto the small table by the door. She dropped her purse beside it, wrapped her arms around Morgan, and rested her head on his shoulder.

"This has been a day," was all she said as she held onto him. She sighed and closed her eyes.

They remained in that peaceful moment for a minute or so before Morgan broke the silence. "I can't believe with all the shit you were going through, you still thought of calling Grace and having her bring over Tiberius. Thanks."

"I knew you were all alone in a strange place and felt you could use some company," Paula answered quietly as she gave him a squeeze. The two stood silently holding onto each other for support.

"I've never killed a man before," Paula said quietly. "Yesterday was my first time. I only ever had to pull my gun out once since being on the force before becoming a detective. Now look. I killed a man yesterday, two people today. Wounded another."

"All in self defence," defended Morgan speaking softly as he held her. "Look, you saved my life yesterday, your fellow officers today and kept yourself alive throughout it all. I know there must be a lot going through your mind, but you did what you had to do. Did what you were trained to do."

Morgan felt her head nod yes against his shoulder. "Was one of them Mitt Pin?"

Paula stepped back and looked directly into Morgan's eyes, "No. No he wasn't. If he was there, he escaped before we busted in."

"I definitely saw him go in."

"He wasn't there."

"Damn! At least we have the name of the detective agency they worked out of."

"Nope. It's been out of business for years. They were just using it to meet up. Not many offices are in use in that building so it wasn't a bad place for them to meet."

"Damn. That sucks. What happened back at the station then? Did you get shit?"

"Oh yeah. I was expecting to. I had to twist the truth a little, leave some things out which I really hate to do, just so I wouldn't be suspended."

"What did you tell them?"

"I told them I took it upon myself to shadow Stutz and followed him into the building. I could hear them talking but couldn't make out clearly what they were saying. They sounded like they were about to leave, so I headed back outside so they wouldn't see me when they left, and

I could continue following them. When I didn't see them come out, I went back in and spotted Stutz's body through the partially opened door."

Morgan considered the story for a moment and decided even though the story was made up on the fly, found it believable. He pulled Paula in and held her close to him.

"Christ Paula. I'm so sorry. Since you met me, your life has become a bit of a mess," Morgan said quietly.

Paula pulled back and looked him with two tired but dazzling sapphire blue eyes. "No ... it's a huge mess! Today I could have been suspended or worse. I lied for my first time on the force to keep it from happening. But Morgan, none of this is your fault. If I hadn't been there yesterday, Tiberius would be gone. You may have been seriously hurt or killed so I'm glad I was there. Taking you with me this morning was a bad call on my part, but we almost got Mitt Pin because of it. God, I hate lying but I had to in order to save my job. I love it too much."

"I know. So, what happened at the house? Did they start shooting to protect Pin?"

"No. We were ready but never expected the situation would escalate the way it did. Turns out there was a high-level meeting between two small drug gangs trying to slice up a piece of the city between them. I guess they thought we were there to take them down in once fair swoop. It turns out we did but as you know, it wasn't our original intention."

Paula wrapped her firm arms around Morgan. He loved the feel of her body pressing up against his.

"Mitt and others are still out there," she said softly into his ear. 'Don't worry, though. I'm going to keep you and Tiberius safe."

"I thought the man was supposed to be the protector ... the hero!" said Morgan as he leaned back to look at her with a smile.

"Welcome to the new world order, Sir!" Paula said before leaning forward and placing her lips against his in a long, warm kiss. She then leaned back and sighed. "It's been a long day and I need to change. Back in a minute."

Paula stepped around him and disappeared into the bedroom. Morgan was quite aware she never closed the door behind her. He then felt a creature rub up against his legs. A purring creature. He looked down to see Tiberius was demanding a little attention for himself. Morgan sat down on the carpet and ran his hand over Tiberius's head and along the length of his back while he kept his eyes peeled on the open bedroom door. He could hear a belt being unfastened and then the sound of clothing and the belt landing on something, probably the chair which was on her side of the bed. He had noticed her clothes piled on that chair before.

His eyes opened wide when she stepped back through the bedroom doorway wearing just a blue satin slip. The soft shiny fabric gracefully played up against her skin and fell over her hips gently hugging and highlighting the outline of her sweeping curves. The patterned lace did little to hide her sensuous breasts, yet enticed him at what they did not allow to show. Morgan didn't say a word. He could only watch, enjoy and desire the perfection of the woman who slowly approached him. Each step she took sent a shockwave of excitement through him.

When she was just a step away from where he still remained sitting on the floor, he lifted Tiberius from his lap and set him to one side. With one motion, she stepped over his leg with her right foot and swung her left leg gracefully over his shoulder. The gentle satin on her slip flowed out over his head while the silky skin of the inside of her firm thigh pressed up against his cheek.

Her aroma was the scent of excitement. Under her slip, she wore no panties. Much to her delight he knew what she wanted. She held one hand against the back of his head while the other hand gripped his shoulder tightly. She leaned her head back and moaned. Her hip thrust out with the movement asking for more and he indulged her. Both of her hands grasped his shoulders held his shoulders and he could feel her fingernails dig in. He eagerly helped to increase her excitement even more until with many gasps, one final groan and spasm, she peaked.

He pulled his head out from underneath the satin and placed it up against the fabric which again hid all her pleasures. Paula stood breathing heavily with both her hands resting on the back of Morgan's head. She was sweating and smiling. After the day she had just been through, it was what she had needed.

Chapter 13

Earlier the same day, Mitt got off the bus at Laird Drive. He unconsciously patted the jacket pocket which held his money, then stuck his hands in his pockets and crossed at the light. As he crossed, he started to feel a little uneasy.

He was on his way to finally pay off a large debt which had been with him longer than it should have been with the money he had just hijacked from Oscar. Once he did, he would finally be free and avoid any physical damage which he knew would be coming if he waited any longer.

The thought should have made him happy however there was something he sensed telling him something wasn't quite right. He slowed down and became totally aware of everything around him. When he came to the corner and turned, he spotted Morgan on the other side of the street.

Oh, fuck! I'm being followed ... wait. It's just some loser asshole yakking on his cell. Shit! All this dough I have on me must be making me jumpy.

He passed the corner house and turned down the driveway of the next one. Reaching the side entrance, he opened the screen door, stepped in to block it from closing and knocked hard, opened the door and walked in. He closed the door behind him, stood on the landing and pounded the wall once. Immediately he heard a gruff voice call out, "Name?"

"I know you saw me on the monitor when I stepped in," he answered.

"Well, damn, looky here. If it isn't Mitt Pin himself," he heard a taunting voice he recognized as a man he knew only as Big Mike exclaim as the door four steps up from the landing opened. Something wasn't right. Big Mike wasn't usually around unless something important was going on.

Big Mike thudded down the stairs, spun Mitt around pressing his face against the wall and gave him a brief frisk. He confiscated Mitts knife and jammed it into his own pocket.

Once finished, he turned Mitt back around to face him. Mike's nickname fit him. He was a heavy set, barrel-chested man whose size belied how quick he was. He took up most of the landing they stood on but Mitt was not about to complain even though he was still jammed against the wall. "So, Mitt. What brings a loser like you to our fine neighbourhood today?"

"Money."

"Looking for more? Damn man, you're so late paying as it is. They're getting ready to fuck you up if you're any later."

"Tell him I have it. I'm here to pay."

"How do you know he's here right now?"

"Because he usually is this time of day. The nocturnal rest during the day and live by night."

"Shit, what's up with all the fancy words?"

"Just feeling good about things. Come to pay off my debt ... in full. Now if you're on the door it means there's some big shit going on right now, but I don't give a fuck. I need to see Henderson and need to see him now."

"Hey, Pin. You ain't in any position to be giving orders. Henderson's in a meeting right now and I don't want to interrupt."

Mitt reached into his jacket pocket, pulled out a small wad of bills, counted off five hundred dollars in twenties and held them out. Big Mike snatched them out of his hand and stuffed them into his pants pocket.

"Wait here," he ordered and headed upstairs.

A minute later, a tall, slim, nicely dressed, redheaded man, appeared at the top of the stairs.

"Well, if it isn't Mitt fucking Pin come to pay me a personal visit. I was just going to get Big Mike here to take the payment and show you some reasons why you shouldn't be late with me, when he tells me you've come to pay in full."

"That's right. Can I come up?"

"No. We'll do this in the basement. Mike, follow him down."

Mitt did not like having to going into the dark basement. He had no idea what Henderson had in mind but reluctantly made his way down. Big Mike joined him at the bottom as did Henderson a few moments later.

Henderson held his hands out in front of him and spread them out. "Well?"

"Nine thousand bucks I think the total is," Mitt said as he reached into a different pocket than the one he had paid Mike from and pulled out a wad of bills. He started to count off what he owed.

"It was nine G's but you know, Mitt. I've had to chase you down for payments. I've just finished making arrangements to have some people pay you a visit to give you an excellent reminder on how you should pay up on time. Now I'll have to take some of my precious time to call them off. I hate inconvenience, Mitt. I do. I really fucking hate it."

Mitt glared at Henderson. He didn't want to lose it all, have it just taken away from him. There was no way out, though. He came expecting to pay up and get out quick. Now he hoped he would be able just to get out.

"Look Mitt, I want to be reasonable. I don't know where you came up with this kind of green and I fucking don't care. So, here's the deal."

Mitt anxiously waited as Henderson paused for effect.

"Ten thousand. I need ten thousand to make me happy."

Mitt sighed. It wasn't as bad as it could be. He went over to a small table he saw, counted out ten piles of a thousand each, came back and placed it in Henderson's outstretched hand. Mitt was about to return the remaining bills to his jacket pocket, when Henderson reached out and gently grabbed his hand.

"Mitt, Mitt, Mitt. What about my boy Big Mike here? You wasted his time too. That'll be a thousand for him."

Mitt hated the huge grin which broke out on Big Mike's face and wished he could bury his fist into it. Instead, he quietly counted it off and handed it to Big Mike.

"At least we've left you enough for one really good hooker," Big Mike joked as he jammed the bills into the same pocket as the five hundred he had received earlier. "Or a whole lot of crack hoes. Probably what you go for anyways, eh Mitt? Quantity not quality."

"I guess we're done here then?" Mitt said, deciding not to reply to Big Mike and choosing to just step around him, go up the stairs and leave. Big Mike took a step to the side to block Mitt's exit.

Mitt stopped, "What now?"

It was Henderson who answered. "We've a lot of important people upstairs. Don't want the neighbourhood seeing people coming and going so you may have come in through the side but you're fucking leaving through the back."

"Didn't know you had back door."

"Original owners had an in-law apartment with a private entrance from the back. Use it and head through the opening in the hedge at the back. There's an empty lot on the other side. Oh, and Mitt," Henderson said placing a hand on Mitt's shoulder, "nice doing business with you. Please come again if you need anything. Now fuck off!"

Henderson turned and headed back up stairs while Big Mike waited to ensure Mitt left. Mitt complied. He opened a door to the apartment. It hadn't been used for years and the musty air was thick. He coughed but kept moving. He wanted out of the foul air and away from those inside as soon as possible.

Fresh air greeted him as he stepped back out into the sunlight. *Those bastards are going to get theirs someday*, he thought as he climbed the crumbled outside stairs up into the backyard. At the far left hand corner of the yard, he saw a small gap in the fence and hedge and made his way through. Mitt crossed the yard and headed up the street.

He walked over to Laird and started south when he saw cop car followed closely by another go speeding by him. For a moment he stopped to watch, curious as to what was happening. Then as more cop cars sped by, he thought it best to keep his head down and get the hell away as quickly as possible.

When he reached the corner of Eglinton and Laird, he stopped and looked back. He saw a cruiser blocking Laird and another north of it doing the same. Except for the traffic on Eglinton, all seemed quiet in the neighbourhood he had just left. He stood at the bus stop and waited. More cop cars roared into the neighbourhood. A few minutes later he heard the unmistakable sound of a shotgun blast, followed quickly by the cracking of gunfire.

Hearing all hell breaking loose from where he had just been, he was delighted to have a westbound bus pull up to the stop at the same time he did. He climbed aboard and sat in a curb side window seat. As the bus pulled away, he looked back to where he had just come from.

Another passenger who was waiting at the stop, sat down beside him and asked, "Did you hear that? What do you think is going on?"

"Hell if I know. Kids and firecrackers maybe."

A huge smile broke out over his face. He turned back to face the front of the bus.

Too bad I paid off the asshole before he got taken down, he thought begrudgingly. *Oh well. At least I made it out of there with some decent cash left. Hmm, maybe Big Mike had a good idea but hell, never a crack hoe? Give me a fucking break! Hey I haven't been with Audrey for quite awhile. Great fucking broad and a quality lay. Think I'll get her for the entire night.*

Chapter 14

Beth arrived home from Halina's. She walked over to a cupboard and opened the door which held her red wine rack. Picking the least expensive bottle, she skilfully removed the cork and poured. She stopped when the glass was about one quarter full, then said to "hell with it" and filled it three quarters the way to the top. Her head spun from what she had heard during the evening. There was much to think about, much to consider and she needed the assistance of a decent merlot.

She was glad Halina at least had not gone insane and decided to kidnap Morgan's cat on what little she had heard from their date. Beth smiled quietly to herself and took a small sip of wine after giving the glass a gentle swirl to aerate. Originally, she had told Halina about the cat, whatever its name was, as she thought Morgan was being an ass, doing the usual guy thing of telling some bullshit story in hopes of somehow getting himself laid from it. She thought Halina would get a laugh out of it. Instead, Halina's company knew of the cat's background but not its name or where to find it. Beth shook her head slightly realizing she had opened the door for her.

At least I've done nothing wrong here, Beth thought. *I really knew nothing about any of this when the cops grilled me. Oh hell, I do know now and I guess that would make me an accessory and I could be charged. The blast I gave Morgan when I left that voicemail though was sincere. I can't see anybody ever suspecting me now of being in on this.*

She walked over to her living room window and took another sip of wine as she watched the lights of the city below. One part of her wanted to help Halina. *Maybe I should text Morgan and apologize for my call. I could suggest we go out again so Halina would have eyes on the inside.*

No Beth. That would be stupid. If Halina gets caught, fingers would start pointing at me. I know way too much already and don't think I could fake my way out of it with the cops. Halina would end up in jail. I'd end up in jail! Hell No. I don't need this. I just need to stay the hell out of it.

Beth had heard too much about Halina's boss, Sturgess, to know he was lying to her. His nice story about needing to keep the cat alive was pure crap. Halina was an animal lover. Sturgess would kill the cat in a second if it would make him a buck and give him the fame he desired. It would break Halina's heart knowing she was the one responsible for handing over the cat.

Maybe I can talk her out of this, Beth tried to reason to herself. *No, Beth believes Sturgess and wants to come through for Shane. She'd likely lose her job if she doesn't come through. Oh, Halina, how ... why did you ever get yourself tied up in all this!*

Chapter 15

When Morgan first opened his eyes, he was groggy and a little confused as to where he was. Once he managed to come fully out of the deep sleep he had been in and focus, the reality of where he was came back to him.

He was laying on his right side on the side of the bed closest to the door. The front of his legs was a little cool as there was just a sheet pulled across his hips and over the hips and back of Paula, who too was on her right side snuggled hard up against him. Although he had only stayed over two nights, he felt they might have already figured out who has which side of the bed. He smiled at the thought.

When he looked over at the clock on the end table on his side of the bed, he was surprised to find it read 10:09 am. It had been such a long while since he had slept in so late. Usually a hungry Tiberius would have him awake way before then. When he looked over at Paula's dresser, he saw Tiberius curled up contently sleeping on a pile of clothes she had left sitting on it. He smiled again. Now she'd find out how cat hair sticks to clothing.

The room was dim as even though the bedroom blinds were closed tight, light still spilled in from the open door to the living room. He looked back to the nightstand to find an empty wine glass sitting there.

After their session in the living room, he and Paula had continued on in the bedroom. He loved her passion and the way she brought out more of his. After they were done and they had laid quietly together for awhile, Paula had gotten up and left the room. Morgan remembered how he had watched as she had exited the room naked and marvelled about how seemingly perfect her body was to him.

He remembered the confidence she had in her own naked form, how she had just glided back into the bedroom with a bottle of white wine and two glasses. After jumping back into bed and pouring them each a glass, she had waited for him to sit up against the pillows before handing him his. They had talked a little about nothing as they sipped on their wine. When the glasses were empty, they had quietly set down their glass on their end tables and slid back down into a laying position facing each other.

Morgan had enjoyed the smell of the wine on her breath. He had moved his head close so their lips came together. They were so soft and warm. The day, though, had been long for both of them. She had put her arm around him, and he put his around her and together they both drifted off into deep slumbers.

Morgan thought briefly about getting up, but she was cuddled up tight up against him and he didn't want to wake her. He also had to admit he enjoyed waking up to that wonderful feeling of closeness, so he wasn't in any hurry to disturb the situation. A few minutes passed until she finally stirred, let him go and rolled over onto her back. He waited for her eyes to open.

"Morning," he said as they did.

"How long have you been awake?" asked Paula before rubbing her eyes. Morgan liked she never bothered to cover up more. Before he could reply, she glanced over at the clock. "Holy crap! 10:16!"

"Yep. Looks like we got a fair bit of sleep."

Morgan sat upright in the bed and grabbed his empty glass. He reached out a hand towards Paula, "Let me get rid of that for you."

Paula grabbed her glass and held it against her. "What? We still have some wine left in the bottle."

Before he could reply she grabbed the bottle and poured them each a third of a glass full, tilted up hers and drained it. She looked over at Morgan, "Come on, your turn. I don't want to be the only reprobate in the room."

Morgan chuckled, saluted Paula with the glass, then did his part and drained it. Hearing the two talking and not wanting to be left out, Tiberius jumped down from the dresser and onto the bed between them as if this was the way his morning had always started. They both started stroking him, which caused him to give off a loud constant purr.

"We can't do this all day long. Time for us to get up and squeeze some fresh orange juice. I figure even though the wine we just had wasn't sparkling, if we have some O.J. now we can call this a deconstructed mimosa, which makes us classy, not skids." Paula spoke with a smile which Morgan found disarming. "It's our day off, so time to get at it. You get to make breakfast. Bacon and eggs are in the fridge, frozen home fries in the freezer."

"Sure, but what do you mean 'day off'?"

"I mean too much has gone on in the past couple of days for the two of us to even comprehend. Hell, Morgan, I've never killed a living being before this week. Now I've killed three men and a woman. You've been attacked, had to fight for your life and your world's been turned upside down. Tiberius has been shuttled off from place to place. We all need a day to rest. A day to recharge or we won't be good for anything. Everything about me, mind, body and soul are screaming to just shut down for a day."

"Yeah, I guess you're right," Morgan agreed.

Paula leaned over and gave him a long warm kiss. She pulled her head just slightly back, keeping her face close to his. "And you know, with everything that's happened we haven't really had time to sit back and get to know one another. Today seems to be a good day for us to do just that."

She leaned even closer and gently brushed her lips against his. Then she suddenly pulled back and gave him a surprisingly short playful peck on the cheek before she turned and swung herself out of bed. "Before I do anything, have to shower." She headed out of the bedroom without bothering to throw clothes of any sort.

"Hey! I like my eggs easy over in case you're wondering," she called back playfully. She spun around and walked back with more instructions, "No broken yolks or runny whites either. Don't blow it."

Morgan chuckled. He looked down at Tiberius and ran a hand along his back. "First I have to make my boy some breakfast. Then I'll worry about not screwing up the eggs."

Tiberius had greedily eaten most of the wet food Morgan had put out for him and was in the living room playing with a stuffed toy, flipping it around and chasing it when Paula returned from her shower. She wore just a robe, no slippers. From what Morgan could tell there was little, if anything, worn beneath it.

"I think you'll be pleased," he said as he set down a plate containing three eggs, four pieces of bacon and a generous pile of home fries on the table for her.

She looked down at the nicely presented plate and then up to him with a questioning look. He shrugged his shoulders and explained, "Sorry. I didn't know how much you usually have for breakfast and didn't want to come up short."

"Wow! Usually I have a decent breakfast but nothing like this. Sure, looks delicious!"

Morgan sat kitty corner form her at the table with his plate holding the same as hers. Paula had already sliced open one of the perfectly done egg yolks and had put together some egg, bacon and potato on her fork. Before she put it to her mouth she asked, "So Mr. Watson. Tell me about your life."

Whoa, interview time, he thought as he stalled for a moment, "Let's see. I might as well start by telling you what I do for a living. I'm the head of purchasing at NIC. It's what we call it anyways, National Insurance of Canada."

Paula interrupted. "So how did you end up there? I always find it interesting to see the choices people made to find out how they ended up where they are."

"During high school I worked part time in a warehouse and loved it. I couldn't see what could be better than driving around in a forklift all day. When I asked my boss about full time, he told me there was no money or future in it. I was a kid. What did I know? I just wanted to tool around in a forklift.

"My last year there, he had me transferred to the company's purchasing department. I was pissed about it but met some great people the first week I was there. The next thing I know is not only didn't I care about running around in a forklift all day anymore but I'm enrolled full time at Seneca College going for a degree in Purchasing and Supply Management. Not a very interesting story, I'll admit."

'To me, it is. You were lucky. It sounds like you ran into the right people at the right time in your life."

They finished up their breakfast chatting about Morgan's job, plus his interest in fencing. Paula was delighted to find Morgan also enjoyed yoga as it was something she did whenever she could find the time for it. Morgan had brewed a pot of tea and poured them each a cup which they took into the living room. By that time, Tiberius had become bored with his toy and was curled up in a chair, fast asleep.

"You know, Morgan, I'm not a cat person. At least I wasn't. Now look at him. How cute is he? I think Tiberius might be turning me." Almost on cue when she had finished Tiberius took a moment to stretch, gave a big yawn, circle his spot, curl up and drifted back to sleep. Paula shook her head at the cuteness she was falling in love with.

They both sat down on the couch. Paula shifted and crossed her right leg over her left which left it exposed. He was surprised to see a scar on her thigh, which sat a couple of inches above her knee.

"Morgan, you're staring. It's a little creepy."

"Sorry. I just noticed the scar on your leg. We've been naked together enough you'd think I would've noticed it before now."

Paula gave a small laugh. "It was usually dark and you're always pretty busy."

"How did you get it?"

"There's probably not a cop anywhere who doesn't have a couple of these. This one here," she explained as she ran a finger along its length and back, "came from a pen. I was a rookie and disarmed a suspect with a knife. I had him on his knees and thought it was over and guess I let my guard down. He pulled a pen from his shirt pocket and well, this is the result. Discovered how anything can become a weapon."

"Ouch!"

"Oh, it hurt but not as much as Jim's lecture afterwards. Both are still with me today."

"How did you end up on the force? Were you a tom-boy growing up?"

"Hell no. I loved dresses, dolls and all that girly stuff. When I became a teen, a lot of my friends took to stealing, drugs, doing bad shit. It wasn't me. I discovered I was a law and order person. My dad used to say there's nothing lower than a thief. They're lazy assholes looking to take something away from a person who worked hard to get it. Drugs, well I just didn't get the whole shooting up, smoking up, snorting thing. I saw it ruining lives of many people I grew up with. Found myself wanting to do something about it.

"I thought about being a lawyer, definitely not a slimy defence lawyer, mind you, but a prosecutor. Then I started thinking I could do more if I were on the streets. Maybe not just take down the assholes but also get involved with communities and maybe help someone not become another asshole behind bars."

Morgan nodded slightly. He'd seen in the past couple of days her dedication to duty. There never had been a moment of hesitation in any of her actions. She had noble ideals and held fast to them. When she finished talking, he could only sum up what she said with a quiet, "I think I understand."

"Of course, it pretty much made me updateable."

"Why?"

"Oh, you know, the weird hours I have and the fact I'm a cop. Guys seem to get intimidated when I tell them."

Morgan leaned over and kissed her warmly. "I'm not."

"I didn't think so," she replied and put her lips back against his. After a long moment, she gently pushed him back and stood up. Her robe had fallen away from her right shoulder which exposed her breast. She flipped the robe back over it. "I'm not trying to tease you. We'll have time later. Right now, how about I change, put on a yoga CD and we stretch out our tired worn out bodies?"

"Sounds good! I haven't done any yoga since the Wednesday night before this all happened." Morgan chuckled a little before he continued, "Actually, it's where I met Beth, the woman who left me that really angry voice mail."

"Beth?"

"Yeah. You're not jealous now are you?"

"No but Beth." Paula's voice trailed off for a few moments as she looked at the floor and pondered. "The message she left sounded genuine. There was too much hate and venom in there for it to be anything else, but what ... what if she could lead us to something, someone. Morgan, it's really the only place we have right now to start."

"Start?"

"Yeah. The only thing we have right now is a name. 'Oscar'. That's it. So tomorrow we're going to spend a very long boring day tailing your ex-friend Beth. Hopefully she can show us another path to follow." Morgan nodded and started to get up, "But Morgan?"

"Yes"

"We start tomorrow. Today, well, we're just going to enjoy ourselves."

Chapter 16

Leo Sturgess sat in his chair at the far end of the long boardroom table and observed while a woman in a white sterile lab jacket, holding what looked like a meter, finished her daily task of ensuring the company's bunker was not bugged in any way. As the room was fairly barren, there weren't many places to hide a small microphone or camera. Still, the inspection took a good half hour each day to perform. Even the handle on the door was disassembled and inspected.

Daily sweeps were an overkill he knew but long ago he had decided to accept his paranoia. It was a decision which made life easier for him. After the woman signalled the room was clean, she held out a form which Sturgess quickly reviewed then signed. After she left, he removed a device from his pocket and gave the room one last quick scan. Satisfied, he sat back into his chair.

He looked at his watch. It was ten in the morning. There should've been a knock on the door, but none came. He opened a folder and skimmed over the pages inside while he waited for the knock. Finally, he heard a rap on the door.

Sturgess got up and walked to the door. He checked his watch one more time before opening it knowing it would be Halina.

"It's 10:02. You're late," he stated.

Only by two minutes, Asshole, Halina thought. She took a breath and tried to explain. "Sorry, but as I was leaving the lab somebody had a question for me and…"

"And you thought what they had to know was more important than our ten o'clock? Dr. Shimon, as you already should be aware my time is a precious commodity and when you ask for a meeting and I grant you one, you are expected to be on time. The next time you are granted a one-on-one meeting, please leave earlier so as to arrive on time. Do I make myself clear on this?"

Halina hated his arrogant authority. "Yes Sir. I'm sorry. It won't happen again."

"Good. Close the door and take a seat," Sturgess directed as he returned to his chair.

Halina closed the door. Knowing Sturgess did not like people behind him, she rounded the table and made her way to her seat adjacent to him. He sat with the chair turned slightly toward the chair she took. He looked directly at her but didn't say a thing. She didn't know if she should start first. Knowing Sturgess, however, she gathered taking the initiative to start the conversation would upset him, as so many small things did.

"Cat," Sturgess stated.

"Pardon?"

"Cat. Feline. Scientific name 'felis catus'. You called this meeting. I was hoping for news on a very important cat. Where is it?"

Halina hesitated for a moment. She had wanted to start by explaining what had happened and then let him know what she needed from him. Her plan changed quickly as she felt him staring right through her. He tapped an index finger on the table waiting. "I need more money. I know you don't want to know the details, but I need more"

Sturgess stopped tapping, removed his wire rimmed glasses and sat them gently on top of the papers in front of him. He gently patted the papers with his right hand, then looked up and stared deeply into Halina's eyes. She wasn't sure but his brown eyes seem to grow darker and their glare unnerved her. She shifted uncomfortably.

"And how much more do you require?" he asked with almost no emotion.

"Sixty. Sixty thousand."

"This cat is starting to become quite expensive, isn't it?" He removed a pen from his lab jacket and tapped it several times on the table before answering. "Alright, I'll make the arrangements, but I don't care what it takes. You have one week, one week only to have this cat in my hands."

"Tonight, go to the Pantages. Arrive at seven like last time. Ensure nothing looks suspicious. Then go into the Stages Lounge and take a seat at a table, not near the bar. Order a wine and wait. The same man you met before for the original payment will join you. This time call him 'Bill'. Stand up and shake his hand, then sit."

"He will talk a little then slide over a paper for you to sign. It's gibberish but this needs to look like an everyday business transaction. Once signed, he will put it in his pocket and hand you a folder. It'll be full of blank pages and an envelope with your money. He leaves. You stay and finish your wine. Then in one week or less, you'll place in our possession one very valuable feline. Again, I don't care how you do it, just get it done. Time is now of the essence."

"Yes Dr. Sturgess. Thank you."

"Don't disappoint me again, Doctor. Now get back to work."

Halina stood up, gave a partial nod to him. Why, she didn't know. It just seemed to be the right thing to do. On her way out she passed Dr. Bakerman, second in charge of the clinic, in the hall just outside the door, She heard the swipe of his card in the lock to the bunker as she made her way back to the lab.

"Let me guess," Bakerman said with a smile as he sat down in the chair just vacated by Halina, "She needs more money."

"Yes, just as I thought she would. Already made provisions for that possibility. I told her she has one week to get it done."

"Leo. I'm a little troubled by all this. The guy who owns the cat knows somebody's after it and hell, even the cops know. If we grab it now with all the trouble which has been caused up to this point and come up with a cure, we are going to be investigated right up the ass."

"No, I'm way ahead of you there. You see, I have a man…"

"You seem to have people everywhere."

"Please. You know I hate being interrupted, even by you. I have a man, a great hacker, one of the very best in the business and he is busy laying out all the evidence the authorities will find upon the good doctor's death."

"You're planning to have her killed?"

"Eventually that will need to occur in order to protect ourselves. I am well aware when this cat disappears there needs to be a trail in place to lead the authorities elsewhere."

"I know of a research facility down in the States, DiaCure, which is doing diabetic work. I hear may be getting close to an oral pill which would replace insulin injections. We can't have them beating us. My man has been planting emails in Dr. Shimon's sent box and recycle bin. He has also been doing the same with DiaCure. After her murder, when the investigators start to dig, they'll find Dr. Shimon had plans to kidnap the cat and sell it to DiaCure. They will find the two have been communicating via secure emails for weeks and Dr. Shimon was to be paid quite handsomely for her work in securing this feline for them."

"From those emails, they'll also find dates, time and places where Dr. Shimon had two meetings with a DiaCure representative. Of course, this person will never be found and when they flash her picture around, she will be identified. When they come to us, they'll find we had hired a P.I. to keep an eye on her because we felt there was something just not right about the way she was acting."

"Don't worry, Bakerman. The guy we hired is legit and he's not in on this in any way. He will, though, have pictures of her taking money at the bar. His instructions are if he witnesses such an act, he is to follow the other suspect to find out whom he might be working for. He'll trail the man to Pearson and watch him hop a flight to the States. If he's any good, he'll find his suspect flew to, yes, that's right, to the same city where DiaCure is headquartered."

"Of course we'll gladly co-operate with the police and hand over everything the detective found. The only conclusion they will possibly be able to reach is our Dr. Shimon managed to kidnap said cat but was murdered after the cat was handed off. They can only conclude the creature is now somewhere in the U.S, probably in DiaCure's procession."

Bakerman took a moment to digest all he had just heard. "Yes, it all sounds well laid out Leo, but I do have just one question."

"Sure, let's have it."

"Do you have it in you to kill?"

"Kill? Of course I could kill a cat, especially for everything we'll gain from it, fame, fortune and of course a Nobel Prize for Medicine. But could I kill an actual human being? No, no I couldn't ... but then that's why I have people. They'll do it for me."

Chapter 17

After Paula laid out her plans to follow Beth most of the rest of the day had been a fun and relaxing one for Morgan. The two had spent a lot of time talking and it seemed to him they had grown closer because of it. They had done yoga, ordered in pizza, and when they played fetch with Tiberius Paula was astounded by the cat's seemingly limitless energy with the game. After going to bed, they had made love a couple of times before falling asleep.

The next morning Paula left early to go to the station to deal with another round of debriefs and internal interviews regarding the shootout. She never did tell Morgan the details of what happened inside the house after she went in but it must have been bad. Morgan had heard officers could suffer posttraumatic symptoms after having to kill but whenever Morgan had looked at Paula before the incident, he had seen a mentally tough and stable woman.

After they had enjoyed a wonderful morning the day before they sat down for lunch. During the meal he had noticed she had become quiet and sullen, plus she hardly ate. When they were done, she excused herself from the table and headed to the bathroom. It was while he was clearing the table and getting ready to wash up when he heard her sobbing.

He had no idea what to do or what she needed from him. Then he realized she just needed space. She needed time to deal with what she had been through. What she didn't need at the moment was him trying to be the "fix it guy", trying to make everything right. It's why she went to have a private moment. She was a strong person, but it came to him even the strongest have an emotional breaking point.

Morgan was glad the others were dead, and Paula had survived the ordeal but he wasn't the one who had pulled the trigger. It tore at him how he had no idea what went on after she had disappeared inside that house. He wanted to ask, was desperate to ask but he knew enough not to. As much he wanted to and as much as he felt he needed to know, he knew it best just to wait and let her tell him about it when she was ready ... if ever.

When Paula returned not a hair was out of place, her eyes were not red and she wore a smile. He marvelled at her ability to pull it all back together.

Paula had received word during the afternoon about meeting with the brass at the station the next morning. As it was a regular business workday, she determined it would not affect any of their plans to follow Beth as she too would be at work. The plan was to follow her from her place of business there when she left for the day.

Grace dropped by at ten to pick up Tiberius and take him back to her place. Morgan was glad how Tiberius strutted over to her quickly when she came in and rubbed up against her legs. Instinctively, Grace swooped him up in her arms causing him to irrupt with a loud purr. He seemed happy to go with her. Although he knew having Grace take Tiberius to a safe place was the best thing for him, Morgan was unsure about the enthusiasm his tabby exhibited at being taken. At least he could have shown a small sign of hesitation before being put in his carrier and carried off. Morgan couldn't believe the slight pinch of jealously which bit him.

Paula returned home at three in the afternoon, dropped her purse in the chair by the door, removed her revolver and embraced Morgan. She rested her head on his shoulder and held on to him tightly. When she finished and let him slip from her grip, he could see by the look in her eyes just how long of a day it had already been for her.

"You look exhausted. How did it go?"

"Pretty surprising actually."

From the tone of her reply he gathered she felt like talking. "Oh? In what way?"

"When I walked into the station thought for sure I leave being either suspended or demoted. I dreaded the thought. I worked so hard to become detective."

She let him go completely and went into the kitchen to pour herself a glass of water from a filtered water jug. After taking a long drink she continued. "My first meeting was with the SIU and it seemed to confirm it too. Taking part of a police operation while off duty, even worse, while on required leave is the direction, they came at me from. They said my mental condition after I killed that suspect at the hotel and discovering a dead body placed myself and fellow officers in danger during the raid. Damn, I really thought that was it for me."

"Something changed?"

"Yes. I came out after two and a half hours of grilling depressed and confused. I spent some time waiting at my desk, going through messages, trying to get some paperwork done even though my mind was nowhere close to being able to concentrate. Then I was called into the Staff Inspector's office."

She took another sip of water before continuing. "It turns out I'm not being demoted or suspended but, hell I can't believe this, I'm receiving a special commendation for my actions."

Morgan noticed she wasn't smiling but looking at the floor as she spoke. "Shouldn't that make you happy?"

She stood in silence for a few moments before she answered. "Two of my people took hits. Jerry was lucky. He took the first shot which hit him in his vest. When he went down he slammed his head against the ground and went unconscious. He has a couple of leg wounds which aren't serious, a broken ankle and a concussion, but Ed ... Ed..."

Paula started to well up. "Ed's lost his eye. Too much glass entered it when the screen door was shot out. Morgan, I was the one who called it in. I should have been at the door. It's my fault those two were hurt. Shit! Ed loved his job and now he has to ride a desk for the rest of days ... and they want to give me an award for that?"

Morgan knew there was nothing to say so he stepped forward and wrapped his arms around her. She clutched him tightly as if she were about to lose him. After a couple of minutes she let go and wiped her eyes, "Okay, I'm going to go pull myself together. When I'm done we're going to go see what we can learn from your Beth Poole."

It didn't take long for her to shower. While she did, Morgan printed off some pictures from his laptop and spread them out on the small dining room table. He glanced up just in time to catch a glimpse of her from behind as she strode naked from the bathroom to the bedroom. He smiled to himself, not at the image he just saw but the thought of the bedroom. Not too long ago he thought of it as 'her' bedroom. Now he thought of it as just 'the' bedroom. He wondered if there would come a time when it would feel like 'their' bedroom.

He could hear hangers being slid across the bar in the closet and at times, some gentle cursing. It took a few minutes for Paula to finally came out of the bedroom, tugging down on her skirt and running her hands down the front of her blouse to soften any creases as she walked towards him. She wore a grey skirt which ended just slightly above her knees, with an off-white long sleeve blouse. The neckline, although open to show of the bare skin of her chest, did not reveal anything else. He noticed she also had a thin smile, so must have been able to shake off, for the moment at least, her earlier upset state.

"Nice outfit. I haven't seen you dress professionally before."

"Oh, I dress professionally everyday Buddy. Just for a different profession," she said with a smile as she stopped and took another moment to smooth out her blouse. "If I'm going to follow somebody, I have to blend in, you know, just another face in the downtown business crowd."

"No matter what you wear, you're too damned good looking to blend in."

She playfully punched his upper arm. "Yeah right but thanks."

"Pretty nondescript colours, though."

"If you're following somebody, you don't want to standout, just blend in. If I wore my bright red or blue skirt, she might just notice me always being around."

"You have a bright blue skirt?"

"Actually, it's a dress. When we finally go out on a proper date, I'll wear it for you," she said as she started to walk over to where he stood. "Anyways, you know what Beth looks like and I don't. We can't take any chances on her seeing you, but I have a way of getting a picture…"

"Like these?" Morgan cut in as she came over beside him and held onto his arm. He swept his other arm he over the table presenting to Paula a variety of pictures of Beth.

"What are these?" She asked looking at the array of pictures. "Any stalking issues you want to tell me about?"

"Nope. What I did though, was pull up her Facebook page and it turns out she doesn't have her privacy settings ramped up. She's also on Instagram and her settings there are set to public. I knew you needed to know what she looked like from all asides so here you go. Beth from every angle."

Paula gathered the pictures together, picked them up and flipped through them one by one. "Good thinking. These are quite helpful. You might even have enough brains to be a cop one day."

He smiled, "Hell no, your jobs way too hard. I'd rather sit behind my desk telling people what to do."

Paula put the photos in her bag and the two headed down to the underground for her car. They pulled out remembering to fill the car with gas and headed downtown with Morgan behind the wheel. As they rolled down the Don Valley Expressway Morgan started to question the wisdom of what they were doing.

"Hey, Paula."

"Yes."

"Question."

"Shoot."

"The other day you were upset you brought me along on a stakeout, saying it was the wrong thing to do but here you are doing it again. What changed?"

"The other day we were tailing a suspect we knew was prone to violence and could be possibly armed. Anything can happen. Anything can go wrong ... and it did. I put you in danger. Today, however, we are not following a suspect who was just bailed out of jail. This is an unassuming woman. My feeling is neither of us are in any danger here.

"Or maybe I just like hanging with you," she added with a smile.

They the ramp off the parkway at Richmond and headed to the downtown core stopping on Queen Street in front of the southern entrance to the Eaton Centre. Morgan pointed up to the white office tower by the entrance.

"That's where she works. There's an entrance to the tower on the left as you go through the doors which takes you to the elevator banks. Like we discussed, when she gets off, she'll probably head straight for the subway."

A car honked at them from behind.

Paula looked back and waved the angry driver around. "Just keep the car moving and circle the block until you hear from me. I'll call you as soon as I see her. Funny, I've heard how in the old days how this would be difficult to pull off. These days I'll be just another idiot with their cell glued to their ear. I'll blend right into the scenery."

She tossed the pictures of Beth behind the driver's seat, pulled her hair back into a ponytail, then leaned over to give Morgan a short peck on the lips.

"Normal stake out procedure?" he asked with a smile as she climbed out of the car.

She stuck her head back inside the passenger window. "Let's just say I really like the guy who I'm partnered with these days." She flashed a smile and headed to entrance to the mall. He put the car in gear and started to lap the mall, right turns all the way.

Morgan began to be able to memorize the names of all the stores on the left side of each street as he circled around the block again and again. If Paula had not been on the phone with him while he drove, he would have been quite bored. Finally, she seemed to run out of things to say as he hadn't heard anything but background noise on her end for a few minutes.

"Hey, Paula. What's going on? Did you set the phone down and go shopping?"

"No. I hate shopping. Just people watching right ... hold on. There she is. She just stepped off the elevator ... Hi Mom. I'm at the Eaton Centre. Is there something you want me to pick up for Dad ... Okay, she just walked by. She's through the doors and in the mall. Looks like she's not heading down to the subway ... No, she's heading towards the south entrance."

Paula followed from a distance and watched as she exited through the doors. Once outside Beth turned to face traffic and held up her right arm.

"Morgan. Where are you right now? Looks like she's hailing a cab."

"Just coming to Victoria and Queen. Stopped at the lights. Idiot in front of me has his signal on but looks like he needs a written invitation to turn. Come on Jerk-face!"

"A cab's pulling over. I have the licence and cab number."

"Great, I just made the turn."

The cab pulled away from the curb and joined into the slow-moving traffic. It only traveled a very short way before coming to a stop at a red light at Bay Street when Morgan pulled up to the curb and Paula jumped in.

"Morgan, I know or hope at least you've never followed anybody before. The trick is to keep some distance but always be able to see them. You don't want to be noticed. It shouldn't be hard in this traffic."

"I've seen enough movies and TV shows in my time to know how this works."

"Maybe but this is for real and harder than it looks."

They kept a comfortable distance as they followed until the cab turned into a neighbourhood north of High Park, where they dropped back a little more. The cab turned down a side street.

"Hurry up in case they turn down another street before we have them in sight. Take the corner easy though. We don't want to lose them but don't want to appear to be chasing them either."

Morgan sped to the corner then braked and rolled around the corner normally as Paula had instructed. The cab made a left onto another street and he repeated the procedure. Half way along the street the cab slowed and made a right turn into a driveway.

"Keep going and drive by. Don't speed and look the other way when you pass them. I don't want to take a chance on her recognizing you."

Again, Morgan did as instructed. They passed the cab and Paula watched Beth reach over the front seat and pay the driver, taking note of the house number as she did. Morgan kept going but had slowed down considerably.

"Alright. Turn into that driveway on the right, the one mostly hidden by a hedge. You're going to turn around and head back the way we came. Don't slow down as we go by."

Again Morgan did as he was told and as they passed the house, he saw Beth facing the front door of the house with her back to the street.

"Nice shack," he commented as they passed the house. Both watched as the front door opened and a woman stepped out and gave Beth a big hug. Morgan didn't dare look back but instead looked over to Paula who was opening her laptop.

"Take a right at the corner, drive until we're out of sight and stop," instructed Paula as her fingers started to tap away at the keyboard. Morgan did as told and in a moment, they were stopped at the curb.

"What are you doing now?" he asked.

Paula held up a finger indicating she would answer him in a moment. She typed in a few more lines before she hit enter. "I'm searching our database to see who lives in that house. Ha! There she is ... Halina Shimon. Do you know her?"

"No."

"Let's see if we can find what she does for a living. Heading to LinkedIn."

"LinkedIn? But she'll be able to see you, a cop has been looking at her profile."

"Relax. We have a bunch of phoney profiles set up. People never know we're looking at their posts. For this one

... yes, there we go, for her we're using a head-hunting firm. She'll be none the wiser."

Paula logged in and typed Halina's name into the search area. "Interesting ... hmm."

"What? What'd you find?"

"It says here she's an endocrinologist with Constance Addison Research labs."

"What the hell's an endocrinologist?"

"Damned if I know. Haven't a clue. Let's Goggle it." She copied and pasted the word into the search bar and hit enter. "Endocrinologist. 'Physicians who diagnose and treat diseases relating to glands. Conditions which are treated by endocrinologists include', well, well, what do you know? Diabetes!

She closed her laptop and looked over at Morgan, "Well partner. This morning we didn't have shit to go on. Now it looks like this shot in the dark of ours may have put us right back into business."

Chapter 18

Halina stepped out the front door and gave Beth a hug. She always enjoyed her Friday nights with Beth and missed it whenever her cousin had a date or went out of town. She motioned Beth inside and when she stepped in, she was met by a running stumbling Shane, who came as fast as he could manage for a hug. Beth swung him up in her arms and gave him what he wanted.

After Beth set him down and gave him his sugarless candy treat, they made their way to the living room where, as usual, a bottle of wine sat chilling in a bucket. Beth walked over to it, rolled it around to see it which kind it was. "In a Gertz mood, are you? Great choice. So am I."

Shane played with a number of toys scattered around room while they talked. He seemed almost ADD as he jumped from toy to toy but Halina had explained to Beth it's the way two year old's act and she would need to wait for one of her own before she'd be able to understand.

After finishing the bottle, another was opened for the Carbonara they had for supper. The conversation may have flowed but each knew there was a much more serious one to follow. After the table was cleared away and Shane was put to bed, they returned to the kitchen where they sat with each waiting for the other to start. Beth reached across the table and took Halina's hands.

"Halina ... look, I know you must be doing this for Shane, not for your own personal glory, but still ... why? If the JDRF had this cat, wouldn't it be better for everyone? Wouldn't they end up with the same result which hopefully would be a cure."

Halina opened her mouth to speak but Beth cut her off, "Cuz, look at the shit you're in already. You're lucky you're not in jail right now. You told me a man is dead. That's on your hand's you know."

Tears started to well up in Halina's eyes. She wiped them and bowed her head.

"God, Halina. I've known you forever. You're a good person. Just let it go. Be done with it. If this cat gets safely to the JDRF and if there is a cure which can be found, they'll find it. Shane will benefit and his mother will be home with him instead of in jail."

Halina lifted her head and looked Beth in the eyes. She took a large gulp of wine, stood up, walked over to her purse and brought it back to the table. She reached inside, pulled out a brown envelope and slid it across the table to Beth.

Beth put her elbow on the table and ran her hand across her forehead. She was scared to open it, scared to even touch it. She looked up at Halina with eyes full of fear, "Halina. What's inside?"

"The reason I can't just be done with it."

Slowly Beth pulled the envelope towards her and picked it up. She slid her finger slowly under the top flap and flipped it open to reveal a wad of bills. For a moment she said nothing and just stared at the contents. Finally, she pulled herself together to ask, "Halina ... how much is this? Where ... what's it for?"

"Getting this stupid beast has become quite complicated and the people I hired want more to get it done. Sturgess arranged for me to get this," she answered motioning to the envelope, "so I could make sure the job does get done."

"Why doesn't Sturgess handle this himself? Don't you wonder why he has you involved in this? It's his lab. I'll tell you why. If anything goes wrong, it's you who'll take the fall. You'll be the one going to jail. Halina, Christ, just call it off. Tell Sturgess he's not getting the cat and let the real Diabetic researchers get on with the job."

"They'll take years. Years of research. More years of compliance testing. Years and years before Shane would get any good from it."

"I knew, just knew you had to be doing this for Shane."

"Of course, I am. Our lab can get things done quicker. When we know we have something and it's safe, Shane will be the first to have it. He won't have to suffer a life like I did, pricking fingers, taking shots, constantly worried about his feet and his eyes. Damn, I lost one of my own eyes. I can't bear the thought of it happening to him. Beth, don't you see why I need to get this thing done."

"With nobody overseeing this, if you do manage to get hold of it, think of how its life will become so miserable. It'll spend its life stuck in a cage all the time and you have to know it'll come to a point when they'll put it down and dissected."

"I was promised that won't happen."

"They're lying to you, Halina. They're lying."

"So, what if they are? If they can find a cure, then what the hell is one cat's life compared to hundreds of thousands of people. What's one cat's life compared to Shane's? Besides, you forget I'm one of the top researchers the place has. Sturgess needs me in on this. I'll make sure its always comfortable and cared for."

"Don't you see you're fooling yourself. You're my cousin, my best friend and I love you. I love you enough to be honest with you. All those promises he made will be broken. You'll look back and curse the day you became involved in this."

Halina bowed her head. She spoke softly. "One of us here will be proved wrong. I pray it's you."

"Me too!"

Chapter 19

Mitt opened his eyes, groaned and closed them again. They hurt. His head hurt. It had been one long, really good bender. He never did find Audrey on the Wednesday night but still never spent the night alone. Thursday, he had slept until two. If he remembered right, he had finally caught up with Audrey later that evening and had one hell of a great time. Booze, coke and although he didn't remember a lot, he did remember a great lay. At the moment, however, he was physically paying for it.

He rolled onto his side and was surprised to find a woman sleeping beside him. It wasn't Audrey, though. He had never seen the sleeping blonde woman before. As he tried to pull the events of the night out of his foggy brain, he heard a tap being turned on in the bathroom. He carefully lifted his head and looked around.

Obviously, he was in a hotel room. It wasn't as run-down as some of the places he had been in. It was a standard room with a queen bed, TV, desk couch and a bathroom by the door but actually looked decent. The tap stopped and he was surprised when the door opened and Audrey stepped into the room, wearing just her red panties.

"There he is!" she declared. "I thought for sure you'd be out for a few more hours. You really had something going on last night."

Mitt gave her a weak smile and looked at the woman still asleep beside him. "I had two of you?"

"Oh yeah and you were quite the stud. Insatiable. There was just no satisfying you. It was Julie's first time pairing up." Audrey stopped and laughed, "Even though there were two of us she's still going to be quite sore today, might even need to take tonight off."

"Shit, she can't miss a Friday night. It's gotta be a good payday for her."

"Friday! Hell that was last night. You've had us for two nights!"

"Two nights, damn" Mitt exclaimed as he swung his legs out of bed and sat on the side trying hard to clear his head.

Audrey walked over, stood in front of him, took his head and pulled it into her breasts. She was in her early forties with died orange hair and considering her occupation, had a considerably firm and well looked after body. Her breasts felt warm and soothing against his face.

"I feel like a bag of shit," he declared.

"You need a line. That was some great blow you got your hands on. I know you got some left. It'll fix you right up. How about it? A line and a real good fuck. What grown man wouldn't want that to start his day?"

She dropped to her knees and took him in her mouth. After a few moments, she removed him and looked up. "Nothing seems to be happening here. Hell, you do need a line."

Mitt nodded and motioned her to the bag sitting on the table beside the bed. After they both took a hearty snort, Audrey stretched out on the bed but was surprised when she saw Mitt didn't join her. Instead he walked across the room and picked his pants up off the floor.

"Hey, Mitt, you're not leaving are you? I thought we had plans on how to start this day."

"I'm not going anywhere. In fact, I can feel all my juices starting to work again. I just wanted to pay you."

Audrey laughed, grabbed a bottle of rye from the nightstand and took a healthy swig, "Asshole. You paid me when we got to the room. It was only for one night but with all the blow you had, I didn't mind hanging around. Besides, it's been awhile since we've hung together. You're always a good time. Cute too."

"It's what I love about you, Audrey. A great fuck and honest too. When did we get her?" He motioned pointing to the naked sleeping woman.

"Julie? You wore me out but wanted to keep going. I needed a rest so I gave her a call. Figured you wouldn't mind. From what you paid her when she got here, she can afford to have tonight off. Tomorrow too."

Mitt dropped the pants, walked back over to the bed and took a slug of whiskey from the bottle Audrey offered. He sat it on the nightstand and watched as Audrey leaned back, using her sleeping partners stomach as a headrest and removed her panties.

She rose up on her elbows, looked over at him and smiled, "That stuff works miracles. Looks like your ready boy. So ready. Come on, let's get it started."

He took a couple of steps and slid on top of her but instead of taking him, she rolled Mitt over onto his back so his head was propped up against sleeping Julie's right breast with her riding on top of him. Although Audrey was quite aggressive and physical as she brought them both to orgasm, Julie never woke.

Once they were done, Audrey fell onto her side, using her female partner's stomach as a place to rest her head. She took Mitt's hand in hers. Mitt took a minute or two to catch his breath, his head still warmly tucked against the side of Julie's breast and enjoyed the closeness of being with Audrey. It was the kind of closeness he rarely felt.

"Audrey. I was just thinking. You've been telling me for some time you're ready to get off the street. I gather you still feel the way."

"Oh yeah. I know I've been lucky so far but feel I've been pressing my luck. Why?"

"Because I think I have a way."

"Really! You're not shitting me are you?"

Mitt sat straight up in bed and turned to Audrey, who lifted her head off her colleague and again rested on her elbows. "No. It just came to me. I've always been looking for the big score. Hit it big and then walk away from this life. Now one comes along and falls right at my fucking feet and, shit, I never saw it. Not until now. I can see it all now, Audrey. It's right there for the taking. The big payday."

"Really? You've got a way to hit it big and ...and you'll take me along?"

"You bet. I may have been paying for you for all these years, but we've always had, you know, some kind of connection, unless you've been pulling shit down over my eyes."

"No Mitt I haven't. The others sure but not with you. I would've been the hell out the door the moment I opened my eyes this morning if you were only business."

"What I wanted to hear Babe."

Just then Julie woke and lifted wearily lifted her head off the pillow. Her face was red, and her eyes were slightly opened slits. "Holy shit, you assholes are really fucking loud! Can't you keep it down, for Christ sake?"

"Back to sleep, Doll," Mitt commanded. The moment he said it, Julie's head collapsed back onto her pillow and she rolled over facing away from them.

Mitt stood up. "Okay, I've got things to do. Time to get this operation rolling."

Audrey smiled and rested her head against the curve of her friend's waist. Slowly she drew her fingers down her neck, between her breasts, over her stomach to her sides. Then she ran her hands along her sides, tracing the curves of her figure to the top of her legs. "Before you go are you sure you don't have one more in you?"

A smile broke out from Mitt's face. He did have one more left and once again Julie never stirred.

Chapter 20

Paula sat at her living room table with a laptop in front of her and some jumbled handwritten notes to the right of it. She liked the papers to the right which made it easier for her to jot down notes which meant she needed to push the notes aside to mouse. It was the only way she could comfortably do both but there were times she wished she were ambidextrous.

When she heard Morgan ask where she wanted him to set down the coffee he just brought for her, she looked up and started to laugh. Morgan stood there with a coffee in his right hand and Tiberius perched on his left shoulder.

"Well there's something I haven't seen before, "she exclaimed. "Just too cute, both of you."

"We haven't done this for awhile. When he was a kitten, he always wanted to be carried around like this. Then suddenly he didn't seem to like it anymore and would jump down right away. Just now in the kitchen, he gave me the same look he used to, so I hoisted him up and he stayed."

"He looks comfortable enough."

"Yep, he likes it up here." He turned his head towards Tiberius. "Okay fella, time to get down. Paula and I have some researching to do. After all, this is all about you."

"No. It's about both of you. I have a bad feeling they no longer care anymore if they have to kill you to get Tiberius or not."

Morgan walked over to the couch and deposited Tiberius on the back of it. He grabbed his coffee from the kitchen and sat down at the table in front of his own notes and ran his finger down them. "So, where do we go from here? Think it's worthwhile to maybe hire a private detective to dig further?"

"What!"

"They might be able to do the kind of digging we can't."

"Morgan! I'm a detective, remember? A real one," Paula said as she gave him a questioning and somewhat angry look. "A damned good one too! We don't need to hire some P.I. asshole which has a tenth of the training I do. Hell no! Jesus, what the hell were you thinking?"

"I…"

"Forget it. We're not going that route, so sit down and let's figure this thing out."

"Alright," Morgan agreed and let the subject drop right away. He sat at the table where his pen and notes lay and gave them a quick look. "So, what do we have?"

Paula tapped her pen on the table as she thought. "Let's break it down. Halina Shimon is a diabetic specialist who does research for a lab run by the Constance Addison Research Foundation. Dr. Leo Sturgess is in charge of the lab and of course, her. She's friends with Beth, who you told about Tiberius. Beth tells Shimon about Tiberius, innocently too from the reaction in her voicemail. The doctor either tells her boss, who decides to go after our boy here or she doesn't tell him and instead is doing this on her own."

Morgan noticed right away how Paula had said 'our boy'. It pleased him. He quickly brought his mind back to the problem at hand. He watched as she tapped the paper with her pen. "Go on."

"Now whoever is after Tiberius must have hired this Oscar guy. The one you heard Pin talking to the day of Stutz's murder. From what you said you heard, it seems Pin, Farely and Stutz were working for him.

"Who's Farely?"

"The guy who attacked you outside your hotel and got himself killed. Damn, Morgan, if we're going to solve this, you have to be able to keep all the events and names straight in your mind."

"Sorry, it's a steep learning curve for me. I work in an office where everyday is the same, remember."

Paula laughed, "Shit, sorry. I'm used to working with people who think the same as me. I shouldn't have jumped all over you."

Unless it's in bed." He saw her smile at the comment before she returned to her notes. "

"Anyways, we have to find out who this Oscar is. The trouble is we don't know what he looks like or anything at all about him. My people at the station don't know about him as I couldn't tell them because you didn't tell me until after my debriefing."

"It seems to me our next step is to follow Sturgess. See what he's up to."

Morgan heard the printer start to run and watched as a page printed out. When it was finished, he grabbed it and turned it over to see a colour picture of Halina Shimon, the one from her LinkedIn page.

"Not Sturgess, the man in charge?"

"No. People don't get to the position to where he is in life by doing things stupidly. If he does know about Tiberius, he'll keep himself well-distanced away from everything. The one thing we do know for sure is Beth knows the doctor and it's highly likely the doctor knows about Tiberius."

"Think the doctor can lead us to him?"

"Let's find out."

Chapter 21

Oscar walked into the basement office of his house, stepped around the large desk, and sat down in the deep leather of his office chair. He leaned back, put his feet up on the desk and closed his eyes. He loved being upstairs with his family but when it got right down to it, he found his office and his chair the most comfortable place to be when he was home.

Although he was physically comfortable, his mind was not. Instead, it was racing to come to a solution to a problem, the problem of what to do with Mitt Pin. He hadn't seen or heard from Mitt since the day he watched Stutz murdered right in front of him and it made him nervous. The moment it happened he thought he might surely be next, and the feeling haunted him. He felt Mitt hadn't just taken the money and left town but instead had stuck around and laid low.

He smiled for a moment. It wouldn't be like Mitt to just stay out of sight until the heat let up. Mitt wasn't the patient type. More than likely he was busy wasting it all on blow and hookers. He laughed quietly at the thought before the smile quickly left his face.

After the money was gone, what then?

He knew the answer right away. Mitt would be back. Now Oscar knew what Mitt was capable of and even with just one good arm, fear ran through him.

Oscar leaned forward in his chair. Maybe Mitt would come grovelling back for another job. He had done it before many times after he had blown all his cash after a job but this time, he doubted it. That was the old Mitt. The one he saw the other day had too much anger in him and not enough control over his actions. Oscar realized he couldn't just sit back and wait for Mitt, be it grovelling Mitt or out of control Mitt. No, he couldn't wait for Mitt to make the first move. He would need to be the one to take action first.

An old saying ran through his mind, 'Keep your friends close and your enemies even closer'. It made him smile. He reached pulled open the right-hand drawer of his desk, pulled out one phone of the many which were in there and dialled. It was time to ensure Mitt felt that 'even closer' feeling. Offering him a well-paying job him should do the trick.

◆ ◆ ◆

Mitt left the hotel after he had finished up with Audrey. As he walked along the sidewalk, he lit a cigarette and began to mumble under his breath between puffs. *Shit should have done another line before I left*, he thought. His head started to hurt again plus his thoughts were scrambled from the past couple of night's activities, but he knew the gist of what needed to be done. He wanted a big score. No, he needed one. The promise of having Audrey all to himself was the thing which drove him now.

Damn it Mitt, you've always been nothing but a small-time asshole even when times were good, he thought. His once lucrative business of home robberies, mugging and grabbing purses just didn't pay much anymore. First it was credit cards but back when he first started, most people didn't like to buy much on credit, and carried cash. Then along came debit cards, chip readers with PINs and cash started to disappear. He'd grab a wallet only to find it maybe had ten dollars in it and a bunch of useless cards. If he was quick, he could use the tap feature on the card to buy a bottle at the liquor store for under the allowable fifty bucks without using a PIN but otherwise the card was useless, even for resale.

He was down on his luck when he met Oscar and started working for him. Oscar gave him small, well-laid out jobs which paid him some decent cash.

Fuck! I'm not going to get rich or make any kind of big money working for somebody else. I need to get hold of a big pile of cash. Then I can grab Audrey and take off south. Someplace warm. I can do it too. Christ, Oscar deals in cash. He must have it stashed somewhere. Somewhere close where he can get his hands on it quick. Oh shit, if I could just find out where and get my hands on it.

Hold on. He probably still hasn't gotten hold of the swordsman's damn cat. Nah, screw Oscar. He'll pay me shit and keep most of job money for himself. To hell with it!

Mitt had been walking quickly in a huff as he had wound himself up thinking about his entire life but began to slow down as a plan started to form in his mind. He tapped on the fingers which stuck out from the cast on his broken wrist with the fingers of his good hand as he planned out what exactly what he needed to do.

Oscar must have something in the works. He wouldn't be so damned horny about getting hold of the thing if he wasn't going to be making some serious green from it. Although Oscar had promised him the job, Mitt knew he just said it out of fear at the time. There was no way Oscar would offer it to him.

"I need to get it first," he mumbled as his pace picked up again in anger. "And the rat bastard who killed Jonny dead. Yeah Asshole, you're going to die! Shit, I don't need

Oscar. I'll just grab it myself, ransom it back to him for one hell of a price. Yeah Mitt ole boy, you're thinking now."

Just then the phone in his pocket rang which startled him.

"God damn it!" he exclaimed as he pulled his phone out of his pocket and answered.

"Mitt?"

Mitt was surprised the voice at the other end was Oscar's, "Yeah. Sorry. I didn't expect for you to be calling."

"Well, I promised you a job. I said I would be calling you about another shot at that cat and you know I'm always good to my word. You have a score to settle and I get it. I really don't care how you do it or who you have to take out to get it done. I just want it. How does twenty-five sound?"

Twenty-five G's? It's not a big score but it sure is a fucking good start. Besides, if I stay on his good side, he'll never suspect the price will be going up.

"Thought you were pissed about... well you know?" he answered back.

"Yeah, I was. Then I got to thinking about it. You know what the thing looks like. You're motivated. Sure, we've had our differences but you've always got the job done for me plus I've always been able to trust you. There's nobody I'd like to have on this job more. So, how about it?"

"Sure."

"Great! Our spot at the train yards on Islington. Two this afternoon." The line went dead before Mitt had a chance to confirm.

"Fucking asshole!" he said as he shook his head and dropped the phone back into his pocket. Even though he was used to calls from Oscar ending abruptly, it always bothered him.

This had fallen unexpectedly right into his lap. He knew he wouldn't get the entire twenty-five grand from

Oscar right away but would get a decent advance on it. Of course, with said cat in his hands, the price would be four times the amount Oscar was now offering.

He was grubby and needed a shower but as usual, Oscar had given him just three quarters of an hour to get to their meeting. Oscar never gave him or anybody any time for planning. It was his way of keeping in control of the situation and Mitt knew it.

Mitt arrived at the meeting spot at 1:50. The train yard was fenced in but built up against the public side of the fence was an abandoned sturdy old soot covered shack. It was hidden from the street by a derelict three-story factory. Mitt and Oscar had met there many times before.

Although he was just ten minutes early, he couldn't very well stand around outside, so he walked to the door and gave it three raps. There was no reply from inside. Oscar was usually early, but Mitt figured must have been held up by traffic or something. The old rusty doorknob and lock had been replaced years before by Oscar with another old one. So although he didn't own the shack, he had full access. Mitt had been given a key so he opened the door and stepped inside the gloom.

He turned to close the door. To his surprise he heard a gun go off from behind the door and the deadly sound of a bullet which punched through the loose fabric of the back of his shirt and embedding itself in a wall.

Quickly Mitt moved back behind the door using it as a shield. The parking area behind the factory was too open for him to try to run. If he did, his assailant would have an easy time gunning him down from behind.

A couple of more bullets ripped through door, missing him, and he heard another strike the wall behind. Although his assassin couldn't see him, he could still shoot him through the door. Mitt acted right away.

A locomotive sounded its horn as it passed just as Mitt pulled out his pistol. He left what little protection the door had offered and took two quick steps inside. Two shots instantly were fired in his direction. Both missed.

Mitt turned to the sound of the shots and hurriedly returned fire. He wasn't the best shot with his left hand and knew it, so he kept firing. His first shot hit his attacker in the shoulder and sent him spinning to the ground. The next two missed, but the three that followed, just as a locomotive sounded its horn again, all found their target and buried themselves deep into the man's chest.

Mitt approached the body cautiously even though it wasn't moving. He could see the three holes in the front of the man's shirt all oozing blood. Mitt bent over and picked up the dead man's gun.

"Asshole. Guess you won't be needing this anymore." He took a moment to examine the gun before he stuck it into the back of his pants under his shirt. "Nice piece. Too bad you were such a shit shot with it."

He gave the dead body a kick. "Worked out for me, though. Thanks, Oscar. You gave some rookie asshole the job of taking me out? Me, Mitt Pin. Look at him! A jerk face loser with no damned patience! If he knew the fuck what he was doing, he would've waited for me to be all the way in before letting me have it."

If anybody had heard the shots, there would have been a huge commotion around the shack by then, so he took a moment to bend over to look at his would-be assassin's face. He turned the man's head slightly so he could see it in the light. It was the same man who had helped him bury his friend, Jonny.

"Oscar, you dirty bastard," Mitt grumbled as he let go of the man's face and stood up. He jammed the dead man's piece into the back of his pants and slid his own gun into it's shoulder holster. "So, you do want me out of the picture, after all? Well, fuck you!"

It was time to clean up the mess. Although he knew the shack was never used, which made it such a great place to meet, he was worried some kids might come along and see the body through a window. After he wrapped his hands in old rags, he pulled out some dirty wooden crates out from under a rack. He dragged the body over to the spot and rolled it under the racks until it came to rest snug up against the wall. The crates were returned back to their original spot, which hid the body nicely. He swept dirt around the floor to hide the blood stains.

Before opening the door he checked himself over quickly to ensure there weren't any noticeable blood stains on him. Satisfied he only looked a little dirty, he listened carefully. When he found he couldn't hear any voices or sounds of any trains approaching, he stepped casually outside. He closed the door behind him, ensured it was locked, gave it a wipe, then made his way back to Islington, walking as if he didn't have a care in the world even though he was boiling on the inside. He arrived at a bus stop at the same time as the bus did and climbed aboard.

I wonder when the little asshole was supposed to report back? Mitt wondered as he found himself an unoccupied seat. Oscar's hit man had changed his plans. *Oscar's probably sitting around waiting to hear that I'm now outta the way. Well, I guess I'll just have to go and tell him in person it didn't go down quite as he had planned.*

Chapter 22

It was a Saturday, a day of the week Morgan almost always slept in on. Instead he and Paula had set the alarm to go off at 5:00 am as they wanted to be up and out the door by 6:30 am. They had left Tiberius overnight with Jim and Grace so they could leave early. He felt quite indebted to the Upton's for taking such good care of his boy, ensuring he was safe and happy.

Paula knew a car rental agency which had a few cars with tinted windows in the side and back and had made arrangements for one. After they switched cars at the rental shop they headed to Halina's and parked six houses down, facing the way they figured Halina would leave if she was driving.

There were quite a few cars parked along the street and they were lucky to find an open spot neatly tucked between two vans which helped to conceal them. Paula poured them each a black coffee from her thermos and fixed hers up with some cream and sugar. Knowing they could be in for a long wait, they hunkered down and made themselves as comfortable as possible.

The two never seemed to have any issues talking and killed the first couple of hours doing just that. They talked about the friends they had, family and sports. Morgan liked the fact Paula was a big time Blue Jays fan and they spent much of the time discussing the season up to that point. Paula told Morgan about some of the funnier moments she had on the job and he did the same.

It was when they started talking about past vacations, they had each taken, the great ones and the bad ones, which got Morgan thinking.

"So, do you have any vacation ideas for this year?" he asked.

"Usually I catch a Jays series in Boston every year. Other than that, I've been toying with the idea of a week up in the Yukon."

"The Yukon?"

"Yeah, the Yukon. Also considering Iceland."

"Come to think of it, not one of the vacations you've told me about has been about heading south, being on a beach anywhere or having cocktails poolside."

"Laying on a beach and catching rays. Wasting a week sitting beside a pool? It's not for me. I'd rather be exploring. There's something about the remoteness of the Yukon or Iceland which has had me quite intrigued for years. I guess maybe its being a cop and seeing all the shit, dealing with more assholes than decent people, makes going to a place with very few people sound like paradise."

"So, it's the Yukon or Iceland?"

"You got it."

"Care for some company when you go?"

As Paula had been talking, she had been staring straight ahead as she kept a watchful eye on their targeted house. With Morgan's question though, she turned her head towards him, paused for a moment and smiled. "Yeah, I'd like that. It'd be fun."

Morgan reached over for her hand and took hold of it. "Me too."

They sat in a comfortable silence for a few minutes with smiles on their faces, holding hands and watching the house.

"Hey! There she is," Paula exclaimed. Immediately she let go of Morgan's hand and started the car. "Damn it! My mind must have wandered. I never saw that cab pull up or her coming out. Okay Doc, come on and lead us to some place good."

When she saw Halina's cab make the turn off her street, Paula pulled out to follow. Once they were on a main street with lots of traffic, Paula began to relax a little as it was easier to keep from being noticed with so many other cars on the road.

"Grab my camera," Paula said more as a request than an order. Morgan reached between them, picked up the camera and removed the lens cap. "Take a close-up of their license plate and another of the back of the cab just in case."

"Too bad she came out when she did," Paula commented. "For the first time, I was actually enjoying a stakeout."

"Yeah, me too."

They followed Halina's cab at a safe distance into a plaza's parking lot and pulled into an empty spot. The cab pulled up to the entrance to a pub, The Empire of Britain. They watched her pay the driver, get out and enter the pub. Knowing Halina had no idea who they were, Paula felt very comfortable following her in. She pulled their car up to a spot closer to the entrance and both she and Morgan went inside.

The pub was a busy spot and a little dark. Morgan had to wait for a moment for his eyes to adjust from the bright sunshine. Paula chose a table by a large supporting pillar adjourned with beer mats of English, Scottish and Irish beers. Morgan looked at them and over to the line of beer taps on the bar. Most were big North American breweries. It seemed to him the place didn't know which country it wanted to imitate.

Paula sat where she had a clear unobstructed view of Halina, who was seated at a small table for two against the far wall. Morgan could only see her if he leaned over but as long as one of them had a full view, all was well. Morgan ordered a rum and coke and Paula went with a soda water. Morgan paid for both.

They watched as Halina ordered herself some kind of cocktail and paid for it immediately when it came. It only took a second for Paula to size up the situation, "I think we're on to something. She didn't come all the way here for one quick drink. No way. She's here to meet somebody."

The Empire of Britain seemed to be a popular spot. Morgan could see the door and watched as people came and went. Fifteen minutes passed and the door opened once more.

"Oh my God!" was all Morgan could say when he saw who had just walked in.

Chapter 23

Mitt sat on the bus still fuming at what had just taken place. He was lucky to be alive and he knew it. But for a bit of luck and impatience it could just as easily been him dead and rolled up behind the empty wooden crates.

Okay, where the hell is that bastard's address, he thought as he awkwardly pulled his wallet out of his pocket with his bad hand and started to fumble through the cards and notes inside. *Damn it, I know I wrote it down and stuffed it here somewhere just in case.*

After a minute of searching he found it and held it up. *Got it! Hey, Asshole, I know where you live, and you don't have a damned clue that I do. Hell, you don't even think I'm still alive so you sure won't be expecting me at your door. Oscar you dick, you've screwed with the wrong guy and now I've got a big fucking surprise for you.*

After changing buses a few times he finally arrived on Oscar's well-kept middle class neighbourhood street. He shook his head and chuckled. *Looks like you've been making a lot of big bucks off of our backs. Shit, we take the risks and you pocket most of the cash. I bet that safe you have hidden at home is just full of green.*

Mitt stopped and took another look at the house number on the piece of paper. He reminded himself he had to look natural, look like he belonged in this neighbourhood. Instead of storming directly to Oscar's he walked over to the community mailbox and acted like he was checking his mail. Instead he was going through a mental checklist like he did before any job. He took a moment to let his anger settle, then started towards his former boss's home at a normal pace,

He saw the front door of Oscar's home open and a woman with two children walk out. The boy looked to be about ten years old and the girl maybe seven. *Oscar has a family? Never would have thought it. Hmm, should give me some leverage.*

The woman stopped on the front step and turned back toward the house. Mitt saw Oscar step outside and give the woman, who Mitt assumed to be his wife, a kiss. He waved at the kids and went back inside. Mitt slowed his pace to allow the family to get in the car and drive off. They passed Mitt when he was two houses away.

Once they turned the corner and were out of site, Mitt casually strolled up the driveway and approached the door. He took a quick look around to ensure nobody was walking down the street or out in their yards. Satisfied no immediate witnesses were around, he slipped on his gloves and rang the doorbell. Instinctively he stepped sideways to the side of the door to put him out of view from the peephole. His surprise at seeing him would most likely cause Oscar to freeze for a second. He'd be ready to take advantage.

Mitt waited full of anticipation for the door to open. He could hardly contain himself thinking of the expression Oscar's face would hold when he pulled the door open to reveal the ghost of Mitt Pin standing before him. It only took a moment to find out. The catch clicked and the door swung inward as Oscar stepped out onto the doorframe. Suddenly the pleasant friendly face Oscar wore when he pulled the door open turned to astonishment and panic. He quickly stepped back and attempted to slam the door closed as Mitt had anticipated.

"Where the fuck do you think you're going, Cocksucker?" Mitt spat as he put his shoulder to the door to stop it from closing and barged in. With his good left hand he grabbed Oscar by his thick gold chain to keep him from running and kicked backwards to close the door. In his return motion he used his leg's momentum to drive his knee into Oscar's stomach. The force of the blow sent Oscar stumbling into a thin wooden hallway closet door which shattered the slates and caved it in.

"What the hell are you doing here?" Oscar seethed as he straightened up and stepped forward in hopes of grabbing and taking down his attacker. Instead he was greeted by the butt of a gun which hammered into the side of his face sending him staggering back against the wall. He knew if he fell, that would be the end, so he managed to remain upright.

"Fucking asshole, you just tried to have me killed!" Mitt hissed as he raised his hand and attempted to strike Oscar with the gun again. This time Oscar managed to block the blow and a hard right sent Mitt sprawling to the floor.

"Mitt, you piece of shit," Oscar growled as he took a couple of steps towards him in hopes of kicking the gun from his hand as Mitt had never let go of it when he went down.

Instead, Mitt quickly raised the gun in time and fired. As Oscar's right arm had been extended towards Mitt when he was in kicking motion, the bullet entered his shoulder from under his armpit and lodged into a bone. He howled in pain and fell back onto a small hallway desk crushing it as he did. The side of his shirt showed he was bleeding profusely.

Mitt clambered clumsily to his feet. He still held the gun in his good left hand and rubbed his jaw with the back of his right hand as he approached Oscar.

"How'd you find me?" Oscar asked with a little panic in his voice as he desperately grabbed onto the broken desk and tried to get to his feet.

Mitt answered with a hard kick to Oscar's stomach. Oscar collapsed to the floor in obvious pain which brought a huge grin to Mitt's face. After a moment of watching him suffer, Mitt took hold off Oscar's shirt with his good hand and hauled him to his feet.

He looked around for a moment and thought of his next move. Oscar took the opportunity to try to push and trip his assailant but was stopped when Mitt delivered a hard elbow to his face.

"You're not going anywhere fuckface. There's a safe in this house and you're going lead me to it. Don't screw with me either. I know you think 'I'm just some stupid asshole but I bet you I can figure out how to get you to do this. Oh yeah, you've got a wife and two kids. All the bedrooms are upstairs so you wouldn't have an office up there. It must be downstairs. Right?"

When he didn't receive a quick reply, Mitt quickly punched him hard in the midriff which dropped Oscar to his knees. "I SAID RIGHT!"

Oscar could only nod wearily.

"That's probably where the safe is. You see I'm not fucking dense now, am I?" Oscar never replied to which he received a gash in the side of his forehead with the butt of Mitt's gun. "Bet there's plenty of cash in there for me too, isn't there. Okay. Let's go!"

Mitt hauled Oscar to his feet and twisted Oscar's chain tight in his hand behind his neck. With three steps to go as they descended the stairs Mitt let go and shoved Oscar sending him painfully tumbling to the bottom. Mitt sat on a step and watched Oscar as he lay in a fetal position holding his hands against his wound, breathing in short pants.

"Not such a big shit now are you? Didn't you call me a fuck-up for not getting that feline for you? Then you tried to have me whacked this afternoon. Asshole. You must have been some fucking surprised to see me standing at your door just now."

"Feline? Mitt I wasn't aware you knew big complicated words. Thought fuck was the biggest word in your vocabulary."

"Still trying to be the big fucking man are you? Well, how about this. You show me where the safe is, open it and maybe, just fucking maybe I'll let you live."

"Fuck you!"

"Okay, Cocksucker. Let's try it from this perspective. Yes, perspective. Another big fucking word. We go to your office, you open the safe and I take whatever I need from it before your family gets back home. Yes, family. It's not a big word but a very important one. Your wife, hell she's quite the beauty and your kids are just, well, they're just too fucking adorable."

Oscar said nothing. He could only glare up at Mitt who sat calmly on the stairs with his gun. He probably was not a good shot with his left hand but was too close to miss. Also, Oscar found himself starting to become a little weak and dizzy from the beating and loss of blood. He knew he didn't have much hope. He knew his best bet was to cooperate and hope something would come along to him an opening.

"Alright, Mitt. Just help get me to my office. The safe's in there. I know what you want and it's all in the safe. Get it then get the hell out. Just leave my family alone."

Mitt never made a move to assist him. "Smart man. You know I won't be hanging around once I get what I want so get the fuck up and start moving."

Oscar tried to leverage himself to his feet with his good arm but collapsed.

Mitt rose and took the last few steps to the bottom of the stairs. "A little weak fucker or are you just working me, looking for a chance?" he asked as he hauled Oscar up and leaned him against the wall. A large pool of blood covered the floor where he had laid.

Oscar used the walls for support as he led the way down the hall to his office. He felt Mitt's hand on his collar and the barrel his gun against his back the entire way. Energy was draining from him fast. The side of his shirt was soaked with blood and when he bunched it to hold against the wound, it didn't help. All he knew was he had to get the safe open before he passed out in order to spare his family. It was the only thing at the moment which spurred him on.

Once at the office, Oscar moved to sit down in the chair behind his desk.

"Where do you think you're going," Mitt asked menacingly.

"I have to sit before I pass out."

"Then sit on the God damned floor!" ordered Mitt as he rounded the desk. He pulled open the unlocked drawers. One contained two handguns and a spare clip. Mitt held them up for Oscar to see. "Oscar! You really do think I'm fucking stupid, don't you?"

He aimed one at Oscars leg then decided against it. Oscar looked to be fading and he needed him to get the safe opened. "Okay, where is it?"

"The wall to your right," Oscar said in more of an exhale than a sentence. He could feel himself becoming weaker by the moment. "Third panel over. Push ..."

Mitt did as instructed and a hidden door sprung open. "Hey nice spot. Might never have found it on my own. Now, the combination please."

The safe used a keypad instead of a dial. Oscar didn't answer. "Oscar! Combo!"

Oscar sat propped against the desk with his head slumped forward. Mitt grabbed Oscar's hair and pulled his head upright. He tapped the fingers of his cast hand against his face a few times. "Stay with me, Oscar. I need the combo?"

In barely audible words, Oscar gave the sequence. Mitt hurried to the safe and punched them in. He heard a whir and a click. A green light on the pad lit up. He yanked the handle downwards. His angry face lit up with a huge smile when the door swung open to reveal stacks of nicely bundled cash.

He grabbed a strapped bag from beside the desk and stuffed the cash into it. A few wads of bills spilled onto the desk. As he retrieved them, he found one of the bundles had come to rest over a note; *H = cat. $60K, 3pm sat.*

"Interesting. What's this all about?"

"You have the money. Just get the hell out."

"No. I think I'll stay," Mitt said sitting down on the floor in front of Oscar. "It's quite comfortable here ... unless, of course, what's in this note gives me some reason to leave. *H for cat. 60K. 3 pm sat.* Something's happening today which can make me a lot more rich. Tell me what it is, and I'll fly the fuck right out of here."

Oscar could barely get the words out as weak as he was, "Halina ... meeting at the ... Empire of Britain ... pub... still wants ... the cat... paying sixty large."

Mitt smiled and stood up. "Thanks Oscar. Time for me to go. You too!"

He grabbed a pillow from the chair and looked at Oscar who nodded slightly. He knew what was coming but was too weak to fight it. Besides, he now could die knowing Mitt would leave right away and his family would be safe. Mitt placed the pillow against his chest, pressed the gun he had found in the desk drawer against it and pulled the trigger. The bullet ripped into Oscar's heart stealing away what little life he had left in him.

Mitt dropped the pillow, walked over to the desk and scooped up the cash filled bag. Just as he was about to leave, he spotted a couple of notebooks on the desk, tossed them into the bag and headed out to the Empire of Britain for his next appointment.

Chapter 24

Morgan stared at the man who had just entered the pub for a few seconds. "Oh my God!" he said in a voice not too much louder than a whisper. Morgan turned to Paula and leaned forward resting the side of his face in his hand as casually as he could, hoping it was enough to keep his features hidden.

"What's wrong?" Paula asked as she took a brief glace over in the direction of where Morgan had been looking. She saw a man pass by a few tables away from them. He seemed to be looking for somebody. She looked back at Morgan waiting for an answer.

"Jesus Christ, it's him, "Morgan answered keeping his voice low. Paula could see a little panic in Morgan's face as he hurriedly spoke. "The guy we're after. I smashed his wrist, we thought we had him at the house."

"Mitt Pin," Paula stated as she watched the man cross the room. His back was to her now so he couldn't see her watchful eyes on him. "Hey! Don't try to look. Just keep facing me. You're in a good spot. The pillars are hiding most of you and you have your back to him. He won't be able to see you and he doesn't know me."

"He must have seen me. He looked over at me when he came in."

"I doubt it. Maybe he looked this way but his eyes probably were still be adjusting to the room after coming in from the sunshine. If he had made you he wouldn't be acting so calm. Probably would have turned and left."

"What's he doing now?"

"He stopped for a moment and is looking around the room," Paula said looking straight at Morgan as if they were conversing. The doctor's the only person here sitting by themselves. There he goes. Just started heading in her direction.

"Okay. He's at her table and saying something to her. She just nodded and sat down across from her. It's definitely Pin. I can see a cast on his right wrist."

"Paula, you've got to go arrest the son of a bitch. We have him. We have him cold."

"No. It's the wrong move. Let's see what happens here first. They're meeting for a reason. We need to find out why." Paula casually picked up her glass and sipped on her soda water. Although she seemed to be looking straight at Morgan her attention was completely focused on the two at the table.

"He just ordered a something from the server and now they are just talking."

"Do you think they are working together on this?"

"Not sure but I doubt it. Something tells me they don't know each other. Wait, the server just returned with a small glass. Looks like a shot over ice." Paula smiled and looked down at the table. She could see the questioning expression on Morgan's face. "Looks like when the drink came, he made her pay. She doesn't look happy about it either. I just found it funny."

"A man doesn't always have to pay you know."

"You just did."

"Well, I'm a gentleman or at least try to be."

Paula reached over, took one of his hands in both of hers and gave it a squeeze. She continued to hold on while she kept watch. "The server's left the table and the doctor's reaching into her purse and ... oh, look ... it's a nicely wrapped small box of some sort. She's passing it to him."

"A present?"

Paula pondered for a moment. "I doubt it. From both their responses it's not. A payment perhaps, all dressed up to look like a present. Wouldn't attract any undue attention. After all, what's more innocent than one person giving another a gift? Happens all the time.

"It's not very big. He was able to put it into his jacket pocket. He's saying something to her. She seems nervous. Now he's getting up. She is too.

"Wait. He walked over to her side of the table and gave her a hug and a kiss on the cheek. It's a good show they're putting on, but I can tell she really didn't like it at all."

"Paula. Come on. When are you going to nail him?"

"I'd really love to see where he goes with this little present, see where it leads us but no, just too big a chance of losing him."

She sighed. "Looks like my best move is to take him down. I'm going to wait until he steps outside to do it. You need to stay here."

Morgan gave her a questioning look. "Why not now? What about her?"

"There're too many people in here and somebody might get hurt if I try to arrest him before he leaves." Paula let go of Morgan's hand. "When he passes on his way out, I'll follow and nail him in the parking lot. You make sure she doesn't leave. Just don't look at him when he passes. He can't see you ... wait, look out, here he comes."

Two tables separated Paula and Morgan from Mitt as he passed them.

"I'll be right back Honey," Paula said as she patted Morgan's hand, stood up and casually followed Mitt towards the exit.

Mitt grabbed the handle of the door and pulled it open. Seeing Paula a few steps behind him he stopped and pulled the door fully open with his good hand and held it for her.

"Ma'am," he said motioning with his injured arm for her to go first. As he did, he looked back across the room. Morgan wasn't sure but it seemed Mitt's eyes had lingered on him for a second.

"Thank you," Paula said innocently as she passed him and stepped outside. Her hand was already on the inside of her jacket resting on the butt of her service revolver. She started to turn around when she felt something hard slam into the side of her face.

The force of the blow sent her sprawling onto the hood of a car parked close to the door. Her head spun and her eyes watered. She hadn't been able to draw her gun before she was struck but could still feel it in her holster.

Inside, Morgan wondered if Mitt had recognized him. Something told him he had to be outside where everything was about to happen. Quickly he stood and moved towards the door. His walk turned into a dash when he heard Paula's painful cry.

As he pulled the door open, he saw Paula slumped sideways against the hood of a car as Mitt brought down another damaging blow against the side of her face with his cast. Even though she had managed to partially deflect the strike with her arm, it still sent a tidal wave of pain through her head when it struck the same spot as the first blow.

As Morgan bounded towards Paula's attacker, he saw her roll onto her back and strike straight out open handed. The heal of her palm slammed into the side of Mitt's face which sent him staggering back.

Mitt roared in pain and anger and raised his cast to strike her again but by then Morgan was there to stop him.

He grabbed Mitt by his left shoulder and yanked him away from her. He fisted up his free hand as he spun Paula's attacker around, but Mitt moved with the motion instead of fighting it and came around much faster than Morgan had expected. Before he could throw even a single punch, Mitts fist lashed out catching Morgan in the jaw sending him sprawling to the ground.

Although Morgan hit the ground hard, he came to his knees quickly, ready to defend himself. All he could see though, was the back of a man rounding the corner of the tavern and disappearing from site.

Morgan looked over at Paula, who was attempting to push herself up off the hood of the car but her arms gave out before she was successful. Afraid she would roll or slid off the car and further injure herself, Morgan scrambled to his feet and was there in a moment to steady her. He leaned over and very gently moved the hair which covered her face and wound. It was bleeding and had white pieces of cast stuck in it. Already the side of her face had started to swell and bruise.

"Paula! Paula, I'm here. You're safe. Everything's okay. How bad are you hurt?"

He heard someone call to him from behind, "Hey mister, lady! I've just called nine-one-one. The police and ambulance are on the way."

"Thanks," Morgan answered, "I appreciate it."

"Morgan," Paula said in a harsh whisper as she brought herself to an upright position. "I guess we lost him, didn't we?" She was unsteady and leaned into Morgan's arms for support.

"Yeah, we did. I really should have been ready for his haymaker when I pulled him off you."

"No, it's not your fault. I shouldn't have let him get the drop on me."

"I think he made me when he opened the door for you."

"Never mind. I just want to get inside and sit down."

Morgan looked over and saw a crowd start to gather round, including the person who had served them their drinks. "Hey, could somebody help me get her inside?"

The server stepped in to assist. Paula was unsteady but the two helped her back into the pub and sat her down in a booth.

"Charlie," the server called over to the bartender. "We need two glasses of water, some ice and a clean cloth right away."

It took only a minute for Charlie to get it all together along with some extra towels. He came over quickly and sat them on the table. Paula leaned forward in her seat and rested the right pain-free side of her face in hand. She attempted to lightly touch her injury, but Morgan softly took hold of her hand and pulled it down. "Leave it alone. Here, let me look after this."

Paula nodded weakly. Morgan wetted a towel and gently dabbed it against the wound to clean it. At times he would stop to carefully pick out a piece of cast from the exposed area. He continued with his work while the server wrapped the bag of ice in a dry cloth. When Morgan was finished cleaning the area the server handed him the wrapped ice.

"This will sting," Morgan warned softly.

"I know. It's not my first time. Hell, probably won't be my last either." She winced as Morgan placed the ice to the wound as carefully as possible.

"Ow, let me do it." She grabbed the bag and turned her head slightly to the server. "There was a woman sitting against the far wall. Dark hair? Did you see where she went?"

He took a sweep of the pub, "Sorry. I guess she left during the ruckus. At least she paid up. Looks like some of the others took advantage, stiffed me and left."

"Bunch of thieving assholes," Paula commented. She leaned back. "Thanks for all your help. I really appreciate it but could we have a moment alone?"

"Sure. I'll be over by the bar if you need anything. Just call." As promised, he left and made his way to the far end of the bar.

"How are you feeling?"

"Like I was hit with a brick. Morgan, listen. The boys will arrive any minute. We have to get our story straight," Paula said in a hushed tone.

"Story?"

"Yes. They can't know we were following the doctor. I've already caught hell for doing this before with you."

"But..."

"No buts. This is our story. We went for a drive and decided to head to the Beaches. We got hungry, saw this place and decided to check it out. Pin came in from out of the blue, pure dumb luck, and you recognized him. We saw him meet with a dark-haired woman who gave him a gift. Nothing else! When he left, I told you to stay behind and followed outside to make the arrest."

"Why?"

As she answered sirens could be heard approaching. "Yesterday I was told in no uncertain terms to stay away from the case. Hell, if they find out you and I were following her they'd bust me back to uniform or worse, I'd lose my badge."

"But we're here together. We met on this case concerning me. Wouldn't associating with me still get you into a pile of shit?"

"Damn it, Morgan," she said in a voice low enough not to be heard. He could hear the pain in her voice and see how she flinched when adjusting her ice pack. She spoke in a determined whisper. "They can tell me I can't bring you along on police business. There's no way in hell they can they tell me who I can be with, who I date and where we decide to eat."

She sat the ice pack on the table and placed her fingers gently against Morgan's face. "I guess this means we're dating ... if it's okay with you."

"Sure but couldn't you have asked me in a more romantic way." He smiled. "Don't worry, I'll stick to the story," He squeezed her hands and shook his head nodded slightly to indicate not to say anything more. He gave her a soft rub on her back as he rose to welcome the four uniformed officers and two paramedics who arrived at their table.

Chapter 25

Mitt's wrist was throbbing when he walked through the door of his basement apartment. He went to the fridge and looked inside. It was almost devoid of food, but food wasn't what he was looking for. Three cans of beer were off to one side and a bottle of rye whisky sat in the middle of the top shelf looking for some company. He grabbed it, screwed off the cap and took a long pull. Before he took another, he slung off the bag he had around his shoulder, tossed it onto the old beat up sofa and flopped down beside it.

"Let's see what we've got in here," he said to the empty room.

He reached in and started to pull out handfuls of neatly banded twenty-dollar bills. Each band read $2,000. Mitt broke out in laughter He zipped each bundle with his thumb before tossing it to the side. After every ten bundles, he would take a short swig from his bottle.

After twenty bundles his wrist throbbed so much, he stopped zipping but never stopped smiling. He took another long swallow from the bottle and continued to count. At seventy-five bundles, he took a moment for a good couple of gulps before continuing. His wrist started to hurt a lot less and after ninety, with another hit of whiskey, hardly hurt at all. His wrist was numb when he reached the one hundred ninth and final bundle of cash.

"Whoa! Two hundred and eighteen thousand fucking bucks!" he exclaimed with a slur. "Christ that's a hell of a good day's work. Shit what a haul!"

He dug his hand back into the bag, couldn't feel what he was looking for, so he dumped out the remaining contents. Before him was the last of the banded twenties along with the books he took from Oscar's study. The gift box was gone.

"Ah damn it! It was the only reason I went to meet the bitch," he exclaimed with a slur. "Sixty thousand bucks fucking gone. Fuck!"

He sighed and reached for Oscar's books. "Let's see what we have in here."

One book looked to be a ledger of some sort. Names and amounts filled each page. He tossed it aside and grabbed the other. He opened it and whistled as he leafed through it. It was full of notes, names, addresses, phone numbers and memos, with some being crossed out either for being completed or not done at all. Each page was set up for particular jobs.

He saw his own name written in on a few of the jobs. Two thirds of the way through he came upon a page titled 'Cat'. His name was listed on it. So was Jonny's but with a line drawn through it. Mitt ran his finger over his friend's name, then drew it down the page scanning the names and numbers on it. Stutz's name was crossed off too as was another he didn't recognize. What he found under Stutz's crossed off name made him smile.

It was the name and address of a cop, Detective Paula Rogers. He knew the guy with the sword had not returned home and now he had seen her and the guy together.

Could she be sheltering him and his valuable pet. It made sense. He laughed, took a long drink from the bottle and closed his eyes. The pain was gone, and he could feel the warmth of the booze flowing through him.

Once again, he was the hunter, not the hunted. He knew having the cat would bring in a lot more cash than he had just lost and laughed loudly when he thought of how big the prize could be for him. Thoughts of revenge mingled with his visions of wealth.

"You're going to die, Fuckface," he called out with a huge slur. "Maybe I'll put a bullet in that pretty little face of your bitch cop girlfriend first just so you can watch her fucking die".

He roared with laughter as he attempted to stand up but instead staggered and fell onto the pile of money on the other end of the couch and dragged the pillow, money and whiskey bottle into a heap on the floor on top of him. Even though his bottle emptied most of its contents on his shirt and pants so only one more sip for him remained, he didn't care.

"Oh yeah!" he wailed as he rolled onto his back. "Your fucking bitch cop slut going to die right in front of you, asshole. She dies for Jonny. Yeah, that's right. Then I'm going to take my best knife, you bastard, slice your damned throat, sit back and enjoy watching you bleed out."

He lifted up the bottle for a final drink but as he was still prone on the floor, he just ended up pouring it onto his face. Moments later he was passed out in a mess of booze, pissed pants and soaked twenty-dollar bills.

Chapter 26

Paula looked at Jim and asked, "What the hell are you doing?" as he pulled out of the hospital parking lot and turned in a direction away from where she lived. He had come down to the hospital the moment he heard what happened and had sat with Morgan while she was being examined. As Paula and Morgan had left the car behind at the pub when they were taken by ambulance to the hospital, they had no car. Jim said he would drive, although his plans were different than Paula's.

"You're coming back to our place," he answered.

"No way. Come on now, just take us home."

"Jeez that sounded whiney!" Jim responded. "Look, I know you passed all the concussion protocols the hospital ran you through but you're still staying with us tonight."

"Jim, come on…"

"There you go again," Jim said cutting her off. "Whiney. The only time I've ever heard you be whiney was when you were hurting, and you can't tell me you're not hurting now."

"But…"

"No buts! You're staying at our place for the night and that's that," Jim said firmly. Paula knew there would be no point in discussing it any further. Morgan, alone in the back seat, knew enough to stay out of it.

Morgan saw Paula working on the bandage which covered her wound. He thought maybe it had come loose and she was fixing it. "Need a hand?"

"No," Paula stubbornly answered as she pulled the bandage completely off. "There. That feels better!"

"Paula, what the hell are you doing?" Morgan asked in an exasperated tone.

"It was bugging me. Besides, I want to have a look."

"They put it on there to keep it clean. Put it back."

"Don't tell me what to do!"

"Hey, Morgan," Jim said looking at him in the rearview mirror with a smile. "If you know what's good for you, just let it go. I'm only warning you because I know how damned bull headed she can be."

Paula pulled down the passenger side visor, flipped on the light and turned her head to inspect the injury. The wound had required three stitches. Although she wasn't vain person, she was disappointed they had to shave an area above her hairline for the stitching. On the other hand, she was happy to see the slice occurred above the hairline, so any scaring wouldn't show once the stitches were gone and the hair grown back. There was bruising and some broken skin on her cheekbone which she figured would heal well.

As she moved her head back and forth to see better, she saw how dangerously close Pin's attack had come to striking her temple. She flipped up the visor and laid her head back against the seat until they arrived at Jim and Grace's.

They entered the house through the side door and into the kitchen. Morgan thought he saw Tiberius, who had been in front of a food bowel on the floor, scamper from the kitchen. When they sat down at the kitchen table, he saw his friend poke his head around the corner. Seeing Morgan was one of those who had come in, he pranced across the kitchen and jumped up on his lap. His purr started right away as Morgan started running his hand along his back.

Grace watched Paula as she sat down. "Oh my, look at you. Does it hurt as bad as it looks?"

"It wasn't before but the pain killers started wearing off."

"Maybe you should take another. Do you want some tea to wash it down?" Grace asked as she rose from the table.

Paula sat at the kitchen table and rested her head in her hand, "Just a glass of ice cold water thanks. Think I'll take your advice, pop another pill and head off. Same bedroom as the last time you brought me back from the hospital."

"Yes," answered Grace with a warm smile. "And if this keeps happening, we'll have to refer to it as Paula's room and not just the guest room."

Paula took her pill and Grace helped her down the hall of the bungalow to her bedroom. Morgan watched them leave and suddenly felt uncomfortable. Being in somebody else's place, should he just assume he would be sleeping in the same bed as her or someplace else? He wondered how to ask and even if he should ask.

"It's been a long day for you too so maybe you should join her," Jim said with a tone which implied it was more an order than a suggestion. Morgan figured being a cop meant always feeling the need to be in charge. "I know Paula passed all the concussion tests but I'm still a little worried so every time you wake up in the night, roll over and give her a little shake to wake her up. Just ask her a simple question. Make sure it's something simple and she can answer it and do so without slurring. Also, if she moans a lot in her sleep, wake her up and come and get me. Same goes for a raging headache."

"I'll make sure," Morgan answered as he picked Tiberius up off his lap, held him against his shoulder, which caused much contented purring as he stood. Even though they were all adults, he was glad to discover the rules of Jim and Grace's house allowed him to sleep in the same bed as Paula. "Don't worry. I'm just as concerned about her as you are."

Grace showed Morgan the way to the guest room. Paula was already on her back sound asleep. Morgan pulled off his pants and shirt and carefully slid in beside her. He rolled onto his side facing her and listened to her breathing. It was strong, steady and rhythmic. He put an arm around her, which she grabbed and held onto tight.

"Don't worry. You and I are going to nail that bastard. He's not getting away with doing this to you," he whispered softly into her ear before falling into a deep sleep himself with her still firmly gripping onto his arm.

They both woke Sunday morning to the smell of fresh brewed coffee and Tiberius fast asleep between them, curled up at their feet. Paula sat up, rubbed her eyes and gently touched her stitches. Morgan stayed on his back and watched her as she felt around to the different injured areas on her face. She sighed, laid back down, reached over and found Morgan's hand which she grabbed and held onto tight.

Having been disturbed from his sleep, Tiberius walked up between them. He stepped onto Paula's stomach and walked up her body before lying down on her chest and poking his nose lightly up against Paula's chin looking for some attention. Paula obliged, took her hand away from her injury and started running her hand along Tiberius's back which, as usual, caused much purring.

"How do you feel?" Morgan inquired.

"Not a hundred percent but a hell of a lot better than when I went to bed," she answered as she worked her way up to a sitting position against the headboard.

"You look great. Even first thing in the morning after a fight."

Paula looked over at him and smiled.

"Thanks. Even though I know it's a lie, it's a nice way to start the day. You did wake up facing my good side though. You might not be saying if you had of slept on the other."

Tiberius scampered off the bed and out the door as Paula raised herself to s sitting position.

"Boy, I had such great plans for us last night too. I figured we would have success in following the Doctor. Afterwards I was going to put on something which would drop the eyeballs from your head. We'd have some bubbly and you were going to get sooooo lucky. But then all this crap happened." She placed her hand delicately up against her wound as she finished.

"I believe we were successful in many ways. We'll just have to put off the festivities for a few nights."

"You never know, Morgan. Maybe even tonight. We'll see. Let's get dressed and go join them for some coffee." They rolled out of bed to change and Paula was happy to find Grace had left her a clean shirt to wear, instead of the bloodied one she had taken off the night before.

"Well, there you are," announced Grace as they entered the kitchen. She was just placing a fresh bowl of wet food down for Tiberius, which he dup into with gusto. "Thought you guys might sleep the day away."

"I see Tiberius has been looked after. Mind if I help myself?" Morgan asked motioning to the coffee maker. When Grace nodded her approval, he asked if anyone else wanted a cup. Paula raised her hand. By now he knew how she liked it. He fixed hers first, poured himself a black one and joined them at the table.

"I trust there was no carrying on under our roof while we slept," Jim said with a grin before being playfully cuffed by his wife.

"No Jim. Too sore and tired. Otherwise, we would have kept the two of you up all night!" Paula responded.

"Alright now that's enough," Grace said.

After a little bit of talk, Jim got down to business, "So, what exactly went down yesterday, Paula?"

Paula related the story. Once done, Jim looked down at his coffee and then back to her. "I thought I taught you better. You would have ended up much worse off if Morgan hadn't of shown up."

"I know," came her reply.

"You may have got a shot in but he managed to save you from a hell of a beating, one you might not have walked away from."

"I know."

"He didn't do well but he got the job done. At least we know Morgan can take a punch." Jim looked over at Morgan with a slight smile on his face as he said it, then back at Paula. His smile disappeared. "Come with me!"

She let go of a large sigh as she pushed her chair back and followed Jim to the living room.

"What's going on there," Morgan enquired of Grace as the two disappeared from site. "Is he going to whoop her or something?"

"It's the something part. You see, Jim figures she should have been able to make a safe arrest but had put herself in bad position instead."

"What, because of me?"

"No. He couldn't figure how the guy managed to be close enough to strike her but after she told her story, I have an idea he suddenly knew. They're just going into the living room to re-enact it all and work out what went wrong. Then they'll run through the drill of how she should have handled it again and again, so she won't repeat the same mistake. They've been going through this for years. She's sore and likely pissed he has her doing this now. I know she's hating it as much as she is appreciating it."

"He does seem to care."

"Oh yeah. Nobody could ever have a better friend than Jim." Grace took a sip of coffee before continuing. "I'm glad they're gone for a bit Morgan. Gives us a chance to talk."

"Sounds serious. What do you want to talk about?"

"Jim told me when he was bringing you here, she told him to, 'Just take us home.' It's easy to see you two have become quite close."

"I think we have, but..."

"Morgan. Paula's a great catch. It's something I've already told you, but I also really like you too. I think you're good for each other. It's why I have to warn you just what you're getting yourself into before this goes any further."

Having eaten most of his breakfast, Tiberius jumped up into Morgan's lap and sat waiting for some attention. He started purring when Morgan started rubbing his neck. "What do you mean?"

"Dating a cop. Living with a cop. Marrying a cop. Morgan, I wouldn't give up my life with Jim for anything but life with a cop can be hard. Damn hard."

Grace was looking down at the table, "Their changing shifts are hard to get used to, but you learn to manage. You learn to not worry about the danger they could be in and all the ugliness they see in the streets. Hard as they try, there's stuff they ultimately bring home with them and you need to learn to live with it.

"Then the first time they're hurt on the job, you're thankful it wasn't worse but when they go back out, your worry is amplified. You worry maybe one day they will get hurt worse. That's when the reality of their job, their lives comes through. You read about a cop getting killed and it makes you worry even more than you ever thought you could when they head off to work."

"As you know, Jim was shot on the job. The pain and worry I went through when I first went to the hospital were unbelievable. Thankfully, cops are a big family and his buddies from the force were there when I arrived along with some of their wives. I was never alone. But still, sitting there waiting for somebody to come out of the operating room to say he was okay was so, so ..."

Morgan leaned over and placed a reassuring hand on her shoulder. She took a moment before continuing. "You know, I'm so thankful now he's not allowed back on the streets. Even though I know how much it hurts him not to be out there. That he's lost a piece of himself. But I'm so grateful he's behind a desk now because you can't get yourself killed working inside a station."

"Grace, I've witnessed what it's all like. I've seen her fight to defend me when I was being attacked. Hell, I even watched as she stormed into a building during a shootout, bullets flying everywhere, cops on the ground wounded and just yesterday watched her being beaten. Really, I do have more than just an idea of what it can be like."

"Yes, but do you know what it's like to sit at home all alone at night, not knowing what's going on and letting your imagination get the better of you?"

"No."

"I think the world of Paula. She's a wonderful person and I don't want to see her hurt. But before you let this go any further, you need to ask yourself if you can handle all the stress. She'll need strength from you, and you'll need it to be able to cope." Paula and Jim returned from their living room session ending the conversation and sat back down at the table with them.

"Get everything worked out?" Grace asked before taking a sip of her coffee.

"As usual, Jim straightened me out," answered Paula touching her hand gingerly to her un-bandaged wound which looked worse than the day before. "It was a lesson learned."

Jim smiled, "Ah, she's a smart girl all right, learns from her mistakes. Okay everyone, let's finish up in here."

"Grace, I'm going to drop Paula off at the station on the way on to take Morgan over to pick up the rental. Hopefully the overnight late charge won't cost much."

Morgan was getting tired of being hauled around and looked after by everyone else and said he would just take a cab. Jim wouldn't hear of it, so all Morgan could do was thank him.

Jim looked at Paula, "Girl, you have some fun times ahead of you today."

"I'm almost getting used to it. The paperwork, getting shit from the brass for even being there. Hell, it's just another day on the job for me now."

While in the other room, Paula had told Jim the truth of why they were in the pub At the table, Jim reinforced to her the same advice he had given her at the time she told him which was to just stick to her story of 'just happening to be there' when Pin walked in and don't let the brass wear her down.

Paula nodded she understood. Wanting to get off the topic, she turned to Grace and Morgan. "We were gone quite awhile. What did you guys talk about?"

Grace looked over to Morgan and smiled, "Why, Tiberius, of course!"

Chapter 27

Halina woke up to sounds of her son playing with his teddy bear in the crib and smiled. In the past, Shane usually woke up tired and sluggish and could be a bit of a bear to deal with due to his high fasting glucose.

Early in the morning, usually between four and eight, a person's blood sugar drops. The liver compensates for this by releasing glucose into the blood stream creating what is known as the dawn phenomenon. Non-diabetics never notice as their bodies release more insulin to combat the rise but diabetics, without a working pancreas, see an abnormal rise in their fasting glucose levels. The high glucose levels caused Shane's sluggish behaviour when he woke up and it would take a shot of insulin to bring it back down.

Six months before, Halina had decided to try Shane with a computerized insulin pump to control his sugar levels. She was happy for both him and her that it worked well as it meant less shots for Shane, from two to three every day to just one every two to three days, plus he was a lot less moody especially in the morning.

She picked him up, bounced him playfully and took him down to the kitchen. After feeding him she carried him to the living room and sat him among his pile of toys. She returned to the kitchen to fetch the mug of coffee she just had brewed. On the way back she tousled his hair as she passed by, sat on the couch and flipped on the TV.

It was always turned on to a 24-hour news channel. She turned the sound down but high enough so she could hear as she read her paper. Her thoughts took her back to the events of the day before, so she sat the paper down and pulled open the drawer of the end table. She took out the wrapped gift package inside and opened it up to reveal the $60,000 it held.

"Oh, Halina," she muttered softly to herself, "What do I do now? Just what the hell do I do?"

She remembered hearing the commotion just outside of the pub just after her meeting with that disgusting man. When some people opened the door to rush out to see what was happening, she saw the man she had given the package to in a fight with a woman and a man. Figuring she had just been seen sitting with him and didn't want to be questioned by the police, she decided it was best for her to leave.

When she had come through the doors ands turned to get away from the fight she was bumped into by a person trying to get a better view of the melee. The impact knocked her to the ground between two cars. As she had lifted herself up on her hands, to her wonderment she saw the package she had just given up, laying a little way under one of the cars. She scooped it up slid it into her purse and left as quickly as she could.

Halina shook the memory of what had taken place from her mind and tried to concentrate on the problem at hand. She stared down at the money unsure as to what she should do. There was nobody else she knew to hire for the job. She had contacted Oscar as he had done some shady clandestine work for her father in the past but didn't know if she could trust him anymore. On the other hand, going back to Sturgess, giving him back his money and telling him she couldn't get the job done was even less appealing.

She would have to go back to Oscar but needed to get some assurances from him to find out why he sent somebody else for the pickup ... a man who obviously couldn't stay unnoticeable and out of trouble. She sighed, looked up and saw a familiar image on the TV just for a moment before it disappeared. Halina quickly grabbed the remote for the PVR, backed it up to the beginning of the story and turned up the sound.

"Late yesterday afternoon, police were called to the scene of a gruesome, bloody murder," a serious looking young female broadcaster reported. The picture switched to show the front of a home complete with a few uniformed officers standing beside the house in discussion and the place cordoned off with yellow police tape. "After dropping her children off to stay overnight with cousins, Alicia Zimmer arrived home only to find the body of her husband, Oscar Zimmer, who had been beaten and shot twice during an apparent struggle and robbery."

Again, the picture on the screen changed. This time there was a still photo of a man which made Halina gasp. It was a picture of Oscar, the same man she was supposed to have met with at the pub.

"Who ... what?" she said confused as she looked down at the money sitting in her lap, then back to the TV trying to absorb what she had just heard. In a low tone she attempted to talk it through so it made sense to her. "The guy I met in the pub, who I gave the money to. My god, he must be the murderer. Somehow, he found out about our meeting, killed Oscar and showed up himself to pick up the money."

She reached for her phone but then abruptly stopped, "Wait. I can't call the cops. Damn it, I know who the killer is and there's not a thing I can do about it without getting myself thrown in jail for God knows how long."

Halina looked over at Shane who was busy examining a big toy truck, "No, Shane. Don't worry, mommy's not going to leave you. I'm just going to keep my mouth shut about the whole thing."

She picked up the money from her lap and held it in front of her. "I guess Monday I'll have to give all this back to Sturgess and hope he doesn't fire me. Damn, what a mess!"

♦ ♦ ♦

In frustration, Morgan let the hand which held his phone drop from his ear to his side for a moment, then returned it back to where he could hear and speak. "Are you sure it's our Oscar? After all, neither of us have ever seen him."

"Oh yeah, we're all sure down here," Paula replied. She was at her station dealing with her run-in with Mitt Pin when she heard the news. "There was a thorough search done of his office, you know, for prints, evidence, clues on who might have done this. Mitt Pin's name was found in several ledgers and notes. It has to be the same guy."

"Any idea why he was killed?"

"His safe was open and empty so we suspect robbery."

"So, where do we go from here?"

"I don't know. If it was Pin and he walked away with a lot of cash, he might just leave town. He's the last one we know of who's after Tiberius."

"Yeah, but we don't know for sure."

"Right. In the meantime, until we get this all this figured out, I think its best you continue to stay at my place."

"Sure," Morgan's replied but a little quicker than he would've liked. Then again, he thought, the two of them had never played games in the short time they had known each other.

"Great! You see Morgan, there can always be found a silver lining, no matter what!"

Chapter 28

Morgan's day brightened when Paula came through the door. He was not one to feel lonely. After all he lived alone but never felt lonely. Some of the times he had felt his loneliest was when he was in a room full of people.

It was how he had felt since he dropped off the car and went back to Paula's. The place felt empty. Paula wasn't there and neither was Tiberius. He was starting to feel a little trapped and wondered if he'd ever get home. As much as he really liked Paula and enjoyed her company, he found her so easy to be with, he wondered about them living together so soon. Of course, there hadn't been any other options and nothing felt better than waking up beside her. He just wondered why he felt trapped.

Paula dropped her purse on the telephone table by the door, walked over to Morgan and put her arms around Morgan's shoulders. She squeezed him warmly, then pulled back and looked him in the eyes, "Hey, is something wrong?"

"No, well, maybe a little. I was just sitting here wondering when all of this will be over and, you know, we can get our lives sorted out. Maybe start having more of a normal life. Hell, maybe even go out on a proper date."

"What, you don't like sleeping with me?" she asked with a smile.

"I love every minute of it. It's the normal I miss. Being able to flop on my own couch. Walk in the door and have Tiberius right there. I don't even know how the cleanup at my place went!

"I guess what it all comes down to is so much has happened lately, most of it out of my control. I'm just not used to it. Life has mostly been played by my rules. I never envisioned needing anyone to watch over me. To keep me safe, shit, to keep me alive!"

She took his hand. 'I understand. My life's been upside down lately too. I'm a cop who only ever drew my gun once. Now killing and death seems to be a regular thing. I don't know how to deal with it. I haven't even had a chance to and I guess when it gets right down to it, haven't really wanted to."

She pulled him close and kissed him deep and passionately, then rested her head on his shoulder. In a quiet soft voice, she continued, "Both our lives are a mess right now but out of all this, Morgan, I met you. Our lives have been chaos lately. It seems I'm constantly putting myself in a position to be knocked back to uniform or out the door and at the moment, there looks to be no finish line. But you know, I wouldn't give any of it up. Because right here and right now, being held by you, I am so happy. So content."

Paula lifted her head from his shoulder. Their faces were so close each could feel the other's body heat. She slid her hands from his shoulders and started to unbutton his shirt. Again, their lips came together as she worked her hands down. Once she had him unbuttoned, she took a small step back and started to unbutton her own blouse while he looked on. When she was completely unbuttoned, she reached up and unclasped the front of her bra and slowly drew the cups away from her breasts.

"My God, Paula. Never has a woman ever looked more beautiful," he said in wonder.

He had seen her naked many times before and could never tire of it. But here, now, he was in awe of her. He stepped forward, placed his hands on her feminine curves and pressed his lips hungrily against hers. Her lips met his eagerly and they slowly sank in each other's arms down to their knees, their lips never parting.

Any thoughts of where the future was going to take then disappeared as they were too caught up in the moment to care.

Chapter 29

Mitt's broken wrist was throbbing when he woke up. His head pounded, his stomach churned, and he was unsteady when he tried to stand. He looked at his cast or what was left of it. It was smashed, bloodied, soft and wet from the booze he had spilled on it. He looked further down to his damp, yellow stained pants.

"Ah shit!" he said as he placed his good hand to his head and headed to the bathroom. He picked up his phone and one of his saved numbers.

"Hey Audrey," he said in a gravely tone.

"Jesus, Mitt. You sound like hell!"

"Yeah, well, I feel even worse. It was worth it, though. I had a really big fucking haul yesterday. We're almost set. I've just got one more thing to do."

"Really?"

"Yeah, babe. I done good but there's still a lot more to come. First, I need some help. Can you come over?"

"Sure. What's up?"

"Just smashed myself up a little and I need you to take me to my boy to get patched up."

Audrey agreed to hurry over. In the meantime, Mitt changed and washed up. There were a few dryer bundles of $20 bills lying around which he unwrapped and jammed into a couple of his pockets. He gathered up all the soaked bundles, put them in his backpack which he tossed behind his couch. The mess he had created the night before was cleaned up before she arrived.

It was a fifteen-minute drive to get to his "ask no questions and cash up front" doctor. Along the way he told Audrey he had managed to get a huge amount of cash for their getaway fund and it was easily over a hundred thousand. He never said how as he figured the less she knew about the details, the better it was for both of them. At first, she tried to convince him a hundred thousand plus was enough money to take off and start their new lives with. When he informed her he would be doubling it by staying longer, she was all in.

When they arrived, the doctor, dressed in jeans and a tee shirt, removed the old cast and examined Mitt's wrist. "Hell, Mitt. It was healing nicely till you went and ruined all my work. The damage isn't too bad, though. It's going to take a little longer to heal but I think it'll still set properly. No guarantees, of course. Like last time it'll be a thousand, cash up front."

Although Mitt had told her about his haul, she was still a little surprised when he pulled a messed up pile of bills from his pocket. He went over to a table and counted off 50 twenty-dollar bills. Plenty of cash seemed to be left over which he crammed back into his pants pocket.

A new cast was applied, and the doctor handed Audrey a bottle of pain killers. He turned to Mitt. "I'm throwing in the pills for free. Be sure to take one every four hours."

"Some fucking free but thanks doc."

On the way to the car, Mitt opened the bottle and popped two into his mouth which he swallowed without water. It wasn't his first time doing it. Once they were back at Mitt's place, he took two more, but this time he washed them down with whisky.

Audrey had poured herself three fingers with an ice cube and took a spot on the couch. She patted her hands on her lap. "Come here baby, lay your head down. You look like you could use some sleep."

He took another swig from the bottle, sat it on the table and took Audrey up on her offer. His head wasn't in her lap for ten seconds before he was fast asleep. When he woke up, his head was on a pillow and the place was quiet. He looked over at the clock on the wall which read 10:32. As the sun was up, Mitt figured he had slept right through Sunday night. He thought Audrey must have got up, made sure he was comfortable and left to go sleep in his bed.

"Audrey?" he called out. He listened for a moment for a reply and when there was none, he called out louder. "Audrey!"

He sat up and immediately felt his wrist start to throb. His bottle of pills was sitting on the coffee table in front of him. He grabbed it, dumped four into his hand and dry swallowed them.

"AUDREY!" he bellowed. Still there was no answer. He got up and stumbled down the hall to his bedroom.

His bed was empty.

Suddenly he had a sinking feeling. He rushed over to the couch and pulled it away from the wall. The backpack of cash was gone. "You bitch! You fucking bitch!"

A moment later he heard the sound of a key being pushed into the deadbolt lock on his door. Mitt watched as the lock turned, then to the kitchen table where his gun sat. There was no time to grab it.

Bright sunlight spilled in when the door opened which made it hard for Mitt to see exactly who it was. The person stepped inside and closed the door enough so he could see who it was. It was Audrey wearing a huge smile as if nothing had happened.

"Oh, Mitt!" she declared happily as she took a step towards him.

"Bitch!" Mitt hollered as he took a couple of steps and slammed his hands up against her shoulders sending her back against the door.

"What the…?" Her words were interrupted by a hard slap to the face which sent her sprawling to the floor.

"Mitt, stop it," she pleaded and held a protective hand up to shield her face. "What the hell's up with you?"

"What the hell's up with me? HEY! Where my fucking money" he bellowed as he raised a hand to strike her again.

Audrey saw an opening and drove her foot up as hard as she could, right between his legs. Instantly he turned pale, grabbed his tender throbbing area and sank to his knees and fell over onto his side. All was quiet for the moment except the sound of his moans and Audrey's sobs.

She drew herself to her feet, walked over to the table where she sat down and rummaged through her purse. She took out her wallet, pulled a key from it and threw it at him. The key bounced off his forehead and spun to a stop on the floor in front of him. He still hadn't moved from his fetal position, where he remained still holding himself.

"There!" she said panting but without the rage he expected. "Want to know what that is? It's protection. You throw a shit load of money behind your couch and think it's safe. Well, I found it in a second. How safe do you think it would be if somebody broke in? If some bastard got even a sniff of it, they'd find it in a goddamned second."

Mitt squirmed and clumsily came to a seated position on the floor. Audrey looked at the whisky bottle on the table, grabbed it and took a couple of steps to the kitchen where she poured two tumblers almost to the brim. She walked over to Mitt handed him one and sat on the floor directly in front of him so their knees touched.

"Thanks."

"Fuck off." She glared at him. "First of all, I thought it was our money, not yours. That's what you said, right?"

Mitt could only nod.

"Well, you certainly weren't looking after OUR money very well, were you? In a bag behind the couch! What kind of stupid dumb ass move is that? I didn't want to lose it due to your stupidity, so I decided to take care of it."

"Where...?" His voice tailed off as he was still in deep pain. He felt like he could vomit.

"In a safety deposit box." She reached over, picked the key up from the floor and flicked it into his face again. "Pay attention! It's why we have the key"

"Good idea."

"No, it's a great idea, you stupid bastard! I was coming here hoping you would be feeling better so we could celebrate. Guess we can't now. You're going to be too damned sore and bruised down there to be of any fucking use. Ha! Now that's funny. Your balls are too fucked up to be of any fucking use to me." Her laugh which followed had an evil tone.

"Christ stop it. I'm sorry. I just woke up and…"

"Oh, just shut up!" Audrey ordered. "You know, I might have jumped to the same conclusion if it had of been me. Still…" The hand which Audrey was rubbing her sore cheek with suddenly lashed out hard and met the side of his face with the loud slap which sent him reeling back to the floor in a heap. "If you ever, EVER, hit me again, I'll choke you with your own fucking balls! Got it?"

Mitt nodded slightly from where he laid, then pushed himself back up to a seated position. He took a generous slurp of whiskey, looked at Audrey and said in a sincere voice, "Yeah. I was an asshole and I'm sorry, truly sorry. I deserved it."

"You sure did," Audrey replied then cuffed him again. This time he managed to remain upright. "You deserved that one too. Alright, come on. Let's get you up and get some ice on that crouch of yours. Ice and a couple of shots of whisky and maybe we still can get your pleasure machine in good working order for tonight."

Chapter 30

Paula's ringing phone woke them both up. They had fallen asleep exhausted, naked and sideways across the bed after a session of lovemaking which took them from the living room to a chair in the kitchenette and then finally, to the bedroom. The phone was in her purse in the living room and she knew she wouldn't be able to reach it in time. She let it go to voicemail rolled over and snuggled up to Morgan.

The phone rang a few more times before it stopped. Paula leaned her face in close to his and whispered, "For some reason I find myself enjoying afternoon naps more than I ever did before."

"Me too," he whispered back. They exchanged a warm kiss.

"I better go see who it was."

"Okay, just as long as you don't put anything on so I can get a good look at that dynamite ass of yours."

"You've got a great one yourself." She laughed and then slapped his bare ass hard.

"Ow, Jesus!" he exclaimed reaching a hand back to where her slap had landed. She quickly rolled off the bed and trotted off to the living room.

He swung his body around so his head was on the pillow and although he wasn't a shy person, threw a sheet over his midsection. A smile came across his face. He finished his pose by placing his muscular arm up behind his head. Hopefully she would enjoy his presentation.

Morgan closed his eyes and listened to her going through her purse. The sounds stopped and he heard her punch some numbers into her phone. All was quiet for a moment. Then he heard her voice, "Now, there's a Playgirl worthy picture. Nice. Very nice. Quite seductive actually."

He lifted his head and saw her holding her phone at her side as she leaned up against the frame of the bedroom door. She was still totally naked. He smiled and patted the bed beside him. "As beautiful as you are standing there, you must be getting a little chilly. Better come back to bed."

She giggled took two running steps, leapt and landed in the spot beside him. Grabbing the sheet, she quickly flipped it over herself and moved in close to him. Instead of snuggling in as Morgan had expected, she rolled her chest on top of his and lifted herself up onto her forearms on him so she could see him better. "It was Grace. They want us to come over for dinner."

"You mean for a normal night?"

"That's right, Sir. A normal night. Something I think we both could use ... unless you're worried about Pin."

"Should I be?"

"I don't think so. His boss is dead so there won't be anymore paydays coming from him. We're sure Oscar was the one organizing the job and he had hired Pin for it. Evidence shows Pin was there. From what we have pieced together, Pin killed Oscar and cleaned out his safe. Probably was a lot of cash in there too."

"So, Pin's probably somewhere in a lot of pain right now from busting up his cast on my face but sitting there with more money in his lap than he has ever imagined. He'd have to know he's a suspect in Oscar Zimmer's murder. His best bet now, his only one really, is to get the hell out of town. So, yes, I do feel comfortable. I believe we're safe."

"Wow! A normal night. Call her back right now and tell her we'll be there."

She rolled off him and hit the speed dial. Grace answered right away. As they confirmed plans, Morgan rolled onto his side and playfully rolled his fingers around Paula's nipple. She grabbed his hand and pushed it away with a smile. Again, his hand moved in and this time it received a light slap. He then moved his hand down between her legs which she grabbed and removed, this time with a bit of a giggle.

"Alright. We'll be there for seven then," she said.

"Great, Paula. We're looking forward to seeing you guys," answered Grace. "You know, something tells me you're not calling from the kitchen."

"Oh, shut up!"

"See you at seven. Now go and have some fun girl!" She ended the call.

Paula turned over to face Morgan and slapped his butt. "You're bad. I think she knew."

"Hey, she'd know anyway by the smiles on our faces when we walk in."

Paula took his hand and placed it on her breast. "You know we don't have to be there until seven. Let's make sure we walk in with huge smiles."

♦ ♦ ♦

Mitt didn't want Audrey to tag along but she had insisted. As they walked together along the sidewalk in front of Paula's condo, he felt it turned out to be the right move. A man and a woman walking together in the evening were very natural. One man alone might draw attention but now they were just another couple out for a stroll.

If the bitch cop and cat lover ever left or arrived, he would be more noticeable to them alone. Even with his ball cap pulled down over his face, he could be recognized. It was better to walk as a couple. Besides, he liked Audrey's company and she had proven she could be trusted.

They stopped by the garage exit to the condo. He noticed Audrey had wrapped her arms around her chest and had her shoulders hunched up. "Everything okay, Aud?"

"Audrey. Don't shorten it to Aud. You've never done it before. Makes it sound that you've nicknamed me 'odd'. I hate that!"

"Sorry, Audrey. It won't happen again. What's the matter?"

"I'm just a little chilly."

He rubbed her arms, "Let's head back to the car then and get warmed up."

Before they could take another step, they heard the garage door start to open.

"Hold on," Mitt said. He pulled Audrey in close and held her tight. Her back was towards the drive the car would be coming up. He faced the opening of the garage with most of his face buried against her shoulder. His cap was pulled down low to hide him but up enough he still had a clear view of the car as it drove up the ramp and passed them.

"Ha. The macho bitch cop won't even let the smuck drive. Guy's a pussy."

"So that's them?"

"Yup. Hold on one more moment until they reach the corner."

He watched Paula turn right at the intersection. "Let's go. I've got their plate number."

He found it quite easy to follow until she stopped to turn left off the busy main street and into an old subdivision of homes built back in the sixties. Flustered, he figured it wouldn't be wise to pull right up behind them and sit there close enough to be recognized. Instead, he drove a little farther along and made a left into a small plaza. He hit the accelerator and raced the short length of the parking area to the other exit and pulled out onto the busy street and headed back to the corner.

Luck seemed to be with him as he saw the car they were tailing had just finished making their left into the neighbourhood. Staying far behind, he followed them through the neighbourhood until they finally pulled into a driveway. He drove by and kept looking straight ahead as he passed by hoping they wouldn't look and see him. From the corner of his eye, he could see them both getting out.

"Looks like they're going for a visit," Audrey surmised.

"Good. It's what I was hoping for. Alright we need to find a way to get close. Have to see who's inside and if the tabby cat is with them."

He turned at the next corner, pulled over to the side and parked. The old neighbourhood lots had large front yards with mature hedges and trees which Mitt could use to his advantage. The problem was it was still too light out to case out the place up close. For the time being, they could only have a look from the road.

"Want to go for another walk?"

"Sure. I'm putting on my sweater this time."

It was red and stood out but, when Mitt thought about it, he figured they sure wouldn't look like a couple on the prowl. They walked holding hands down the street. Audrey looked down at his hand in hers and commented, "You know, Mitt. You've screwed me so many times in the past, but this is the first time you've ever held my hand."

"Because we need to look like a couple."

"Really?"

"Yeah... um no, not really. Look, I'm not very good with words but yes, we ... we used to screw. Now it's more than ... it's just more." He stopped and lifted the hand he was holding up in front of them. "What I'm trying to say is we're not just playing a couple here. We are a couple and if this all goes the way I want it to, well, we're going to be a much richer one."

They walked past the house but saw nothing. After walking by a few more homes, they turned and made their way back to the car. Mitt decided they needed to wait till nightfall before they could sneak up to the house and get a good look in the window, so they went for a coffee.

An hour passed and they spent their time mostly discussing what city they should move to once their business was completed. Finally, Mitt figured it was dark enough so he moved the car and parked it on the street in front of the house next to the one they needed to check out. It appeared no one was home as not a single light was on.

Mitt looked at Audrey. "I need you to sneak up to the house and have a look inside. We need to know how many are in there. I'd do it but if they spotted me, they'd know I'm onto them."

"And if they spot me?"

"Don't get spotted," he half joked. He saw she took the comment more seriously than he intended. "Look, if they do see you and want to know what you're doing, claim to be homeless or, hell I don't know, come up with some story."

"Don't worry. I'll get it done," she responded with some enthusiasm. She found this a lot more exciting than hunting Johns. She removed her bright sweater and got out of the car.

Mitt watched her disappear into the shadows the hedge cast from the streetlights. His fingers tapped nervously on the bottom of the steering wheel as he waited and listened intently for any sounds of trouble. There were none.

Finally, she returned and climbed back into the car. The street was very quiet. It appeared this was not a busy neighbourhood, one where people walked, jogged and biked. Instead, it seemed to be a place people just settled down in front of their TV's for the night. As a result, Mitt felt no need to move the car right away.

"So?" he asked.

"That was quite exciting. You know, in the past I've found guys sneaking up and hiding so they could watch me getting screwed by a John or giving some head, so I just loved being the one doing all the sneaking."

"What did you see?" Mitt asked again, this time a little more impatient.

"There are four of them. The two we followed and another couple. The couple are older, maybe in their fifties. Oh, and the older guy has his arm in a sling."

"Did you see a cat?"

"At first I only saw a bowl of food and water on the floor. Then just as I was about to come back, I saw it. I saw the cat. Sure 'nuff, it's a tabby."

"Excellent! Just what I wanted to hear. Great job! Now come here," he said as he leaned over, grabbed her neck, pulled her over the console and kissed her hard.

"Mitt," she said pulling back a little, "Thanks for bringing me. This has been thrilling. My juices are running so damned hot. She pressed her lips against his again, this time even harder, "You are going to get so laid when we get home boy. So laid!"

With a grin he let go of her, started the car and pulled away.

"Where we going?"

"Not sure but we can't be hanging around here."

"What about them?"

"We know where they live and know where they are. Before we do anything, we need a plan. If we can pull it off, that tabby will put a shit load more money in our pockets to start our new life. We'll never want for anything!"

Audrey laughed then reached over the console so her hand rested in his lap. She leaned over, kissed him lightly on the check as she carefully pulled unzipped his pants and reached in as he drove.

Chapter 31

It was the kind of night both Morgan and Paula had yearned for. Although the night was supposed to be a relaxed one, free of the issues of the past few days, the conversation started right away when Paula and Morgan walked into the house and Paula removed the red fleece vest she wore to reveal her gun and shoulder holster.

"You brought your gun?" Grace asked in an incredulous voice.

"She told me we were safe but wanted to bring her gun anyways. I feel better she did." Morgan answered.

Paula set the holster on a hook by the door. "With everything that's happened I didn't feel comfortable leaving home without it."

"Good move," replied Jim. "Better safe than sorry, that's what I always say."

"And so have a great many other people too," Grace added with a smile.

Jim ignored her comment. "Pin's likely long gone but until we can confirm that, you guys need to always be careful. What are your plans now you know Oscar's dead?"

"Well I thought..."

"I think they came over for a nice evening without talking about this and it's just what I plan to give them," Grace cut in. "We're not discussing this anymore, so drop it. You can talk about it tomorrow but tonight's all about having a good time and getting to know Morgan a little better."

They all agreed, and the subject was dropped for the night.

Morgan and Paula had not been eating very well, except for breakfasts which Morgan excelled at making, so they both enjoyed the aroma and taste of Grace's slow cooked roast beef. It was accompanied by a big bowl of garlic mashed potatoes, sautéed mushrooms, and peas. Morgan was not surprised to find out Grace also baked when she presented lemon meringue pie. He devoured two pieces.

Afterwards, the cards were brought out for a game of progressive euchre while seventies rock played loudly in the background. The game ended and they talked some more until it was after midnight when they all decided to call it quits for the night.

"Well, guys, it's late and if you like you can sleep here," Jim offered.

"No, but thanks," answered Paula. "I want to get home and wake up in our own bed."

Grace smiled, "Jim, I think they just want to get home, go to bed and maybe not sleep right away."

Paula, who was standing beside Grace, slapped her shoulder playfully.

"Hey, we were young once, "Grace offered.

"Still are." Jim said then walked over and put his arm around his wife. "So, what are you two up to tomorrow?"

"Not sure," Paula answered. She noticed Tiberius had been picked up by Morgan which seemed to make them both quite content. "As we don't really know where we stand right now and tonight was so great, I think it might be best to just take tomorrow off and rest. I think Morgan and Tiberius might enjoy some time together too."

"And maybe it's time to get Tiberius over to JDRS and have them take a look at him," Morgan suggested. "If there is an insider there after Tiberius, his contacts on the outside are mostly gone. So many people now know about this now I'm sure he'll be safe there. Plus, while he's there I won't let him out of my sight."

"Me either," Paula chimed in. "Of course, we could always do it the day after tomorrow." She stepped close to Morgan and ran her hand along Tiberius's back which resulted in some loud purring.

"I think the day after tomorrow is best. You've both been through hell lately and could use a rest," Grace commented. "Jim, go get the carrier for them."

"I'll go with him and grab our jackets," Paula said and followed Jim to the other room.

When they returned, she had her red vest on and the carrier in hand. Jim followed with Morgan's jacket and waited while she opened the carrier's door so Morgan could slide Tiberius inside. "You went in easier than usual," Morgan remarked as she sat the carrier on the floor. "Must be looking forward to going home."

Jim handed Morgan his jacket. "When this all started and she let you stay with her, I wondered if it was a good idea. Once I got to know you though, I felt comfortable with you staying there. Paula always had good instincts about people."

"Thanks Jim," Morgan replied sliding on his jacket. "It's great to hear that from you knowing how close you two are."

They all said their goodbyes with handshakes, hugs and kisses. Morgan picked up the carrier, took Paula by the hand and headed for the car. Grace and Jim stayed in the doorway with the door open and watched them.

"They're a cute couple," commented Jim.

"They are. You know, when I watched them together tonight, I think it's possible he just might be the one."

"Really?"

"Really."

When they were close to the car Morgan let go of Paula's hand. He took an extra quick step to get to the car door first. With the hand which was not holding the carrier, he opened it for her. Paula smiled at the gesture and turned around to Grace and Jim.

"Ha! Looks like I've found myself a real gent..." She stopped in mid sentence when she saw a figure emerge from the shadows by the side of the garage.

"Gun!" she yelled. A shot rang out which missed both of them and smashed through the backseat window. Tiberius screeched in panic. In an instant, Paula had her gun in hand and as she stepped in front of Morgan to shield him was raising it to fire.

The muzzle of the attacker's gun flashed twice more, and their barks filled the night air. This time the shots were accurate. Both slammed into Paula's chest with the impacts knocking her back into Morgan sending them both crashing to the ground. Morgan landed on his back beside the car with Paula falling backwards on top of him, her gun falling from her hand.

Jim reacted quickly. He pushed Grace back into the house and charged the attacker who had his back to him. After only a couple of steps, the attacker turned and fired. Jim swore as the bullet struck him in his left shoulder and sent him reeling to the ground. Grace ran out to him screaming.

The assassin wheeled around back to his original targets to complete his work. He saw Paula lying motionless on top of Morgan, who was still pinned underneath her. He smiled. They were like a big turtle on its back. He stepped forward and raised his gun but never noticed Morgan had managed to get his hand on Paula's fallen revolver.

Three shots rang out from it in rapid succession. Only one missed. One slammed into the right side of the attacker's chest while the other completed the job and blew a hole in the left side of his skull which toppled him to the ground in a lifeless heap.

"Oh Jesus, Paula," Morgan cried out in a panic. He rolled Paula off him and onto her side. Now freed, he then rolled her onto her back. She looked very pale. "Paula, Paula. Oh my God, Paula. Please don't die. Please, please."

Paula started to cough. She grabbed her chest and took a couple of deep breaths. She coughed again and, in some obvious pain, said to Morgan, "How's Jim? You have to get over and see how he is. Kick the gun away from the body first. If he moans leave him. You have to see to Jim."

"What about you? You've been shot."

"Morgan, I'm fine," she replied coughing and clutching her chest. "My vest's lined with Kevlar. It stopped everything. I'm just bruised and it's a little hard to breath. Just go kick the gun away, don't pick it up and see if Jim's okay."

Morgan stood and went to the lifeless body and as told, kicked the gun away. After he did, he heard Jim call over to him. "Morgan! Don't move the body at all but have a look. Is it Pin?"

"Jim, you okay?"

"Yeah, just peachy. Damn it. Just check if it's Pin!"

Morgan bent onto one knee for a closer look. The face of the unknown man was turned sideways with only the bloodied hole in the side showing itself. There was nothing in it he could recognize.

"Morgan!" He looked up when he heard Paula call out to him. She had risen to her knees, something he was quite happy to see. "Morgan! Is it Pin?"

He looked back down the man's body but before he could say anything, a car pulled up to the curb and a woman jumped out the driver's side.

"Bastard! You fucking bastard! You killed him," the woman screamed.

"Hey lady..." Morgan rose and took a step towards her. He suddenly stopped and dove to the ground when he saw she had a gun which was pointed at him.

She pulled the trigger repeatedly, shooting until the gun was empty. One shot smashed the light by the front door, another shattered the living room window. Morgan heard the frightening sound of a slug whizzing by his ear and landing with a sickening thud in the dead body behind him. Two more kicked up dirt around him. He turned his head from where he lay in time to see the woman pull away with the tires screeching.

"Morgan!" Paula shouted, "Morgan! Were you hit?"

He didn't answer right away. The sound of bullets just barely missing him and the whole scene in general had unnerved him.

"Morgan!" He heard the fear in Paula's voice as she called out to him. He came up to a sitting position and saw her clutching her chest as she stumbled towards him.

"I'm okay, Paula. Thankfully she missed." He turned his head and saw Jim struggling to get up off Grace. It was obvious Jim had dived on top of Grace to protect her. The man's a hero he thought. "Jim. Grace. You guys alright?"

"Sure, as long as there are no other damned surprises for us," Jim replied. Grace was already taking off his shirt so she could tend to his wound.

Paula reached Morgan, dropped to her knees and threw her arms hard around him.

"Doesn't it hurt when you do that?" Morgan asked.

"It'd hurt more not to."

They held on tightly to each other, both glad the other was alive. Morgan finally broke the silence between them, "You wore a bullet proof vest to a euchre game?"

"Sure. You know how they can get out of control," she answered with a laugh which made her wince and grab her chest. Morgan looked concerned and was about to say something, but Paula removed her hand from her chest and placed it on his. She smiled. "I only wore it because it looks good on me."

She shifted, coughed and grabbed her chest. Her face was a canvass of pain.

"You sure you're okay?"

"Yeah, I'm alright. The vest stopped the slugs but I'm probably pretty bruised." She looked down and grimaced. "Damn it!"

"Shooting pain. Maybe you have broken ribs!"

"No. It's my vest. Look, it's ruined!"

"Sure glad you wore it though ... and brought your gun!"

"Shit!" Paula held her chest as she spoke in short gasps. "It's only a couple of months old. I got it in case I needed to wear one discretely. A thousand bucks and now it's unwearable. Damn it!"

"It did its job and don't worry, I'll split for a new one." He leaned in and warmly kissed her cheek. "At least we don't have to worry about Mitt Pin anymore."

"Really? You sure? Did you see his face?"

"Yeah. When that woman hit him with her shots his head rolled over. Also, I saw his cast. Looks brand new. He must have got it today. Not that he'll be needing it anymore."

Paula started to laugh but the pain made her stop and clutch her chest. A few tears trickled from her eyes. His too. They were holding each other close when the police arrived with their sirens wailing.

Chapter 32

It was almost four thirty in the morning when Paula, Morgan and Tiberius arrived back at Paula's condo. Morgan hung his jacket in the closet and watched as Paula gingerly set her purse on the telephone table by the door. The jacket she had been given at the station, as her own vest was being held as evidence, she tossed on the seat of the small table. The jacket didn't land fully on the table and fell to the floor. Paula looked at it, sighed and left it where it landed. Exhausted she crossed the room, put her hand against her chest and tenderly eased herself onto the couch.

Morgan sat the carrier down and let Tiberius out. He fixed him a fresh bowl of wet food and water and then joined Paula on the couch. The moment he did, she grabbed his hand and held it tight.

"My God, Morgan. I thought for sure you were going to be killed when I saw Pin came out."

"Thanks to you I wasn't. You saved my life, or should I say, you saved it again."

"No. This time you saved mine. When I was hit, I couldn't breathe and didn't have my gun. Damn it! How could I ever have let it go?"

"You were shot, remember ... twice!"

"How could I forget? The jacket stopped the slugs but didn't absorb the impact. Oh God, I felt so helpless when I saw Pin standing over us." She closed her eyes for a moment and Morgan could see tears starting to form. "Thank God you had the presence of mind to grab my gun. I thought for sure we were both dead."

A couple of tears appeared and slowly made their way down her cheek. Morgan wanted to hold, hug and comfort her so bad. He didn't because she held onto his hand so tightly, he knew it was what she wanted, what she really needed at that moment. She raised his hand held it to her lips and kissed it.

"A couple of weeks ago I never even knew you. Now, damn it, I don't know what I would do if I ever lost you," she said quietly.

"I know. I feel the same way."

She let go of his hand, placed her arms around him and put her lips on his. He could taste the salt of her tears. She rose gently from the couch, took his hand and led him to the bedroom. Together they laid on top of the covers and held each other close. It was the way they remained until they both fell into a deep sleep.

Five hours later Morgan was awakened by Paula's voice. "Oh shit! They look as bad as they feel."

When he opened his eyes, he found he had rolled onto his back during the night and Tiberius had taken the opportunity to use his chest as his own personal bed. He looked over to Paula who was standing topless in front of the mirror of her vanity running a finger around the edges of two very large overlapping bruises on her chest.

In the mirror's reflection, he could see the outside edges of the bruised areas were nearly black with the middle seeming to be a mixture of different tones of red and blue. It all encircled a white area, the place where the bullets had struck her. The middle of one of the bruises was located almost dead between the top of her breasts. Her left breast had been struck in the shooting and the entire inside area around the area of impact was mainly blue.

"It looks so painful!'

"Oh yeah. Hurts like hell. I can't believe it didn't break any ribs." She turned around so he could see them better. This time she had a slight smile. "They're so unattractive too. It'll be awhile before I put on a bikini."

Morgan chuckled at the comment. He pushed Tiberius off of him, got up and went over to her. She was still looking down as she traced her finger around the edge of the injury. He was afraid to hold her so instead he looked down at the huge bruise and drew his own finger lightly along the outline for just a few seconds. Then he reached out and grabbed both of her hands. She leaned in and kissed him warmly.

"The good news is we're both still alive today," she said softly. Then in a little louder voice she added, "But the bad news is, I don't think we'll be having any sex for the next few days. Not that you'd want to. I mean look at me. My face looks like it's been dragged across concrete. My breasts are like a baboon's ass. Want to know a secret? I'm not vain, at least I don't think I am, but I used to be proud of my chest, my face, my body. Now it looks like I've been pulled through farm equipment."

He laughed and held onto both her hands. "Are you kidding? Even as banged up as you are, you're still one hell of a beautiful woman."

She leaned in again and their lips met tenderly, "Thanks. I really doubt it but thanks."

Morgan carefully helped her put on a button-up blouse. Hand in hand they walked into the living room where he helped her lower onto the couch. He took an icepack from the freezer, wrapped a tea towel around it and gave it to her to help bring down the swelling. She held it against her chest while he made them breakfast.

They ate quietly. Morgan could see Paula was having difficulty finding a comfortable position to sit while she ate. Every once in awhile she would wince and hold her hand against the soreness. After they were finished, she returned to the couch. She winced as she leaned back and again when she placed the ice pack against the area.

Morgan felt it every time her face scrunched. He asked if she had any painkillers in the house. She told him where and he returned with couple and a cold glass of water. She asked for one more which he dutifully retrieved. He sat down beside her as she gulped them down.

"So finally, it's all over," he surmised.

"No. Not until Shimon's behind bars."

"Can't your buddies at the station pick her up?"

"We never told them about her. You weren't supposed to be with me, remember, so we decided not to mention it to them."

'Oh yeah. So ... what do we do?"

"Before we do anything, we have to go to the station first. You've been through this all before but not for killing someone. It'll probably be tougher and longer. Last night they were easy on us knowing we were traumatized by the whole thing. Then I want to go see Jim. See how he's doing."

"What about Doctor Shimon?"

"Oh, we're going over to see her right after. Damn it, Morgan. She's the cause of all this. People are dead. Jim's been shot. You were almost killed and now you've had to kill. You've no idea how that's going to mess with you.

"And it's all because of her. What kind of doctor sets off such a trail of death? You know what? No matter how much pain I'm in, it'll be all I can do to keep myself from beating the damned bitch half to death for a confession before I drag her ass down to the station!"

Chapter 33

It wasn't the way Paula marched up Halina Shimon's driveway in angry determined steps which made Morgan nervous about what might take place once she was face-to-face with the doctor. It was the way she acted before she got out of the car.

Paula had hardly said a word in the car after they left Jim's place. He was going to be fine and had even joked that Pin had shot him in the wrong shoulder, the one attached to an arm which didn't work. Jim had wanted some time off work and now he had the excuse to take it with pay but it didn't lighten her mood any.

As she drove, her jaw was clenched, and Morgan could see she was grinding her teeth. It must have bothered her facial injury as every once in awhile she opened her mouth to stretch it. Then she would lightly press the palm of her hand against the bandage before returning it back to the steering wheel and setting her jaw again.

Each time they rounded a bend or took a corner, she would take her hand off the steering wheel and press it to her ribs. Morgan surmised the motion to turn the steering wheel must aggravate her bruised ribs.

"You sure you don't want me to drive?"

"No!" was her terse reply. Morgan wisely decided not to ask again.

Paula pulled the car up to Halina's house and parked so it blocked the driveway. He wondered about her motive when he saw her quietly draw out her revolver, pull the ammo clip to ensure it was full and snap it back into the handle.

When she flipped the gun onto its side and glanced at the trigger, he asked what she was doing and became even more anxious with her answer, "Ensuring there's a bullet in the chamber ready to go."

Every move was deliberate. Every move calculated. Every move put him on edge.

She slid the gun back into its holster, took out a bottle of pain killers, tossed three tablets into her mouth and washed them down with a swig of water.

"Let's go," she said in a low purposeful tone. Her eyes glared at the house. She reached for the door handle, but Morgan placed his hand on her shoulder which stopped her.

"Paula."

"What?" she retorted in an exasperated tone as she turned to look at him.

"You never answered me when we left Jim's but isn't having me go inside with you going to get you into a shit load of trouble?"

"Of course it will. In fact, they may end up busting me back to uniform but right now I don't give a shit. I want to bag this fucking bitch and I need a witness to back up anything she says. I'm not calling in anybody else who might fuck this thing up. I'll ask for forgiveness after I haul her in with a fucking iron clad confession. Now come on. Let's go!" She opened the door and with long determined steps, started up the drive.

Morgan sat shocked for a moment. He had heard her swear before, but this was the first time she had used the "F" bomb around him. She wasn't just angry. She was enraged. He clambered out the car and caught up with her as she arrived at the door.

"Alright. Remember. I do all the talking. You're only here as a witness. Got it?"

He nodded. She pounded on the door. They heard sounds come from inside and a few seconds later Halina opened the door.

"Police!" Paula didn't wait for any reply. She held up her badge as she barged past Halina into the house with Morgan right behind her. "Halina Shimon. I'm Detective Rogers and this is my partner, Watson. We're here to ask you some questions."

Halina was so shocked she never thought to ask for his ID. Instead she closed the door but kept it unlocked and turned to greet her uninvited guests. She attempted a smile. "Officers, how can I help you?"

Paula was about to speak when she saw a young child playing with toys in the living room. She paused for a moment. "Is there a place we can speak away from the child?"

"Yes, yes, of course. Let's go into the kitchen." Halina led them to a very large kitchen and once there turned on a children's monitor. Satisfied she could hear Shane, she turned to face Paula. With a smile, she turned her palms up and spread them out slightly from her side in what she hoped was a welcoming gesture, "So..."

"You were at the Empire of Britain Saturday and met with a man, Mitt Pin," Paula stated in an even but forceful voice. She paused for a reaction.

Even though she had years of experience, Morgan was still somewhat surprised she was so in control of herself. In her rage as she stormed up to the house, he had half expected her to have a gun in Halina's face by now but was glad he was wrong ... at least so far.

Halina paused. She wondered just how much they knew and considered how she should reply when an impatient Paula broke her train of thought. "I'm not asking you a question. We know you were at the Empire of Britain with Mitt Pin two afternoons ago."

"Yes. Yes, I was."

"And what was the purpose of you two getting together?"

"I ... I was ... I was giving him a present." Halina knew she had to be careful. She didn't know who had seen the two of them together and until they met, she never knew his name. "He's a friend."

"Why did you bring him a gift?"

There was a short pause. "Because ah ... because his birthday's coming up."

Paula took an intimidating step towards her. "You mean the birthday that's still five months away."

"Yes ... no. I mean ... please, what is this all about?" Halina asked as she took a couple of short steps backwards.

Paula stepped forward to keep in Halina's space, "What was inside?"

"Inside what?"

"Inside that goddamned gift box you gave him," Paula bellowed. In the other room Shane started to cry. Halina turned slightly to tend to him, but the tone of Paula's voice stopped her cold, "Leave him. He's okay."

Halina stopped for a moment but knowing Shane had been frightened by the detective's outburst, she turned to go. Paula's calm firm tone stopped her cold. "You leave this kitchen and I'll haul your ass down to the station and we can go over all this there. Think your boy would enjoy seeing his mother hauled away in cuffs? Think of the lasting affect that would have on him."

"You have no right to speak to me like that. To come in here, try to intimidate me, scare my child. You may be a cop but what gives you the right…"

"THIS!" Paula shouted and tore off the bandage on her face. The wound was still quite scabbed and heavily bruised. The bandage peeled off a small piece of scab which caused some blood to start to ooze from it. "Your friend, Mitt Pin, received a package from you then jumped me in the parking lot. This would have been much worse if my partner hadn't been there. Now, what the hell was in that package?"

Halina stood in silence and buried her face in her hands. *Think Halina. Think. Oh God, what can I tell them? They can't know everything, or they would have arrested me by now.*

She lowered her hands which uncovered her eyes which looked ready to burst with tears. "I'm an endocrinologist. My son has diabetes. I've been in diabetic research for years trying to find a definitive cure but with no luck. I heard of a lab in the U.S. which has an experimental drug, one which will regenerate the pancreas. A year of shots once a week and the pancreas, once again, is fully functional. The need for insulin is gone. It won't be through all the approvals and on the market for years. Inside the box was payment for the treatment which he was supposed to appropriate for me."

Paula looked at her in disbelief. Halina continued. "Look. I don't know why he did to you what he did and I'm sorry. It looks so painful. But truthfully I was paying him to bring me what could be a cure for Shane."

Paula reached into her jacket pocket and pulled out her business card and a pen. She crossed out her number at the station and wrote her personal cell phone number on it instead. "I'm not around the station much but when you fell like telling me the truth, call me on my cell and I'll be here right away."

"But I just told you..."

"Bullshit!" spat Paula. She stepped in closer to Halina, so she was close to her face. "Here's what I know. First of all, if you hadn't figured it out already, my partner and I were the ones who saw you hand a package to a man who minutes later beat me, a cop, in the parking lot. But here's the kicker. Last night he tried to kill the two of us."

"Oh my God! What ... how? I... I don't know anything about that." Paula could see by the stunned look on the doctor's face she was telling the truth. "I'm so sorry but I had nothing to do with any of this. I don't know why he…"

"Just shut up and listen. Late last night he made one last attempt to get the cat and shot a great friend of mine in the process. Oh, and you won't be seeing Mr. Pin again. He's on a cold fucking slab down at the morgue."

Halina stared blankly at the floor dumbfounded by what she had just heard.

"That's a huge pile of shit you've been trying to give us just now." Paula took her business card and jammed it into the pocket of Halina's blouse. "When you feel like telling the truth, call me."

Halina's jaw dropped. Although she said nothing, the look on her face told Paula all she needed to know about her.

"Listen. People haven't died because of this cat. They haven't died because of the secrets it might hold. They ALL died because of you!" Paula glared at her for a few seconds before she spun on her heel and left with Morgan close behind.

As they headed down the driveway, Morgan felt he could speak, "I'm not sure what she does know about Pin, but I sure believe she's the one behind trying to get Tiberius."

"Oh, you can bet your ass she is! We'll just have to find a way to get it out of her. For the time being, we'll just let her sweat and see what happens."

Inside the house, Halina went into the living room, picked up Shane and slumped into a chair. Having to go to Sturgess and give him back the $60,000 was the least of her problems. It sounded like everybody involved in her scheme was dead and the police were on to her.

Halina sat Shane down beside her and picked up a throw pillow. She buried her face in it and cried for hours.

Chapter 34

Morgan and Paula, each with a bag of groceries, stood in front of the bank of elevators waiting for one to arrive. Paula was deep in thought and had not said much on the drive back to her place. Morgan too was quiet as there were of things running through his mind.

He was wondering about his future with Paula once they were done with Halina and this entire episode was behind him. "I'm wondering if this feeling will ever pass," he said breaking the silence.

"What feeling?"

"Worry. It's the first time Tiberius has been left unguarded since this has started."

"We've only been gone thirty-five minutes. Like we discussed, Shimon will be too busy figuring how to cover her ass and knowing we're on to her, she's not likely to try anything. We just saw her a couple of hours ago. Even if she wanted to, she wouldn't have the time to put anything together.

"We needed groceries and hey, you're the one who brought up leaving him alone. It was nice getting out with you alone without fear of being attacked even if it was just grocery shopping. Don't worry. It'll get easier leaving him behind. Remember, it's my turn to cook tonight and I promise it'll be a great supper."

Morgan smiled. With his free hand he reached over and gave her free hand a squeeze. He went back to the original question which ran through his head. Where would the relationship take them once they were finished with Halina? Since he met her their lives had been filled with stress, mayhem and danger. With all of it removed would they be able to keep a relationship?

Oh Christ, stop it! I'm starting to think like a teenage schoolgirl.

"What do we do now with Shimon?"

"I've been thinking about it since we left her. She's not talking ... not yet anyways but I'm sure she will. She looked ready to crack. But the more I think about it, the more I think it's best for me to go to the station, tell them everything I know and let them handle her from here. They can get this all nailed down quicker than you and I."

"But wouldn't that put you in a pile of shit."

"Oh yeah." Paula let go of his hand and pushed the elevator button again. "I'll take my lumps. Hopefully I'll get a reprimand or a suspension and not a demotion. In any case I do think it's the right move ... yes, definitely the right move. With her gone, we'll all be safe."

Paula grabbed Morgan's hand again and kissed him lightly. "I don't think we need to worry about the woman who took a shot at you last night. She was acting on emotion. I don't think she ever fired a gun before. She was too wild."

"Too wild? I heard bullets whiz by my head."

"And everywhere else. She's a runner and we won't see her again. Until we have Shimon in custody, though, I think you should stay with me. You don't mind, do you?"

She smiled and still holding his hand, kissed him again.

"Not at all. Tiberius and I are enjoying our stay."

"Who knows? After I take a couple more pain killers, there might be something else to help you enjoy your stay." She closed her eyes in obvious pain and winced. "Definitely after a couple of pain killers, though."

The elevator arrived and holding hands they rode it up without saying another word. They got off at her floor and started down the hall but stopped when her next door neighbour stepped into the hall with a bag of garbage in her hand.

"There you are," the woman exclaimed seeing them. Morgan took her to be in her late seventies.

"Mrs. Jazinski. How are you? Can I take that garbage to the chute for you?"

"Oh, no dear, I can manage. Say, what was all that racket at your place this afternoon?"

"Racket?"

"Yes, about ten minutes ago. Loud bangs against the wall and a crash."

"Oh God." Paula dropped her bag and ran to her door with Morgan right behind her. She grabbed her keys from her purse and drew her revolver.

Mrs. Jazinski stepped back towards her own condo unit. "Ms. Paula. What's going on? Should I call the police?"

"I am the police Mrs. Jazinski. Just get back inside and you'll be safe. I think we were broken into. They may still be inside." Mrs. Jazinski hurried back inside her place. Morgan could hear her door being locked and bolted.

Morgan saw Paula motion him to step aside and wait. He was hesitant to do so as he wanted to be there in case she needed help but when she motioned more forcefully to move, he did so. All was quiet. He watched as she carefully placed her key in the lock, gave it a quick turn and flung the door open. He had expected her to charge in but instead she stepped to the side of the doorway.

"Police! Anybody in there?" she called out and listened quietly for a moment. Not hearing a reply, she took a deep breath, motioned for Morgan to stay put and stepped inside. She checked the living room, kitchen, bedroom and bathroom. "Morgan, it's clear!"

Morgan stepped inside. Paula's dining room table was turned on its side and her shelf of pictures and knick-knacks were toppled over. A sickening feeling churned inside of him. There was no tabby to be seen.

"Tiberius!" He looked left and right, but no tabby came out to greet him. Twice more he called out as he checked each room.

"Morgan," Paula said stopping his frantic search by grabbing him by his shoulders. "They got him. I don't know who, but they got him!"

"Oh my God, no! What are we going to do?"

Paula jammed her revolver back into its holster. "We go back to see Shimon. Only this time we'll be getting some answers from that fucking bitch!"

Chapter 35

With the siren wailing they raced back to Halina Shimon's home. Fear ran up and down Morgan's spine. Not from the weaving in and out of traffic or the hard squealing tire corners Paula took but the thought of what might happen to Tiberius. Paula never shut off the siren as the turned onto Halina's street and skidded to a stop in front of her driveway.

"Want me to watch the back of the house?" Morgan asked as they quickly moved up the lawn. He was worried their noisy arrival might spook her.

"No. You stay with me. There's no way she's going to run. She's not about to abandon her kid."

Morgan quickened his pace and reached the front door first. He pounded his fist on it. Paula, behind him, took a look inside the large front bay window. She saw Halina standing in her living room looking out at them.

"Hey Doc!" Paula pointed at the door. "Open up this damned door before I kick it in."

Paula watched Halina disappear from the window and a moment later the door opened. It was obvious from her puffy red, watery eyes she had been crying. Paula hoped it meant she was ready to talk. Halina said nothing but swept her hand indicating for them to step in. Morgan was in first and led the way to the kitchen followed by Halina with Paula taking up the rear.

"Look, I told you…" Halina started before being cut off quickly by Morgan.

"Your people have Tiberius!"

"What?" said a surprised Halina.

Anger filled Paula's voice. "Your people! They broke into my place and grabbed Tiberius, the cat you've been after."

Halina started to weep, "But I don't know what you're taking about. What people?"

"Your fucking people!" Morgan yelled and took a step towards her.

Paula stepped in between the two and placed her hands on Morgan's chest to stop his menacing advance. She turned to face Halina. The doctor bowed her head and started to cry uncontrollably. Her hands shook and she seemed to be losing control. Paula knew with the right words and some tact, the woman would break.

She had to take a moment to allow her own anger to subside before she started. "Doctor Shimon. We've been following you for some time. It's how we ended up at the same pub as you. We know where you work and your relationship with Beth Poole."

Halina lifted her head, her swollen eyes opened wide with surprise before her shoulders slumped and her gaze headed back to the floor.

"We're also aware you know Tiberius's secret. More importantly, we know you were the one behind the attempts to kidnap Tiberius. I guess all the glory and accolades you'd receive for finding the cure was just too tempting but now with everything we know, you're going to jail. For how long depends on how much you cooperate with us."

"It wasn't for the..." Halina stopped herself. She looked up at Paula and then back to the floor again, "Yes, I know about your cat and yes, I told my boss, Sturgess, about him. He's the one in charge of my lab. That's all I know. You can't put me in jail for that."

"Oh, for fuck's sake, I've had enough of this shit," Morgan groaned and tried to take another step towards Halina. Paula had leverage on him and managed to hold him back. He was surprised at how strong she was.

"Morgan ... Morgan!" Paula said loudly as she leaned against him. She noticed he had stopped pushing against her and she had his attention, so she lowered her voice. "Look. She's not going to tell us anything. The best we can do right now is to head on over to the lab and hope to catch him there with Tiberius. The longer we stay here trying to get her to talk, the less of a chance we have to get him back."

"Last chance," Paula said firmly. She stepped towards Halina, "You're in so much deep shit right now, you have no idea. You need to help us. Where is Tiberius? Damn it, woman. If you help us, then we can help you. Where did they take Tiberius?"

Halina kept staring at the floor in silence.

"Come on Morgan," Paula turned and headed towards the door. "Let's go get your cat. She can stay here and figure out who's going to raise her child while she's in jail. Maybe she'll be out in time for her son's graduation!"

Halina walked to the window and watched as the two cops drove off. She heard their siren fade away as they sped off into the distance. For a moment, she felt sorry for herself and the situation she had put herself in. Then a feeling of anger began to take over.

If all the people she knew of were dead then Sturgess must have hired another crew on his own. But why? He couldn't have known Oscar was hired for the job or he was the one who hired Mitt. Their deaths may have made the news, but they should have meant nothing to him. Then it hit her. Sturgess had been watching and now all the evidence was pointed at her, he was taking advantage of it. He'd grab the cat and let her take the fall.

She picked up the phone and punched in the number from the card Paula had given her. After three rings, Paula picked up.

"Detective, this is Doctor Shimon."

"You have something for me?"

Halina thought for a moment. She had to help but couldn't give herself away.

"Hello? Are you still there? Do you have something for me?"

"Sturgess needs the lab. He'd have the cat taken there," Halina said carefully. She knew how the drop would go but had to explain it like she was guessing even though the detective quite likely would see through it. In any case, she felt she had to help.

"Christ! We've already figured that out. Now stop screwing us around."

"What you don't know is Sturgess would never use the main door in front because of the cameras. There's a door out back. Nobody ever uses it. It's in the middle of the building. There's a camera there but it's been broken for some time. Sturgess knows about it but never had it fixed. That's the door he'd use."

"Thanks."

"One more thing. The back is a mess of skids and crap. It's like a junk yard. They keep a driveway cleared close to the building. A security guard takes a drive around twice an hour, on the quarter hour. He never gets out of his car when he's out back. Sturgess is a precise man and would make any exchange either on the hour or half hour."

"Anything else?"

"He'll do it at night when it's dark as there aren't any working lights out back. The light above the door has been burned out forever and I don't think the ones in the lot have ever worked."

"Thanks. Anything else?"

"No." Halina ended the call and tossed the phone onto the sofa. She looked out the window and saw it was already dark. It was a moonless night. But for the streetlights it would be pitch black. She closed the drapes and wondered if the black night would help or hinder the two cops. Then she wondered what would be the best outcome she could hope for.

Suddenly it occurred to her. The female detective had called her partner, Morgan and when they leaving had said to him, "Let's go get your cat." She knew the cat was owned by someone named Morgan. Maybe he wasn't a cop after all but the cat's owner. It's why he was so angry when they came back. She hoped it was something she could use against them if they survived the night.

She turned around to go to the kitchen but when she did, she found a gun pointed in her face. Halina gasped and took a step backwards, but it was too late. She never saw her attacker or heard her son's terrified scream from the sound of the gunshot which woke him and ended her life.

Chapter 36

Not wanting to be seen, Paula had pulled into the parking lot of the building next door to the lab. She told Morgan to stay where he was and pushed a button on the side panel of her door which popped the trunk. She left for a minute and returned with a radio and extra bullet clips for her pistol.

She leaned in Morgan's window. "Sorry. This time you're going to have to stay behind. It's time now for me to bring the cavalry in on this."

"You can call your pals at the station but I'm coming with you."

"No, you're not. I can't do this and worry about you at the same time. It'd get both of us killed. I need to know you're safe. What I need right now is somebody trained for these situations to have my back. Morgan, please, stay out of the way. Let me do my job."

Paula reached in and placed her hand on his shoulder to reassure him. She leaned in the window where their lips met for a long moment. Her eyes closed quickly, and she winced in pain as she pulled herself back to an upright position and grabbed onto her chest.

"Don't say a damned word. I'm alright." She drew her service revolver and with hand over wrist, pointed it towards the ground. She looked at Morgan one more time.

"Stay here and keep out of sight. No matter what you hear, don't come to help. I'm calling for back-up now. Next time you see me, I'll have Tiberius." She smiled at him one last time before she disappeared quietly into the darkness behind the building.

They had arrived at 10:20 pm and when they did, they had noticed the security car just leaving the lab's parking lot. She was hopeful if there was an exchange it would take place ten minutes from then, on the half hour. If not, it could make for a long night or worse. They might have missed it altogether. She knew backup was on its way and when they arrived, they would be quiet and stay out of sight until they heard from her.

Once she reached the back, she found the chain-link fence which separated the two yards had a gap in it in the back corner. It was wide enough for her to slip easily through. In the darkness, Paula could still see the parking lot behind the lab was a mess of old skids and crates as she had been told. It made it easy for her to find a hiding place fairly close to the door. She hunkered down and waited.

After five minutes, she heard rustling and footsteps from the same side of the yard the gap in the fence was. Her heart sunk a little. If he came in the same way she did, could they have come upon Morgan and done anything to him. The thought quickly exited her mind when even though darkness surrounded her, she could make out a shadowy figure carrying a box. When she heard a cat's muffled cry, she knew she had found Tiberius.

Once at the door, the man stopped and waited. He didn't knock or call out. Instead, he just stood there quietly until the door opened. Light spilled out into the lot and Paula saw a man who she recognized as Leo Sturgess, step outside.

With her gun raised, she carefully, quietly approached them, knowing she had them cold! Nothing ever presented itself in a court case better than catching suspects in the act.

"Police! Everybody freeze. Nobody move."

The two startled figures in the doorway turned quickly in her direction. When they saw her with a gun pointed directly at them, they did as they were told. "You with the box. Put it down carefully then stand back slowly keeping your hands where I can see them."

The man did as he was told and set the box on the ground. With his hands extended out from his sides, he straightened up and turned slowly around to face her. Paula started to lift the radio to call in her backup when she saw the man start to smile. An instant later, she felt the barrel of a gun press up against the back of her head.

"Drop the gun and raise your hands!" After taking a moment to consider her options, she reluctantly let the gun drop. As she raised her hands, she felt her radio being ripped from her hand.

She saw Sturgess smile and reach down for the box. The voice of yet another man broke through the night behind her. "You with the gun, drop it! Sturgess! Get away from that box or I'll fucking blow your head off!"

Even though she was in deep trouble, it was a voice she didn't want to hear. It was Morgan's.

Chapter 37

Paula's voice was calm. "I'm calling for back-up now. Next time you see me, I'll have Tiberius." Morgan felt a little reassured by Paula's smile and confidence as he watched her disappear into the darkness of the black parking lot.

Her reassurance, however, wore off quickly. He hated waiting and did it impatiently. Paula was right though. If he was there, he'd be in the way and a distraction she didn't need. But as he sat slouched down in his seat, his mind ran rampant with all the horrible things which could happen to her. He cursed the fact he had no way of knowing what was happening.

After a few minutes of staring, his eyes had started to adjust to the gloom of the back lot. He finally found he could make out shapes and silhouettes. Suddenly, he spotted what looked to be movement. He straightened up in his seat and leaned forward in an attempt to see a little more clearly.

Although it was difficult to make out much in the darkness, he was sure he could see a couple of shadowy figures down near the back corner. One disappeared through the same area of fence Paula must have used. The other hung back for a minute before he headed through the gap.

Shit! She's got two guys coming up behind her. If she's dealing with the first one, she may not realize there's another. Morgan tried to figure the best way to help.

He reached across the driver's seat and hit the button to pop the trunk. As quietly as possible, he got out of the car and went to have a look inside. As he had suspected, Paula carried an extra weapon in it. Thankfully it was a shotgun, something he had used before, which was sitting in a gun case. He grabbed it, checked to be sure it was fully loaded, and dumped a handful of extra shells into his pocket. She may have told him she didn't want him there but now he felt the need to go. He dashed as quickly and as silently as possible down to the opening in the fence.

After he had pushed his way through the gap, he could see light streaming from a doorway with two figures standing by it. His eyes swept the area trying to find Paula among the mess, but he was unable to until he heard a man's gruff voice. "Drop the gun and raise your hands!"

Morgan heard something clatter to the ground and assumed it was her gun. He stepped around a pile of skids and headed toward the sound of the voice. What he saw horrified him. It was the silhouette of a man holding a gun to the back of Paula's head.

"You with the gun, drop it!" Morgan called out. "Sturgess! Get away from that box or I'll fucking blow your head off!"

He watched as Sturgess straightened up and stepped away from the box. The man holding the gun to Paula's head never moved.

"I said drop the fucking gun."

"Or what? You'll shoot me? You do that and I'll be dead but so will she."

The man standing with Sturgess reached inside his jacket and pulled out a pistol. Morgan never moved. His shotgun was trained on the one holding a gun to Paula's head. He felt helpless. He didn't have a clue what his next move should be.

Paula's assailant turned his head slightly to glance at Morgan. As he did, his motion caused the gun to move away from Paula's head. Immediately, she lashed back and up with her right arm striking the man's gun arm which caused it to point in the air just before he fired. With a spin, she drove her left elbow into his face which sent him sprawling backwards against a pile of skids.

The man stumbled forward still holding his pistol but was quickly dispatched by Morgan, who slammed the butt of his shotgun into the side of the man's skull which sent crashing to the ground.

Paula reached down and scooped up her revolver just as a couple of shots rang out from the man at the door. One bullet smashed into a crate beside Paula while the other could be heard striking a metal object far back in the yard.

Paula dove for cover behind a pile of skids which allowed Morgan a clear shot at the man by the door. He pulled the butt of the shotgun to his shoulder and pulled the trigger only to hear it land with a sickening click onto an empty chamber. Although he had checked to make sure the safety was off, he hadn't looked to see if there was a cartridge in place ready to fire. A gun was usually carried with an empty chamber to ensure it didn't fire accidentally if dropped or jarred.

The man by the door smiled. He took a step forward and raised his pistol. Morgan pumped a round into the chamber and quickly fired at the exact same time he saw a burst of flame erupt from the other gun. He saw the man violently thrown back against the wall by the impact of Morgan's blast and at the same time felt a searing blast of pain as the man's bullet slammed into his left bicep up by his shoulder. Morgan cried out in pain as he stumbled backwards into a stack of empty drums but never letting go of his shotgun.

"Morgan!" Paula cried out as she saw him take the hit. She looked back to the building to ensure the man at the door was down for good. Satisfied he wouldn't be causing them any more trouble she crouched low and quickly made her way to Morgan.

The man, who had held her hostage moments before, had recovered enough from Morgan's strike to bring himself up to one knee. He saw Paula's body silhouetted by the light of the open door in the distance behind her and raised his gun to fire.

From the corner of her eye she spotted him and was much faster than he was with the trigger. She whirled around and let go a couple of quick shots. Both found their mark in his chest twisting his body and sending him face first into the pavement.

Another shot sounded which ricocheted off the ground in front of Paula. Morgan looked over towards the open door and saw Sturgess holding the box against his left side and a revolver in his right hand, aimed directly at him.

Sturgess had dove for cover the moment the first shot was fired and stayed out of sight. When he had saw both Paula and Morgan were distracted by the other gunmen, he slid over to the lifeless body by the cat's box. The dead man's gun was on the ground beside him. He picked it up along with the box and stood up. Seeing he hadn't yet been noticed, he aimed at Paula and pulled the trigger. His first shot had missed and, in a panic, he fired once more, again with the same result. By then Paula had ducked behind some cover.

"Everyone's dead, Sturgess, but you! You're under arrest. Now drop your gun and raise your hands!" Paula shouted. She kept her gun steadily pointed at Sturgess. With her hand, she motioned for Morgan to take cover.

Morgan ignored her. Sturgess never moved and kept his gun pointed in their direction.

"Sturgess, it's over. Put the box down and give yourself up!" Morgan hollered. Although in pain, he swiftly pumped a round into the chamber.

Instead, Sturgess snapped off two quick shots at Morgan, one which he heard go screaming by dangerously close to his ear causing him to duck. Paula stepped out and returned fire. She watched as the bullet slammed into Sturgess left shoulder. The impact caused him to drop the box but as he spun around, they saw he had never dropped his gun. A cat's shriek came from inside the box as it hit the ground.

Morgan and Paula saw him raise his gun and never wasted time. Simultaneously they fired. Neither missed. Blood burst from Sturgess chest and side as he was thrown against the wall behind him. His eyes were empty, and his back left a long bloody red streak down the wall as he slowly slid to a seated position on the ground.

Paula's eyes swept the yard looking for any more signs of danger. Once she felt it was all over, she turned her attention to Morgan. "Oh my God. You were shot. How bad is it?"

Morgan grabbed the wound and gave it a slight squeeze. Searing pain raced up his arm and he did his best to fight off any urge to yell or swear. He removed his hand and in the faint light of the open door, could see it covered in a sticky red mess. "They got my arm. It's bleeding and hurts like hell but I can seem to move it. Shit forget about me. What about Tiberius? God, I hope he hasn't been shot."

Just then police stormed through the door from the inside and also streamed around the outside corner of the building. Orders were shouted telling everyone not to move.

"Over here!" Paula called out. Lights from numerous flashlights lit up to reveal her standing with her arms raised, her revolver in one hand, her badge in the other.

Cat howls cried out from the box and its sides flexed as Tiberius tried to force his way out. One of the uniformed officers bent over to investigate.

"Don't let the cat out," Paula called out to him. "It's valuable."

"Really?" was the sarcastic reply.

"Yes, really! You've no friggin' idea. Make sure he doesn't get out."

Tiberius kept howling but the banging against the box's sides stopped.

Two officers with their guns still trained on them made their way over to Paula and Morgan. One checked Paula's ID as she ripped the sleeve off Morgan's shirt to wrap his wound. At the same time, she explained the reason Morgan was with her. Of course, it wasn't all entirely true.

"I want to see him," Morgan said as he tried to pull himself away from Paula and get over to the door where the box lay. He didn't like the sounds he was hearing from Tiberius.

"Okay, you will. You will," Paula replied. "Just take it easy. You've lost blood and might become dizzy."

An officer helped steady Morgan to ensure he wasn't about to collapse as Paula finished up. "Hey, I'm alright. I need to check Tiberius!" Morgan said as he pulled himself out of the officer's grip.

"Thanks. I've got him from here," Paula said to the officer. She grabbed onto Morgan's good arm. "Come on. I've got you in case you become lightheaded."

When they reached the box, Paula instructed one of the officers to take it inside. More police arrived in the yard, checking the bloodied bodies and combing the yard for bullet casings and evidence. Morgan never noticed the commotion as his focus was entirely on Tiberius, who sounded like he was in pain. Morgan's only concern was to get Tiberius out of his cardboard prison and make sure he was wasn't hurt.

Morgan sat on the hallway floor and the officer placed the box carefully in his lap. When the flaps were opened, Tiberius leapt out and ran down the hall. He stopped, turned and hissed at them.

"Tiberius! Hey it's okay boy. It's me," Morgan called out. For a moment Tiberius was confused. He crouched on his haunches as if he didn't know whether to go to Morgan or flee. "Come on, Boy!"

Tiberius raised himself up and started towards Morgan and Paula. Then to their horror, his backside seemed gave out and he howled in pain. Paula raced over and scooped him up. She talked softly to calm him while she quickly checked him over. Again, Tiberius cried out in pain.

"He hasn't been hit anywhere I can see," Paula said as she went over him once more. Tiberius shrieked again and squirmed in pain.

"Is there an ambulance here?" Paula asked.

"Three. But they're for people, not for cats," a fresh young recruit retorted.

"Really? You don't want to be fucking with me right now, so just get the hell out of my way. I'm already in enough shit so I'm not worried about adding hijacking an ambulance to the list of things which are going to get my ass fired from this force."

Chapter 38

The wailing siren of the ambulance didn't do much to calm Morgan or Paula's nerves. It also terrified Tiberius, who shook and whimpered in great pain. Morgan held him tightly to his chest with his injured arm and stroked him with the other in an effort to calm him.

Paula had already called the station to find out where the closest emergency animal hospital was. Then she called Doctor Everingham, Tiberius's vet, on his cell and explained the situation. The doctor had given Morgan his private cell number when he had called to inform Morgan about Tiberius holding the key to the cure. A squad car was on its way to pick him up and take him over as quickly as possible.

Everingham asked Paula to pass the phone to the paramedic to help assess Tiberius's condition. Morgan listened to the paramedic repeat the instructions but had problems following the medical jargon being used. He understood, though, when the medic instructed him to hold Tiberius firmly while he gave him a needle. In a few moments, Tiberius stopped wriggling and rested his head on Morgan's arm. Paula stroked his back as the ambulance raced along.

When the driver insisted they should be taking Morgan to a hospital first, then go to the animal hospital with Tiberius, the suggestion was shot down quickly and firmly by both Morgan and Paula.

"Guys. I'm good."

"You haven't even let us look at the wound."

"It's more important you get Tiberius to the vet as fast as possible. You can patch me up when we get there." Morgan leaned forward towards the driver. "We end up anywhere else and you'll be bloody sorry!"

"Morgan! That's enough." Paula could see he was seething and needed to settle down. "These guys are taking us to the vet now. It was just a suggestion. They're concerned about you but we're going to the vets. No need to get pissy with them."

"Yeah, you're right. Sorry, guys." He stopped to take a deep breath. "We've been through a hell of a lot to keep this fella alive."

"Don't worry about it," the driver replied. "I'm getting the idea he's more than just your cat. What's so special about him?"

Both paramedics were stunned and amazed by Paula's explanation.

"I guess that'll keep you out of hot water for grabbing this wagon," commented the driver. "When they called in more than one ambulance, we didn't know what to expect when we got there. We only knew there was a fire fight going down. I never expected to be rushing a cat to a hospital. A cure for diabetes you say? Wow!"

The attendant at the back with them cut in, "Yeah. As it turned out, tonight our boys are taking more to the coroner than the hospital. Apparently only one of the three you were dealing with survived."

"Hope it's not Sturgess," Morgan muttered under his breath. He felt Paula bump his shoulder. When he looked over at her questionably, he saw her put a finger to her lips to keep quiet about it.

"What?" he whispered.

"Keep it to yourself unless you want the line of questioning you're going to get centering on whether you shot him in self defence or not," Paula whispered. She knew it was self defence and didn't want anything to distract from the truth.

Morgan nodded he understood and looked at the two paramedics. They were talking and thankfully seemed to not have heard what he said.

Finally, in what felt like forever, they arrived at the animal hospital. The paramedic opened the rear door and Morgan rushed inside with Tiberius held close against him. A nurse took Tiberius from him and exited through a pair of swinging doors. Morgan attempted to follow but was stopped by a doctor.

"Sir. We have it from here," he said then disappeared through the same doors.

Morgan could hear a police siren wailing as it approached. He breathed a sigh of relief when he saw Doctor Everingham come through the doors. The vet quickly shook their hands and headed through the same doors the others had used.

The room had suddenly become uncomfortably quiet. Morgan slumped into a chair. One of the paramedics tried to take a closer look at Morgan's wound but he angrily pulled away.

"Morgan. We can only wait," Paula said softly, "I know there is no way in hell we could ever drag you away from here so let the man take a closer look at that mess and fix you up the best he can until we can get you to a hospital."

He nodded and held out his arm. As much as it hurt and bled, nothing vital looked to have been struck as he still seemed to have full use of it, although every movement he made jolted him.

While being worked on, the outside door swung open again and a woman entered.

"Hi. Are you Morgan Watson?"

Morgan nodded.

"My God, look at your shirt!"

"It's been a busy night. Can I help you with something?"

"I'm June Farnsworth with the Canadian Juvenile Diabetes Research Foundation. Doctor Everingham called me on his way in. Where might I find him?"

With Morgan having his arm looked after, Paula led her through the same doors the others had used. When she returned, she sat down beside Morgan and grabbed onto his good hand.

"Looks like Tiberius is getting the best of care in there," Paula said trying to comfort him. Until he saw Tiberius, she knew nothing would make him feel better.

With his wound cleaned and dressed, Morgan tenderly felt around the area, suddenly grateful for the treatment he had received. The paramedics received another emergency call on their radios and headed out, which left Morgan and Paula alone in the waiting room. Together they held hands, sat and waited in silence. At last, the double doors swung open and Doctor Everingham came into the room.

"How is he?" Morgan asked as both he and Paula rose to their feet. They stepped towards the doctor to hear the news but had to hurriedly jump back when the double doors burst open again and June Farnsworth rushed by them with a cooler held firmly in hand.

"What ... what's going on Doc," he asked hesitantly.

The doctor sighed, put his hands together and cleared his throat. Paula's fingers dug into Morgan's good arm.

"The first thing I want you to know is Tiberius is alright. He was never shot."

"Oh, thank God. I thought my shotgun blast might have hit him."

"No, he was never struck," the doctor continued. "He was in pain, though, and we did have to operate. Please have a seat and let me explain."

Both returned to their seats while Everingham grabbed an office chair from behind the counter and wheeled it over in front of them so he could sit and face them as he spoke.

"He is okay, right? You said he was okay?"

"Oh yes. Right now, he's still out from the anaesthesia. He'll be groggy when he wakes up but he's going to be just fine. Let me explain what just happened."

Both Morgan and Paula nodded for Everingham to continue.

"That little rascal of yours, Tiberius, did something quite remarkable. Miraculous even. You see somehow, someway, his body managed to grow another organ."

"What?" they replied in unison.

"He grew another organ, nothing we had seen before. While we were monitoring him, we detected another hormone in his bloodstream, something we had never seen before. We didn't know what is was, how it got there or what it really did. It was tough to detect early on but was becoming more and more prevalent with the samples we took over the years.

"When I called you to say we felt he did have a cure, those hormonal readings had become very strong. We wanted to get Tiberius over to JDRF right away for tests. With all that's happened since, I realize your reluctance to do so.

"Tonight, when you brought him in, he was in quite a bit of pain and had some bruising so we had to go in and have a look. What we found was an organ we had never seen in any animal before. We feel that this organ had somehow grown in to replace the pancreas and was producing that new hormone but somehow ruptured. Are you aware of Tiberius being struck or mistreated in any way?"

"I don't believe they would have purposely harmed him in any way before our altercation," Paula answered. "The box he was being held in, however, was dropped at least once, maybe even kicked during the exchange."

"It could have caused the rupture. The organs were pretty crowded in him as it was, what with him having an extra one. We surmise the new one still hadn't fully developed. Maybe the rupture was caused by all the rough handling or it burst on its own as there wasn't any more room to grow.

"When we removed the organ, we found a high concentration of this hormone in it. June is rushing it to her lab to see if she can save it or at least learn as much about it as they can. We're wondering if this could be an evolutionary event and if so, has this occurred in other felines?

"As far as Tiberius goes, he's going to live a long and healthy life. Sorry, Morgan, but he's back to being diabetic once again. You know what that means. Test strips, needles, daily glucose tests and insulin shots."

"Doc, I'll take that over what might have been," Morgan said as he closed his eyes and fell back into his chair. Paula wrapped her arms around him "Oh yeah, I'll take that in a heartbeat."

Chapter 39

Morgan sat on the sofa in Paula's condo and was having a problem adjusting the ice pack on his arm. He had grabbed a fresh icepack when he changed the bandage and saw the wound remained swollen, but he was having issues getting the bandage tight enough to hold it in place.

In the kitchen, he could hear the sound of Tiberius's neck cone scrapping the floor and banging up against his plate as he tried to eat. When he was done cleaning his dish, he wandered back into the living room and sat on the floor in front of Morgan. It was a signal he wanted up on the couch.

Tiberius's stitches made it too painful for him to jump up himself so Morgan had spent his last couple of days picking him up, putting on the couch, putting him back down onto the floor, picking him up, putting him on the bed, putting him back down again. He was told by Everingham it could be up to a week before Tiberius could do it all this on his own. Morgan, although he grumbled about it at times, was happy to comply.

He carefully scooped up Tiberius and set him on the sofa beside him. Knowing Tiberius liked the back of his ears scratched he reached inside the cone setting off a very loud purr.

Paula returned home from another trip to her station. Wearily she dropped her keys in the bowl on the telephone table and slid her gun and holster into the drawer. She headed over to the fridge. "I see you two are doing fine."

"Not entirely. We're both still sore. How about you?"

Paula didn't answer right away. Instead, she went into the kitchen and grabbed an icepack for herself. She came back into the living room and gingerly sat so Tiberius and his cone was between them. With a sigh, she placed the icepack against her shirt. The cold emanating from the pack stung her bruised chest but helped to ease the pain. "My chest hurts like hell. Oh, look at the three of us here! A family of walking wounded!"

They both laughed but the pain in doing so caused Paula to lean forward and grab her chest with both hands. "Hell, look at me. I can't even laugh."

"Would more ice help?"

"No but thanks."

Morgan sat up and fought to secure his icepack again with the bandage but with little success. Paula seeing his difficulty, put down her own and made sure his was bound firmly in place. He thanked her and sat back. She did the same but with her icepack pressed tight against her ribs.

"How did it go at the station?"

"Interesting, to say the least."

"Really? What happened?"

"When I went in, I thought for sure I was going to be busted back to uniform and I was prepared for it. Can you imagine my surprise when I was told they can't award me for bravery, going above and beyond ... yada, yada, yada ... then demote me?"

"So ...?"

"So, for six months I'm riding a desk, visiting schools, manning booths at public events. You know, all the shit I hate."

"Then back to duty?"

"Then back to duty."

"So, they liked your story."

"I don't think they bought the idea entirely that you followed me to the lab without me knowing. Oh, and that you just happened to have a set of keys to my car so you could get in the truck. But because of the results, they seemed content not to look too hard. They never even questioned how you managed to get there without a vehicle."

"That's good to hear. Oh, and hey! Congratulations on the award!"

"Thanks, but there's more news too." Paula sat up a little and moved her ice pack from one side to another. "The guy who survived? He was the one who had the drop on me until you came along and saved the day."

"Enough of that. You and I were quite the team out there."

"Yes, we were but if you weren't there, I likely wouldn't be here. Anyways, he talked."

"He did!"

"Oh yes. I'm so glad he didn't die. He spilled everything he knew. It was enough for us to go out and get a warrant. One which was good not only to search the lab and Sturgess' home for physical evidence but one for cyber forensics to go through his personal and company computers."

"And?"

"Our boys found some interesting things. When the investigators pieced it together with what they already knew, they came to a surprising conclusion. In their opinion, the late Doctor Shimon didn't have anything to do with this. She was being set up to take the fall by Sturgess once he got hold of Tiberius."

"But we know that's not true."

"I know but it sits well with me."

"Really? Why?"

"Because she's dead and as much as she really deserves to be, she has a son. People have died because of her. You and I came close to being killed. But that boy, that innocent young boy, had nothing to do with any of this. You know, he's going to have enough emotional issues in his life dealing with the fact his mother died violently. I'm glad he also doesn't have to deal with the truth his mother was an accomplice to multiple murders. None of it was his fault. I'm glad he'll never be exposed to that part of her life."

Morgan nodded. "Alright. As much as it surprises me coming from you, a cop, I guess I can see that."

"With what was found allowed us to arrest Bakerman, Sturgess number one man, on a couple of charges. Accomplice to murder, conspiracy, withholding evidence and all of it will stick. Our evidence against him is rock solid."

"I love it!"

"It also turns out Sturgess did have someone inside JDRF. We managed to bag the little prick. Although we can only get him on theft of information, which isn't much, they fired his ass out the door."

"Excellent!"

"I think so too. Did you hear anything from Everingham?"

"I did. The Tiberius organ, it's what they are calling it now, well, they couldn't keep it alive. It still may shed some clues for a cure in the future but how it functioned or developed might never be known."

"Damn and after all this."

Paula carefully rested her forearm on Tiberius's back, reached over and took Morgan by the hand. They both laid back and rested their heads against the sofa while Tiberius kept up a long and steady purr.

"Did your friends ever figure out who the woman was who shot at us at Jim's?"

"Shot at you, you mean?"

"I still shudder when I think about it. Yeah, her."

"No idea. The boys found out where Pin lived and asked around. It seems Pin enjoyed the whores when he had the money but was basically a loner. Pin's place was quite a mess up when they got there. It was as if somebody was searching for something. If he was seeing somebody, she's likely long gone."

Tiberius stood up and looked at the floor then over at Morgan who immediately and gently placed him onto the carpet. Paula took the opportunity to slide over close to Morgan. She turned to lean in to kiss him and winced at the movement. Then with one hand pressed up against her bruised chest, she used the other to hold onto Morgan's arm for support but without thinking had grabbed onto the bandage covering his wound. He grimaced in pain.

"Whoa," Morgan said with a bit of a gasp. "Let's not try that move again for a few days. Alright?"

"Agreed." Paula pressed her icepack hard against her chest while Morgan readjusted his. They both laid their heads back again. She smiled. "When we are all healed we're going to lock the door, turn off our phones and spend a couple of days in bed ... and there might not be much sleeping going on."

♦ ♦ ♦

Audrey once heard a joke on an old TV show. "Money can't buy you happiness, but it can buy you a car to drive around and look for it." She had thought about that joke often, usually when some rich ass client was handing her a night's pay for a blowjob in his Lamborghini.

As she took another stack of bills from her safety deposit box and placed them into her old beat up backpack, she smiled. No longer would money be a worry for her. Armed with over two hundred grand in cash and perfectly crafted fake IDs, that bad joke and her old profession were now already fading far into her past.

She thought back to the night when she saw what she thought was the key to her future lying dead on the grass on the front yard of house in some strange neighbourhood. The feelings of the deep anger she had felt inside her reappeared as she remembered climbing out of the car with the gun Mitt had given her before he left and fired again and again at man who had taken him from her. Finally, she relived the emptiness, the tears and gloom she was left with when she jumped back into the car and sped off. Right at that moment she thought her future was done.

Audrey smiled as she grabbed the last few bundles of cash and held them up against her chest. When she had arrived back at Mitt's that night, all those earlier emotions left. It all became clear to her. The promise of a great new future wasn't the one with Mitt. It was with the key which Mitt had tossed into a bowl in his cupboards. The key to over two hundred grand. She found over ten thousand more spread around Mitt's apartment and when she left Mitt's for good, she knew what to do.

She placed the last of the bills in her backpack, zipped it closed, locked the safe deposit box and called in the clerk. He took the now empty container, slid it back into place and they both locked it tight. She thanked him, made her way up the stairs and out into the cool fresh air and sunlight.

It was about a ten-minute walk to Union station and along the way she stopped and ducked down an empty alley. She stopped and pulled out her old Ids. With a lighter she set them on fire and held them until she could no longer finally letting the flaming pieces fall to the ground.

"Good-bye, Audrey Spence. You know, I am going to miss you a little," she said quietly to herself. She looked inside her purse and saw her new driver's licence, just one part of the set she had received, and smiled. "Hello, Emma Clark. Look out girl. We have one hell of a great life ahead of us!"

Satisfied the old IDs were well destroyed, she left the alley, walked the rest of the way to Union Station and boarded her train for Halifax. It was time for her to find out if money could indeed buy her happiness.

Chapter 40

It took seven months for the paperwork and legalities to be finalized and approved by the courts. Halina Shimon's home and assets had been successfully transferred to her son, Shane, in trust of Beth Poole. A substantial annual allowance was given by the estate to Beth in order to leave the job she hated and become Shane's full-time guardian.

The documents had been signed and the transfer of assets had been completed the same day the sale of Beth's old condo closed. Beth had made a healthy profit on the sale and with the estate allowance, was financially set for life.

All was quiet within the house. Beth had the TV and the radio turned off. Shane too was quiet as he was fast asleep upstairs enjoying his afternoon nap. Beth walked in from the kitchen with a cup of Earl Grey tea and sat down in a chair by the window. Although she didn't feel at quite at home yet, the chair in which she sat seemed to provide some comfort.

Beside the chair was a small table which was just big enough to hold a decorative lamp, her cup and saucer, and a framed picture. When she lived in her condo, she drank her tea from a mug. Here, in a house which still felt like Halina's, she felt almost duty bound to use a cup and saucer like she did when she visited.

Beth took a sip, sat the cup back in the saucer and picked up the picture from the table. She had never really looked at it before. Inside the carved frame was a photo of Halina and her holding Shane between them when he was just six months old. Her eyes started to well up.

"Why Halina?" she sobbed. She placed the picture in her lap, put her face in her hands and started to cry uncontrollably. "Why did you have to go and get yourself mixed up in all that? Oh God Halina, why?"

♦ ♦ ♦

Tiberius bounded from the couch and over to Paula as she came through the door.

"I still can't get over the greeting I get from him when I get home from work, "she commented.

"It's the whole ritual thing you have with him now," Morgan answered as he stopped practicing his lunges and leaned his fencing sabre up against the wall.

"How're your moves coming along?"

"My arms still stiff. It's frustrating. It's been over six months and I'm still looking at a couple of months or more before it'll be in any kind of condition for a tournament."

"Patience, my dear, patience."

Tiberius looked up at Paula and gave a squawk. It was the only time this particular kind of sound ever came out of him. She put her hands on her hips and looked down at him, "My you're impatient. I guess you want the "Tiberius Song" don't you?"

Morgan chuckled when he heard Tiberius answer back with another squawk as it sounded like a 'yeah'.

"Alright, here we go." Paula bent over and ran her hands one at a time across his back as she started singing a silly song she had made up about Tiberius done to the tune of Lady Gaga's '*Judas*'.

During the last couple of lines, he fell over onto his side as if on cue so she could stroke his belly.

"There. That should hold you for awhile."

"Hmm. At one time didn't you say you didn't like cats?"

"How can I not love this guy? Not only is he so sweet but he's the one who brought us together." She straightened up and walked over to Morgan. "Now it's your turn."

Even though they had been together for many months, their greetings at the end of a workday were long and passionate.

"Soooo, how did it go?" she asked.

Morgan picked up a paper from the coffee table and held it out for her to see, "Look at this. I nailed a ninety-six!"

"Ninety-six percent on your exam! Wow, you aced it! Look at you. You're now a full fledged licensed private eye, dick, sleuth…"

"Alright, alright, that's enough. Actually, the proper term is Private Investigator but you can call me detective."

"To hell I will. Remember I'm the 'real' detective around here," she said with a laugh emphasizing the word 'real'. "Are you trying to downgrade me to your level or elevating yours to mine?" They both started to laugh.

"I think now I may have more certifications than you."

"Not quite but it's nice having a gumshoe license to go along with your Security Specialist license and Commercial Drone certification. You've been a busy boy."

When Morgan had finally returned to work, he found he could no longer stand the nine-to-five paper pushing. The sameness of the day-to-day routine, the same one he used to love, he had come to hate. He became bored.

When he had first discussed the idea with Paula, she was against it. It was a profession she had little respect for. She tried to explain being a 'P.I.' was not as exciting as it was on TV. Her thought was he should instead train for the police force. It was a route he was unwilling to take at his age.

Paula had known he needed something different and was restless. She was pleased when he told her he wasn't intent on being a private eye but wanted it as an option.

Although he had never flown a UAV, Unmanned Aerial Vehicle, he was determined to learn about the field. His intention was to be fully trained for the new drone industry which was opening up. Not knowing where it might take him, he gained his certificates in investigation and security. Next up would be aerial photography, a subject which was only touched upon in his previous courses.

"Well, congratulations, Sir, "she said he still holding onto him, "And I suppose there is some bubbly chilling in the fridge?"

"You bet."

"So, what's your plan from here?" she asked. She let him go and headed to the fridge with Tiberius following after her. He didn't answer and when she looked back, she saw him sitting on the sofa. She returned to the living room, handed him his glass, tinged it with her own and sat beside him.

"You never answered. What's your plan?"

He sighed. It was time to talk. "Alright, hmm, how to go about this? Let me ask you, how many times have Tiberius and I stayed over here for the night? Wait. Maybe it might be easier to answer this way. How many times have I gone back to my condo to sleep in my own bed?"

"I guess the only time is when I'm on night shift."

"Exactly. So here's what I'm thinking. I sell my condo, buy into your place, which makes it officially our place and we live happily ever after."

It took only a split second for Paula to respond. "I love it. Actually, I was thinking the same thing myself but wondered if you were holding onto your condo, you know, um, just in case this all didn't work out. I was scared to bring it up."

"The thought never crossed my mind."

"It's a great idea. The money from the sale would keep you going while you put your new career, whatever it may be, in motion. You know I have your back in every sense of the word while you're doing it too. It's a fabulous idea. I love it. I absolutely love it."

She pulled him in close and pressed her lips hard against his. They quietly held onto each other tight for another minute before she let go. Tiberius took the opportunity to jump up and spread himself across both their laps.

Paula laughed at Tiberius's stealth and reached for her champagne. She held it out for a toast. "To us, to your new future and especially to Tiberius. After all he was the one who brought us together."

Acknowledgements

It's impossible to write a novel in a vacuum. Authors need support in so many ways, which I am indeed fortunate to have.

First of all, I would like to thank Robert Morgan at BookLand Press. He took a chance on me with my first non-fiction book, *Defending the Inland Shores*, and is doing so again with *Saving Tiberius*, my first work of fiction. I enjoy working with him.

To my friends, some who I've known for decades and a few who I've shared my life with since Grade 4, I say thank you. You've always been behind me, supportive and continually asking me for updates on my work, which helps to drive me. I love how you've shown faith in my work by ordering my books in advance of publication.

I also have to thank my cats. Morgan, our late tabby, was the inspiration for this book. Crumpet and Muffin support me in their own way by joining me in my writing room while I work. They may sleep most of the time but when I need a break or become frustrated, I turn to watch them curled up so cutely on the futon or in the window. It brings me a certain peace.

And of course, to my wife, Teena. We've been great together for almost 20 years. She is my biggest fan and critic. As my editor, she contributes so much to make my work better than it ever was. It's easy to work with somebody who is supportive, smart and honest of my work, always constructive in her criticisms, never negative. Well, except for the many times she's come to me, manuscript in hand, to sigh and to tell me with frustration, "Gord … will you please learn how to use a comma properly!" Sorry, Dear. I'll try to do better in the future.

To all of you, I hope I've done you proud.